MW01246075

WHITE MOON

WHITE MOON

BY MOONLIGHT SERIES BOOK 3

CHELSEA BURTON DUNN

4 Horsemen
Publications, Inc.

White Moon
Copyright © 2023 Chelsea Burton Dunn. All rights reserved.

4 Horsemen
Publications, Inc.

4 Horsemen Publications, Inc.
1497 Main St. Suite 169
Dunedin, FL 34698
4horsemenpublications.com
info@4horsemenpublications.com

Cover by J. Kotick
Typeset by Autumn Skye
Edited by Blair Parke

All rights to the work within are reserved to the author and publisher. No part of this publication may be reproduced, stored in a retrieval system, or transmitted in any form or by any means, electronic, mechanical, photocopying, recording, scanning, or otherwise, except as permitted under Section 107 or 108 of the 1976 International Copyright Act, without prior written permission except in brief quotations embodied in critical articles and reviews. Please contact either the Publisher or Author to gain permission.

This is a work of fiction. All characters, organizations, and events portrayed in this novel are either products of the author's imagination or are used fictitiously.

Library of Congress Control Number: 2023941267

Print ISBN: 979-8-8232-0255-8
Hardcover ISBN: 979-8-8232-0257-2
Audio ISBN: 979-8-8232-0258-9
EBook ISBN: 979-8-8232-0256-5

DEDICATION:

To anyone who wants to be masters of their own fate. Keep pushing. Keep striving. Every stumble is a lesson to make you stronger. Don't give up. You'll get there.

TABLE OF CONTENTS

WHITE MOON

PROLOGUE

He shivered at the scent of her. The taste of her in the air seemed to sizzle on his tongue as he envisioned how the nuances of her aroma would translate to his palate. How would she differ from the one that came before? Would she taste even better?

It didn't matter. He just *knew*, based on her scent, that she would taste divine.

Rumors had spread throughout the area about the odd, little locksmith who could feel emotions, who could tell if one was preternatural, and he simply had to know.

Dangerous.

Dangerous for the community as a whole, but more dangerous for him.

This scent was so familiar, the way it clung to any place she went, lingering there despite how incredibly

unassuming and almost human it was. It was a sure indication she was like the woman he had known years ago. No, this woman wasn't the same woman. But she had a little extra in her, and the scents of Fae, Witch, and a little something more were masked, but he could still taste them in the air now that he knew what he was looking for.

That woman years ago would have been his downfall, had she not disappeared on him. He knew now that he had gotten a handle on his unquenchable desire that only someone like her could fulfill; she, as that woman before, had brought forth a monster within him. He shuddered with both delight and disdain, touching the door of the quaint locksmith shop he was standing before. The lights were off at this late hour, with only still shadows behind the glass.

Fiona.

She had done locks too, but she had told him she did many things over the years. Quite the crafter she had been. And quite the beauty. Her eyes seared in his mind; their large emerald depths pulled him in and captivated him. He had wanted to keep her forever. To be able to stare into her eyes, smell her scent, taste her every day for eternity.

A car passed by, with its headlights reflecting off the smooth glass of the locksmith's door, pulling him back to the present.

Vee.

That was the name of this new woman whispered in the shadows from those that were Other—preternaturals. Her scent was so prevalent there at the shop, as if it were her home. He had come here out of curiosity, just to see about this strange, new woman in their community, but what he got was so much more than he had anticipated.

Yes, he had to have this one. He had to keep this one. This time, he wouldn't let her slip through his fingers.

He let his nose follow a path that she had taken many times, though not recently, leading him to a blocky apartment building. He could see there had recently, within the last year, been work done to some of the exterior bricks, and the door had been replaced, not quite matching the look of the structure. His eyes glanced over all the lit windows, resting briefly on a cat that sat staring at him from a window on the second floor, before they travelled up to the one darkened window at the top left.

That was the one.

He knew he couldn't go in, nor could he expose himself by climbing the face of the building to peer inside, but he wanted to know where she was. He wanted to see into her life and learn, so he could find out how to lure her, to keep her. He knew she had given herself to the Werewolf leader, but perhaps he would be able to seduce her away from the beast.

The cat scratched menacingly at the window screen, as if it knew that he was hunting after its former neighbor. He narrowed his eyes at it, baring his teeth slightly and letting his fangs show. He was the predator here. A tiny cat should not have made him feel like he had to assert his dominance. However, its eyes glowering at him made him angry.

A woman came to the window upon hearing the cat, her hair dyed a vibrant blue. She placed a hand on top of the cat's head.

"I miss her too, Midi," she said, her voice carrying to him from the open window.

Interesting ... this girl knew the woman he sought. He would keep that information tucked in his mind. Perhaps she would be useful to him as he developed his plan. He just needed to know more first. He couldn't let himself get swept up in the utter lust he felt at her scent.

No, not this time.

Last time the lust for blood had failed him, his frenzy didn't let him focus on what he needed to do. Last time the woman slipped away, disappearing without any trace he could follow. Her magic had been so potent, so clear, so pure ... his body tingled at the memory of it running through his veins.

The old addiction resurfacing inside filled him with an odd sense of excitement, as he moved swiftly through the night back to his home. The pull was there, but he could be patient. He didn't need to let the madness ruin it as it had before.

CHAPTER 1

This lock was being difficult. Years of wear had stripped the screws holding it in place, not to mention the rust crusting it to where it sat within the door. The house was a little over one hundred years old, like a majority of the buildings in the area. But while most of them had been updated, this particular house had last seen an update in the late sixties, so, therefore, this lock had not been replaced in many years.

Vee struggled with the lock, a fine layer of sweat collecting on her forehead as she continued to work at the metal carefully. She was also having a harder time holding back the sickly feeling she got from the minds below, her brain feeling like it was being doused in ice water repeatedly. Not that the minds were feeling anything bad necessarily, but she just so happened to be changing the locks on a Vampire nest.

Now that she had been ousted to the preternatural world as a true Empath, she had been getting more and more clients of all varieties. Vee didn't mind the extra income, but she did mind the unease she got each time she had to make a house call. In the last few months, she had made house calls to several small Witch covens and a Fae, who had recently moved and needed the iron fixtures removed from their home. (She had done more than just locks in that house: hinges, cabinet pulls, and she even hauled away a wrought iron handrail, giving the Fae her favorite renovation company's card for the replacements.)

Now Vampires.

They all made her uneasy. The Witches especially, given her fairly recent negative encounter with a coven, but the Fae and Vampires were not much better. Not only was it potentially dangerous to be surrounding herself with more and more preternaturals, but she also hated that if Shane knew about it, she had to take a bodyguard with her to work.

It had been about six months since Shane, the leader of the local Werewolf pack, had claimed her to protect her from Others, and she had gotten increasing call after call to help the Kansas City area's unexpectedly large preternatural community. Cities tended to have higher preternatural populations, since much like humans, they flocked to the more densely populated areas; it's easier to hide in a crowd.

Despite Vee being able to feel the presence of Others, she would have never known the extent of the community's size had she not been exposed as one of them. She assumed the knowledge that she was preternatural herself appealed to them, either because they were curious about her or because they didn't have to hide who they were, like they would have for a human locksmith. She knew better than most how hard it was to constantly hide what you were, but it didn't make her feel any safer about stepping over the threshold each time she got a preternatural call.

The heat and humidity of mid-August pushed at her from the open door, but the blasting air conditioning and the Vampire minds continued to make her shiver from behind her. She finally managed to get the lock out after twenty minutes of struggling and breathed a sigh of relief, pulling it from the wood and looking it over. It was a beautiful lock. Clearly, it had been made by hand probably over fifty years ago. She looked at the inscription on the side, where the old locksmiths used to put their initials.

F.O.

She stared at it for a long moment. It was most likely a coincidence that the inscription had the same initials as her birth mother, but she couldn't help the strange feeling that came over her while looking at the letters there. Just touching the inscription, Vee felt like there was something familiar about the piece. As she stared at the carefully carved letters, the metal seemed to tingle under her fingers. She was transfixed, eyes moving over the inscription over and over, waiting, as if they would tell her something more.

But Vee was broken out of her thoughts as a human mind approached, emotions mixed somewhere between exhausted and bored.

"Are you nearly done?" This was said by the woman who had greeted her at the door when she arrived, leaning on the archway of the small entry that led to the rest of the house. She was human, but barely at this point, one of the Vampires' intendeds. They were humans who offered their blood and services for a time, in the hope that they would be turned one day. From what Vee had heard years ago, most of them didn't make it through the transition.

The woman was young, maybe in her twenties, though it was hard to tell which end of the decade she was in. Her hair was dyed black, and her pale skin was smooth, as it pulled over her thin frame. It was the tired eyes peering back at Vee, when she turned to look at her, that aged her by about ten years. Vampires weren't the only things in this house, Vee knew. She could also feel the hum of the other sleeping humans; the woman before her was the only one awake. She must have been with them for some time to be trusted with this task. After all, Vee was encroaching on this Vampire resting place when they were in their most vulnerable state.

"Finally got it out. It was a tricky one. We're replacing?" Vee asked, more as a confirmation, holding up the lock for the woman to see.

"Repairing…?" the woman grumbled in response, as if Vee should know, despite how completely vague the original request had been earlier on her answering machine that morning. Vee recalled the message this woman left simply asked for Vee to come "see about the front lock," never clarifying her request when Vee called back to set the time. So, the way her tone suggested, that Vee should have just known this was a repair, made Vee swallow her instinct to snap at her. She curled her fingers back around the lock, as if holding onto it tighter would keep her mouth from causing her trouble.

"I can't do that here. I'll put a replacement in and repair at my shop," Vee told the woman a little sharper than she would have liked, as she began digging through her bag to find the replacement lock she had brought.

"They're not going to be happy about that," the woman sneered, crossing her arms and staring at Vee indignantly.

"Well, there's nothing that can be done about it. The supplies I need to repair it aren't things I can take out into the field," Vee said, still not looking at her, as she assumed her expression would give away her irritation. She was trying very hard to keep her tone even, but it wasn't easy given that the intended's emotions went from bored to irate with Vee's explanation. It wasn't really her fault though. Vee knew she would have to explain to her Vampires why the lock hadn't been fixed upon their rise at night. Thankfully, she would be too long gone by then to give any sort of explanation.

"They'll have to decide if they want to pay you. I'm not giving you anything until they tell me it's okay," she murmured snottily. Vee held back from rolling her eyes at the woman. Of course, she'd have to wait for the Vampires' approval before she would get paid.

"That's fine," Vee said, her tone clipped as she put the replacement lock in with ease, even with the woman standing over her. She screwed it in, giving it a

good wiggle before she closed the door and made sure the deadbolt lined up with the hole in the doorframe properly. It did, but a little shakily. It would just have to hold for a day so Vee could come back with the fixed part. "Is there a time tomorrow that works better for you?" Vee asked, standing up from her crouching position on the floor after she had gathered all her tools.

"Same time works for me," the woman said with a yawn. Apparently, watching Vee work wasn't exhilarating, or she was up past her bedtime. Probably the latter.

"Okay, I'll call when I'm heading back here," Vee told her, digging in her bag, once again, to pull her little calendar out and scribble the time on there. If she didn't keep track of the appointment, for some reason it would die in the back of her mind, especially now that she had more than just herself and her work to focus on.

There were benefits to having more people in her life to worry about other than herself. She didn't tend to miss meals quite as often, she was far less bored, and almost always had someone to talk to. She felt busier, not just with her actual business, which was good and bad. But of course, she also had Shane. She let the image of him in her mind come into focus for a moment, warming her. His dark hair, very slightly dusted with grey, olive skin, square jaw, straight nose, and warm, brown eyes took over her thoughts.

She had woken up before him that morning, only taking a moment to look upon his beautiful, still sleeping face and gone into the shop early to finish a few custom pieces before the day truly began. Now she was wishing she had skipped the custom pieces and let her body mold against the hard plains of his body in bed a little longer.

Vee may have sat there a beat too long, lost in her own recollections, before the icy feeling from the Vampires below snapped her back to reality. Without a second glance back at the intended, whose glare Vee could feel on the back of her head, she walked back to her van, bags in hand.

The sleek black van with tinted windows was not something she would have ever chosen for herself in any normal situation, but she had finally retired the old, unreliable Lumina for the van at Shane's behest. As she started it, she realized the clock already read noon. She would barely make it back to the shop before her designated thirty-minute lunch was over, being that she was in Brookside already, and the shop was clear over in Westport.

With a sigh, Vee pulled out her phone, dialing Lori's number. Lori was part of the reason Vee was in this particular predicament with the preternatural world in the first place. Vee had saved the sweet teenage girl from savagely murdering her friends when she'd unexpectedly turned into a Werewolf one night, a little over a year before. Vee had exposed herself to protect people she didn't even know. She'd upended her own life in an unthinking moment, letting her instincts guide her to save the group of teenagers, and protect the secret of the preternatural world. Many times, over the course of almost a year and a half since it had happened, she thought about why she did it, and if she should have. Vee always came to the same conclusion:

she wouldn't have done anything differently if she had to do it all over again.

Lori and Patrick were diligently watching the shop as she went on her run in the field. Patrick was Shane's younger son, and her almost-stepson. The two teen-agers had worked for her all summer, as they had the summer before, and there was only a week left before she only had their help after school and on Saturdays.

"Hey, Vee. What's up?" Patrick answered on the second ring.

"I thought I called Lori," Vee said, raising her eye-brow, not that he could see it, but she was sure he'd be able to hear it in her voice.

"I was closer," Patrick said, a grin in his voice. Vee could hear Lori's giggle in the background, even though she had clearly tried to stifle it. The two of them weren't officially dating, but there was certainly a spark between them. It made sense; not only were they close in age, but they were also both Werewolves. They didn't have many friends to confide that particular part of their life in. Vee had also caught them kissing a few months earlier, so she kept a keen eye on them. Werewolves lived a long time, too long for them to make certain life-altering decisions so early.

"I'm not going to make it back to the shop before lunch is over, so I'm just going to grab something quick at your house before I head back," she said, taking a few turns and stopping at a four-way stop.

"You mean 'home,' Vee?" Patrick asked, his voice not hiding the smirk she could imagine forming on his lips. She rolled her eyes.

"Hard habit to kill," she said, still uncomfortable calling Patrick and Shane's house hers, even after six months. Patrick loved to remind her of it.

"We'll close down for lunch and see you in a bit. Everything is good here."

"We're fine, Vee!" Lori added from the background.

"Okay, okay..." Vee murmured, hanging up the phone as she pulled up to Shane's house.

She had somehow made the space in front of the house hers, Shane and Patrick usually parking in back. The pack even steered clear of parking there, so she'd have a place if they arrived before she did. She climbed out of the van, wandering through the grass to the front door, always feeling uneasy as she looked at the large colonial from the outside. It was still so strange that she was coming here of her own accord, instead of being summoned. The structure seemed to loom over her. Memories of her unease from those times before living within its walls, over the more practical part of her brain, which quietly tried to assure her that she *also* lived there now.

But as she placed her key in the lock, the unease seemed to melt away, causing her to feel much more comfortable once she stepped through the threshold. The house had definitely taken on some of her attributes: a few books stacked on the side table in the living room, her little planter where she'd stashed her keys at her apartment previously, sitting on a narrow table just inside the door, and the sturdy hook that Shane had installed right by it for her to put her bag on were all small indicators that this space held her things.

It still wasn't *hers*, which was part of the reason she felt such an aversion to calling it that. She was comfortable there, yes; her things stayed here, yes, but the general feel of the house was still definitively Shane's.

She paused to listen, hearing Shane's voice up in the office. He must have been on the phone with a client. She felt a little of his excitement and mild confusion at her coming home in the middle of the day through their connection, but she decided not to bother him, going to the kitchen to grab some leftovers from the refrigerator instead. She took the food with her, wandering to the dining room to look over the papers she had left out from the night before. Most of her papers from the adoption packet her sister, Eliza, had given her were upstairs. She had needed to see some of them in a different light, a different area of the house, because maybe then they would start making more sense to her or put some pieces together. So Vee had brought a few pages down to the dining room, further spreading the chaos of their research a few days before.

Frank, her sister Eliza's husband, and Cormac—a Watcher that had turned against their purpose to try and eliminate her—had done just enough digging to find out her birth mother had some known aliases. It seemed she didn't usually go by what they assumed was her given name, Fiona O'Morrigan. All the names listed had been used long before Vee was even a thought, unfortunately. She seemingly fell off the map once Vee had been given over to the Malones, the human family Vee had always thought was her blood family.

The revelation that Vee wasn't truly a Malone had been hard enough, but the added mystery of not knowing who or what her true parentage was seemed to set both a pit of worry in her stomach, as well as a burning need to find out more.

She was taking her first bite of the cold pasta she had made the night before, leaning against the counter, when she felt Shane, now off the phone, asking her through the bond to come up to the office. She hesitated a little, knowing the scent of the Vampires' house was probably still lingering on her, but she made her way up there anyway, cold pasta in hand.

The door to the office was open. Shane was sitting behind his desk, busily typing when she entered and sat across from him in one of the large leather chairs.

"Lunching at home today, I see," he said, stopping to look at her. His dark brown eyes examining her movements. She was pointedly not looking at him, which of course drew his attention.

"Had a house call close by," she said with a shrug, gathering another noodle on her fork. He took in air through his nose, his eyes instantly changing to gold when he got the faint smell of Vampire. She knew it was coming so she didn't react, continuing to eat her pasta and keep her eyes focused anywhere but his face, which was a feat. She normally had a hard time *not* looking at his face ... and especially when he was angry. She fought back a shiver.

"House call where?" he asked in a grumble.

"It was a Vampire den. However, it *is* daylight. No danger afoot," she said, trying to reassure him, keeping her voice light and hopefully carefree. It did not work.

"I could have had Tommy come with you," Shane said, fist clinching next to the computer mouse. It was

 WHITE MOON

good his hand hadn't been resting on it; he lost a lot of equipment that way.

"Tommy's doing that security detail for that art installation, isn't he? We can't just pull him away every time I have a house call, Shane," she said, raising her eyebrow at him and finally meeting his gaze. Her irritation was clear through the bond. He put his hand up to rub his forehead in frustration. Her stubbornness and need for independence were part of her appeal, but it didn't make it any easier when she put herself in danger.

"I just want you to be safe. You've been getting so many more preternatural customers now that they all know," he murmured, trying to calm himself. She was right about the daylight, but he still didn't like her walking into a Vampire's home without someone to protect her. He didn't like her walking into a Vampire's home at all. If he couldn't even keep her safe when she was doing her job, what good was he? But he knew that keeping her guarded at all times was much more than just a toe over the boundary she had set. He knew she hated being treated like a fragile thing, even if she was in comparison to him.

She set the container of food on the small table between the two chairs and sighed, looking him over and assessing his feelings. He was frustrated, worried, protective, and possessive. She would feel that way too if he had put himself in a potentially threatening situation, and she wasn't a Werewolf. His protection instincts were far more overwhelming than hers.

"I wouldn't do a job alone if I didn't think I could handle it. Sleeping Vampires in the middle of the day don't really concern me," she told him, leaning forward on the chair to take his still-fisted hand in her hand. He relaxed it, letting their hands fold together on the desk.

"I know that … I don't particularly like you smelling like that though," he told her, looking up from their hands to meet her eyes. His eyes hadn't returned to brown; instead, they only became more vibrant, his wolf wanting to correct the way she smelled. She could feel that little tendril of desire starting to build up within him, a need to reestablish himself as hers and she as his. She stood, moving around the desk, still holding his hand, but coming to stop before him.

"It will go away soon. Just superficial," she murmured, touching his face as his other hand came to rest on her hip.

"Or it can go away now," he suggested, pulling her onto his lap and running his nose along her neck. She shivered a little at the contact, her heartbeat getting erratic.

"I have to go back to the shop in a minute," she whispered.

"Patrick and Lori will be fine for a little while longer without you," he said back, his voice gravelly as his lips took the place of his nose on her skin.

"They'll know," she said, though still not pulling away from him.

"And?" he asked, letting his fingers travel under her shirt, touching the soft skin of her back.

She pushed him back a little in the chair, preventing his lips from continuing their trail along her face and neck. She stared at him in the eyes for a moment, truly

wanting nothing more than to just clear his desk of all his work and climb on top of it with him, but they both had work to do. Briefly she thought of how interesting it was to desire him like she did. Before him, she barely thought about sex, and now...

"How do I smell now?" she asked huskily. He took in a breath, eyes turning more golden as he did so.

"Like you're mine," he growled.

"Good," she said, leaning forward to brush her lips over his before starting to stand from his lap. The flabbergasted look on his face was priceless.

"What? You're going?" he asked, reaching out to grab her hand again and stopping her before she moved too far from him.

"If we do this now, I'll have Lori asking me when the wedding is for the rest of the day. I don't think I can handle fielding those questions when we can just anticipate all sorts of fun we can have later," she told him, giving him a playfully seductive look.

"Or we can do both," he said, pulling her back to him and clutching onto the backs of her thighs. Vee laughed a little, looking down at him from where she stood and bending down to kiss him. It was hard to resist him. But just then the phone on his desk rang, startling both a little.

"You're being summoned, and I need to get back," she said, trying to push aside the pull within her to ignore the phone and continue what they had been doing. Shane squeezed her a little and then released her with a sigh. She gave him one last kiss on the cheek as he picked up the phone and put it to his ear.

"Shane Keenan," he answered, his eyes still glowing as he watched her walk around his desk. She snatched her leftovers, giving him a grin, and padded back down the stairs, taking a few more bites before she wandered back to her van.

CHAPTER 2

Vee pulled up down the street from the shop, in front of the laundromat. Wistfully, she was pleased she no longer had to relinquish useless and wasted hours of her life getting her clothes cleaned there. Now that she lived with Shane, who had not one but two sets of washers and dryers (Werewolves dirtied a lot of clothes), she never seemed to get down to the undesirable and uncomfortable clothes she'd always seemed to have to reluctantly wear prior to laundry day.

As she got out of the van, she felt the thrum of a Fae. She knew before she came around to the sidewalk what Fae it was. The same Fae-woman she had encountered and narrowly gotten away from a year ago. Since that day, she had actively avoided the old woman, seeing her in the neighborhood quite often now that she was aware of her. The old-looking woman stopped, having noticed Vee when the van pulled up, waiting for Vee to come around the car, eyes trained on her like a hawk.

"You are the one they call Vee," the old woman said, hunched over her little wire pushcart that held her small bundle of laundry. Vee hesitantly turned her eyes to meet hers. As she looked, the Fae's glamor shimmered and parted like her human skin was made from smoke. Vee knew she was the only one who could see the beautiful and dangerous true skin beneath the magic, but her eyes glanced around them anyway to see if there was anyone too near to see or hear.

"I am," Vee confirmed, trying to keep the tight feeling in her stomach from showing her anxiety outwardly.

"I knew something was different about you. I see it better now," the Fae woman said, her eyes narrowing with suspicion despite the sure smile on her lips.

"You know how easy it is for some to only see what they want to," Vee said, raising an eyebrow at the Fae, who simply grinned. "I mean you no harm. Leave me be," Vee continued, her voice low and ignoring the smile that sent a chill down her spine. She didn't want to threaten or offend the Fae, but she wanted to make it known she didn't want to play games either.

"I mean no harm either, child. I see your splendor now that the shadow of doubt has fallen. You have blood of my kind in your veins. Ask for me, and I will come. I seek nothing from *you* in return," the Fae woman told her, reaching out her hand. Vee was struck by the Fae's words. She knew Fae couldn't tell lies, but carefully crafted truths often hid their true intentions.

This woman's words had little to hide. She had said, "I seek nothing from you in return," and that settled Vee, but only slightly.

Between two fingers, the Fae woman extended a card to Vee. It was a white card, heavy stock, but it shimmered in the midday light. There was a number with the local area code and the name "Nessa" embossed in silvery letters. Vee reached out and took it, careful not to touch the Fae's skin as she did so. The only things Vee had been feeling from her were amusement and curiosity, but there was an undercurrent of more. She wasn't sure she had any desire to amplify that by touching her.

"I'll take it into consideration," Vee said, carefully avoiding thanking the Fae, who grinned broadly.

"Smart girl," Nessa said, before she turned her cart and headed the other direction, away from Vee's shop.

As Vee suspected, Lori was all over her with questions as soon as the two teenagers had gotten a whiff of her once she entered the shop. It was obvious that things had become a little heated over lunch, and Shane's scent was clinging to her like she had doused herself in *Eau de Shane*. Lori had visibly perked up the moment Vee walked back into the shop at least ten minutes after the clock hit 12:30. Very un-Vee-like to be late.

"Are you going to secretly get married?" Lori asked, as Vee set to work on fixing the Vampire's lock.

"No … we just … haven't decided on anything yet," she murmured back, feeling Lori's eyes on her as she carefully laid the Vampire's lock on top of a towel, turning it over to see how bad the corrosion was.

"They literally haven't talked about it at all," Patrick said, as he came out of the back room.

"What? Not at all? It's been six months!" Lori said, her face strained.

"One, you don't know everything we talk about, Patrick." Vee shot him a sharp glare that had him smiling even wider. "And two, what does it even matter, Lori?" Vee asked in frustration, turning her attention back to the lock as she carefully applied some chemicals to eat away at the rust buildup.

In actuality, she and Shane had talked about marriage, but only to decide they wouldn't be making any sort of plans until they had come to some sort of conclusion about Vee's past. So much change had happened for her in such a short period of time that the idea of getting married, and all the planning that came with that, was a bit much to add to the mix currently.

"Because! It's great that you're bonded and all, but … don't you want a *wedding*?" Lori asked, resting her head on her chin as she stared at Vee from the counter. Vee looked up at the teenage irritant. Lori had recently dyed her hair bright purple, and while a bit jarring, it complemented her darker skin beautifully. Vee was certain her mother, Cora, had had a field day about it. She thought about bringing it up, as punishment for her pushiness, but decided Lori had gotten enough from her mother to last a lifetime, even if Vee hated the idea of being barraged with questions.

"I don't know, Lori. It's not like I told him to ask me or anything," she said sarcastically instead. If her

tone hadn't given away the sarcasm in her words, the look she gave Lori certainly did.

"You told him to ask you?" Lori asked confused.

"Does Patrick not fill you in?" Vee asked, turning her head to glare at him again from where he was leaning in the doorway to the inventory room. He smirked confidently, making him look even more like a younger version of his father.

"Apparently not," Lori hissed, turning hate-filled eyes toward him as well briefly, before turning back to Vee. Patrick flinched at both of their searing looks, his momentary confidence falling away. "Well? Tell me about it!"

Vee sighed, setting her magnifiers on the counter beside the lock. The chemicals needed time to eat away at the rust anyway; she didn't need to watch it happen.

"Before we renewed the bond. It wasn't anything crazy. He asked me if I would accept the claim again and try to renew the bond. I just told him to ask me in a different way," she said shrugging.

"And then he proposed?" Lori asked, her voice and eager eyes urging Vee to give out the details.

"Yep. He proposed," Vee said, very matter of fact. Part of her was uncomfortable retelling such an intimate moment between her and Shane, and part of her fully loved torturing Lori with the lack of details.

"Why do you make it seem so underwhelming?" Lori whined, appearing to deflate at Vee's words.

"He didn't get down on one knee or anything. He just held me and asked me," Vee murmured, leaving out the fact that moments before that, she had been crying uncontrollably into his chest. Vee had just realized her apartment had been destroyed by the Witches who had been hunting her down to steal her magic … and her soul. She was quite the mess when Shane had told her, but even with the bond and claim being broken, he would not leave her; that her mess was his.

Lori's emotions flooded with that swell of euphoria, imagining the romance. It wasn't romantic in the traditional sense, but it had been to Vee. Just thinking about it again made her body tingle, and she quickly tamped that down to avoid the two teenagers becoming aware of the sudden desire she felt. Maybe she should have been a little later coming back to the shop…

"So why aren't you planning the wedding yet?" Lori asked, snapping Vee out of her own thoughts.

"We've been busy with other things," Vee said, donning her magnifiers once again to rinse the chemicals off the lock.

"They've been researching," Patrick said, when Lori shot him a confused look. "Into Vee's past," he clarified when her face only deepened its confusion.

Most nights recently had been filled with research. Durran had even left the city, seeking out more from some of the leads that Frank and Cormac had gathered in the packet. They hadn't even gone through all the papers that were in there yet, each one seeming to add more questions than they answered. At this point, what Vee knew for certain was her mother's name, Fiona O'Morrigan, and that she had given birth to Vee in Ireland originally. How they managed to change her birth certificate to one from the United States, with her adoptive parents' names listed, was beyond Vee,

given that there was no record of adoption anywhere to be found. She assumed it was magic.

Fiona seemed to have decided to give Vee up after having her for about nine months. The adoption had been arranged quietly. One note in Frank's messy scrawl mentioned there was no record of involvement with social services; despite that, he still seemed certain he'd be able to keep Vee from having any sort of claim on *his* family's money. Oddly, none of Frank's plans did him any good, since he ultimately died by the hands of the Watcher he had allied himself with.

Vee didn't want Frank's money, but all his work did nothing when his Last Will and Testament left everything to Eliza, and she, in turn, had left everything to Vee. He never had the chance to file anything legally keeping Vee from it, so therefore when his lawyer reached out, saying everything was held up due to the unsolved nature of their deaths, Vee was surprised. Not only was she technically entitled to whatever money he'd had, but based on what he dug up about her birth mother, Vee realized she hadn't truly been abandoned. It seemed like Fiona's intention was an attempt to keep her safe. Or at least that's what Vee liked to imagine.

"The research hasn't gone very far," Vee admitted, looking over the lock with her brow furrowed, as she saw some more intricacies that had been hidden behind the buildup she had just washed away.

"But after?" Lori asked.

"I don't know if I'll actually find out the truth. Honestly, we should probably give it up at some point. I'm not sure that I *want* to know everything. Whatever I am and whoever I come from already seems quite complicated," Vee said with a sigh. Complicated meant dangerous. Vee had spent so much of her life trying to avoid that, but this past year and a half had been one dangerous thing after another. She knew, deep in her bones, that the further she looked, the more dangerous it would become.

"Well, there's a week before school starts. Maybe you and Dad could find out more information if you go looking, instead of relying on the internet. Lori and I can run the shop," Patrick suggested, coming closer to lean on the counter beside Lori. Vee looked up at the pair now shoulder to shoulder, or more Lori's shoulder to midway up Patrick's arm, and laughed.

"This coming from the two of you? I thought you wanted me to start an online shop to sell my custom pieces, and now you're telling *me* to not rely on the internet?" Vee asked, raising her eyebrow questioningly. The idea of the online shop had intrigued her, but only so much. She had even less time to work on passion projects now that she had people in her life, no longer wanting to stay at her shop into the late hours or leave Shane in bed in the early morning. Odd how quickly her priorities had shifted.

"From what you and Dad have been saying, I don't know how much you're going to find out about your mom from here. She doesn't seem to have left a very good paper trail to follow," Patrick murmured.

It was true; Fiona's paper trail seemed to go cold not long after Vee was handed over to the Malones, but she couldn't help feeling suspicious of Patrick's motivations. He had been helping them off and on with the research, better at scouring the internet than

even Shane, but she got the feeling that wasn't the only reason he wanted them out of the house.

"I can really trust you two to run the shop while I'm gone?" she asked with narrowed eyes.

"We would run it like a dream. You wouldn't even know the difference when you came back," Lori said with confidence.

"House calls?"

"We would just have to tell them you're on vacation or something," Patrick said, nodding vigorously and smiling. Vee continued looking suspiciously at them, testing out their eagerness, which wasn't fully out of a need for helpfulness. No, there was no way Vee would entrust the shop for them to man alone for a period longer than an hour or so; and the idea of leaving Patrick and Lori to their own devices, given the desire and tension she felt between them ever since that kiss she'd happened upon months ago in her wrecked apartment, seemed like a bad idea.

"I don't think so," Vee said, turning back to the lock, ignoring the way their faces faltered. "I have to finish this so I can reinstall it tomorrow," her tone dismissive now. They were up to something, but the idea intrigued her nonetheless. It would make much more sense to go out searching and see what they could find, however hard it was for her to leave her work behind.

Vee had sent Patrick and Lori home a little early so she could have the last hour of closing the shop to herself. It was about the only amount of true alone time she seemed to have anymore and she relished in it, taking her time to put everything away and reconcile her register. It wasn't that she didn't like having people in her life but having been on her own for so many years, she found these small moments of alone time to be cathartic. It allowed her to parse through her own thoughts, without the influence of others' emotions. The familiar routine of closing down the shop seemed to relax her.

She picked up the newly cleaned and refurbished lock from the counter to put it in a box for tomorrow's reinstallation, running her thumb over the engraving there one last time.

The initials on the lock were most likely not her mother's, but it still made her wonder.

Who was her mother?

That was probably the biggest question on her mind as of late. This mysterious woman seemed to be eluding everyone. The idea that the initials carved there were possibly *not* a coincidence had now seared itself in her head. It would be extremely unlikely that she and her birth mother were both locksmiths. Although, doorways held a lot of significance in magic. There were doorways to other worlds hidden everywhere; you just had to have the right key. At least that's what she had gathered from fairytales.

Vee's eyes lit up at that.

A key.

She had a key. A key she had owned for as long as she remembered. It didn't go to any door in her home growing up. She had a vague memory of trying it out in each keyhole and being disappointed it didn't fit. She

used to dream she could use it on her closet and disappear into another world like the kids in *The Chronicles of Narnia* did with their wardrobe.

It was a silly thought though. That old, silver key had never unlocked any doors, but she suspected her fascination with it had influenced her chosen career path.

The heat hit her hard when she stepped out of her shop into the evening air, instantly making her sweat. August in Kansas City was humid and heavy with its unrelenting temperatures. When she turned around to get into her van, she wasn't startled seeing Durran, her best friend and Watcher, there in her usual black duster to mask her wings. Vee had felt her presence before she even turned around, pushing her thoughts of fairytales and keys to the back of her mind to consider later.

"I see you're back," Vee said with a smile, opening the passenger door to stash her bag but closing it to lean against the van beside Durran. The black car was blazing hot from sitting in the summer sun, but she carefully kept only her clothed parts touching it.

"Just barely. I think I found out Fiona's last known whereabouts. I could be wrong, but the name seemed to be in the same vein as her other aliases," Durran told her.

Straight to business. Vee wasn't surprised. Her relationship with Durran had been strained for the last year, ever since the Werewolves had become a regular addition to Vee's life. That, and the fact that Durran had been forced to confess she loved Vee—and not the best friend-love Vee felt for her—by the now-dead Watcher, Cormac.

"I missed you too," Vee said, smirking. The three days that Durran had been out of the city was the longest they had been that much apart from one another since Durran had been assigned to Vee by the Elder Watchers. Somehow, Durran had seemed to come to grips with the fact that Vee was safe with Shane, at least for a few short days. "Who watched your apartment for you while you were gone?"

Durran raised a questioning eyebrow at Vee before smirking and turning her eyes back to the windows of the shop. Vee had never known or been privy to Durran's living arrangements and just assumed that Durran had to live *somewhere*.

"Did you get through the rest of the packet?" Durran asked instead of answering Vee's question.

"Not yet. I feel like I should just get through it tonight, so we at least have all the information laid out. Only a few pages left." Durran nodded, eyes looking off into the distance briefly, worry evident as it rolled off her to Vee.

"The Elders have called me back to the realm. They want an update," Durran murmured, after the silence between them had made it obvious there was clearly more she needed to share.

"We don't really have anything yet," Vee said, concern flashing across her face. She knew the Elders wanted answers about her, but even with six months of looking into it, they still had very little to go on.

"No, that's the problem," Durran said, gaze turning back to her, letting her eyes show what Vee could already feel. The same worry that was creeping into Vee's bones. Vee sighed. No giving up on the search then.

"When do you have to go?" Vee asked.

"In just a moment, actually. I wanted to see you first," Durran said, looking back up at the darkening sky.

A silence came over them. Durran had told Vee everything, finally, not long after the incident with Gwen, the Black Witch, and Cormac months ago. Vee now knew that Durran had been assigned not only to protect Vee, but to also find out what she was. Vee found it shocking that even the Elders had never come across someone like her. She was completely unique, and that was almost more daunting to think about. In the preternatural world, unique meant powerful, and power was either seen as a threat or something to gain. Both meant danger.

Along with that knowledge, Vee was still trying to grapple with what she had done during the attack. She had no idea what power she wielded. No idea what else she could do with the abilities that lay inside of her. The blast of magic she had put out to defeat the Black Witch had been just as shocking to her as it had been to everyone else.

It was strange to know that she had spent nearly thirty years thinking she had abilities that mostly just hindered her life, remaining a weak creature in comparison to other preternaturals. Now she had not only saved herself, but the pack, and she didn't even know how she did it, really. Not that she'd had much time to explore her abilities since that incident. They had been far too busy with the packet from Frank and trying to readjust to her new life for any testing. Shane had suggested she try the next time they went to the property, to push herself and see if she could harness some control over her abilities, so it wouldn't simply be an explosive reaction like it was before, but they hadn't strayed far from the city in months.

"What are you going to tell them?" she asked, turning to Durran once more, whose eyes were still trained on the sky above.

"I can only tell them the truth, that we haven't gotten far. They aren't going to like that," Durran whispered. Vee sighed again.

"Maybe we need to go searching," Vee said, thinking back to her conversation with Patrick and Lori earlier. They weren't wrong; the internet had given them about as much as it could at this point, so they needed to go searching for her mother. It was the only way they'd find anything new.

Durran turned to Vee, surprise evident on her face. She knew that was the only way they'd find out more, but she didn't think Vee would be receptive to leaving the city and her shop to do it. Yet there she was, being the one who offered it up. Durran wouldn't have to try to convince her or team up with Shane to do it, which had been the real reason she hadn't voiced that opinion yet. Her hesitation with Shane had lessened over the past six months, but only so much. Durran had resigned herself to the fact that Vee loved him, and both her duty to Vee and her love of Vee couldn't fault her for finding love. Durran couldn't fault Shane for loving Vee, either.

"That might be the only way," Durran confirmed.

"I'm sure it will be interesting," Vee said with a smirk, thinking of Durran and Shane on a road trip together, assuming they would both join her on this

adventure. But she wouldn't just be a fly on the wall. She would, unfortunately, be in the middle of it, and she assumed the two of them together for any long duration would lead to fighting of some kind.

"I'm sure Shane will be delighted," Durran said, chuckling lightly, her thoughts having gone down the same path as Vee's.

"I'll have to prepare some things."

"Yes, but the plan in place…" Durran sighed. "That may buy me some time with the Elders," Durran said, seriousness evident in her tone once again.

"What will they do if we don't find out anything?" Vee asked quietly.

"I don't want to speculate on that," Durran said, shivering a little at the thought. The Elders could inflict a lot of pain on Durran, but she worried more about what they'd do to Vee. Durran wasn't sure of the extent of the Elders' abilities, but she was certain that there may be … *ways* to extract the information they desired from Vee. It just wouldn't be very nice.

"We'll figure it out," Vee said confidently, reaching over to clasp Durran's hand comfortingly.

The more she dug into her past, her parents, the more confused and overwhelmed she became, but it no longer was just about Vee. Not only would they potentially bring the wrath of the Elders down on them, but she had to know what she was to protect the people she cared about for the inevitable trouble her lineage would cause. She had already been targeted by Witches. For all she knew, more would come in search of her.

They parted ways, and Vee watched as Durran pulled away from where Vee stood beside her van,

wishing she could come with her to meet with the Elders. Not that Durran would ever let her, but she wished she could at least try to appeal to them. Perhaps she'd be able to make them see how her past was so lost and confusing because of the passage of time, that it took quite a bit of digging to pull it all back up again.

CHAPTER 3

Vee once again pulled up in front of Shane's house.
The whole ride over, Vee had felt a distinct uneasiness creeping through the bond. She had felt it before,
a similar pit in Shane's stomach, when he mentioned
the Sha. There were no other cars around; the houses
on the street that held other pack members didn't have
visitors either. So, the Sha weren't physically there,
though an unexpected visit wouldn't have surprised
her. She got out of the van, slinging her bag over her
shoulder, and trudged to the door. Whatever awaited
her in there, it wasn't going to be good.

She could tell Shane was in the office still as she
set her things down and moved to the kitchen. Patrick
was there, worry consuming his emotions as well, as
he stared into the refrigerator without seeing what
was in there.

"What's going on?" Vee asked, grabbing a glass from the cabinet to pour herself some water. The house was frigid in comparison to the outside heat, but she had sweat so much standing outside the shop talking to Durran that she could already feel the dehydration setting in.

"Dad's on the phone with Min ... the Sha," Patrick said, his voice a bit shaky as he said it. Well, at least she got the feeling right. Vee's ears perked up as she tried to listen to what was being said. The soundproofing on the office was doing its job, so she could only pick up the tone in his voice. "The little I heard when I was up there, they're finally wanting some answers about you." Shane's worry became her own, souring her stomach. No wonder Patrick was standing there looking at the food that no one would be in the mood to eat.

"Don't we all," she grumbled.

Without another word, she headed upstairs to the bedroom. There was no way she planned on interrupting Shane while he was on the phone with Min, but she had to do something productive. The only thing she could think of was to continue looking at the packet, the one thing they had that she knew may hold some answers. The open space on the floor between the flanking dressers had become her little investigation station. Most of the papers from the packet had been laid out, with notepads full of notes set beside various sections of information. The only ones missing had been the pages she'd left on the dining room table the previous night. She picked up the last few pages that had been left untouched at the center to start looking over.

Elders were demanding answers, and now with the Sha as well, there wasn't any more wiggle room for her to put off the last bit of information waiting to be known. But as she took in a deep breath, preparing herself to pull out the top page that had listed several cities with no context, she heard Shane emerge from the office the next room over. The light mood he had been in that afternoon when she'd left him was gone, as if it had never been there.

"Vee?" he murmured from the hall, knowing full well she was in their room.

"Thought I'd finally look at these last few pages," she said in return, eyes remaining firmly fixed to the top page. She could feel his worry and hesitation, but she wasn't sure she wanted to see it on his face just yet.

"The Sha called," Shane said quietly, stepping into the room and closing the door behind him.

"Patrick told me," she said, still not looking up from the papers in her hands.

"They want to see us," Shane murmured, moving to stand behind her. His words were heavy, solidifying the stone that was forming in both of their stomachs.

"When?"

"As soon as possible." His arms snaked around her waist and pulled her back against his chest. The touch eased them both for a moment. Vee leaned her head back onto his shoulder and took a deep breath.

"And why is that?"

"They've heard the rumors. They feel it's important to know the truth about one of their leaders' mates," Shane said with a heavy sigh. He had been hoping to avoid this as long as possible. At least until they knew more about what she was. It was hard to be forth-coming when they didn't even know the whole truth themselves.

"Durran is seeing the Elders. She stopped by the shop," Vee said, continuing to lean against him, their collective anxiety giving way to the comfort of each other's touch.

"On all sides, then," Shane murmured into her hair. She took in a deep breath. Yes, everyone was demanding answers, and she hadn't even managed to get through these papers yet. Partially out of procrasti-nation, partially out of fear, she had been putting it off, unsure if she wanted to know everything. Ignorance was bliss, after all.

"Let's see what these last pages have to say then," Vee grumbled, refocusing her eyes on the words. The top page she had looked at already, so she leaned over to set it with the other pages and notepads that had Fiona's aliases on them.

Underneath the page was a handwritten letter. It was on thick stationery, the top of the page embossed with the Smith family label, and the curly, elegant script was unmistakable. Eliza had written this. Vee's eyes welled with tears looking at it. It had been six months, but it still stung every time she thought of her. Every time she remembered that Eliza had died because of her. Shane tightened his hold on her, reas-suring her both physically, and through their bond, that he was there.

 WHITE M⚬⚬N

Victoria,

I slipped this in here. Frank doesn't know. I need you to understand, I didn't want any of this. Even though I can't see you or call you, I don't want you to ever think that I don't love you. When Mom and Dad brought you home, you became ours. You were one of us. It doesn't matter whose blood runs through your veins. You are my sister.

If I could change things between us, I would. I was young and selfish. I didn't understand things like I do now. But it's not just you and me anymore. Mary needs me. I know you understand that.

With this note, I put the letter that Mom held onto for you. She was given it by your birth mother when you were handed over. She had always planned on giving it to you when you turned eighteen. After Mom and Dad died, I planned to do the same, but you were gone before I had the chance. I didn't think I'd ever see you again. When you came back, I already had Frank. I'm sorry it took me so long to make this right.

I think Mom had already given you the trinkets that came with this letter. I remember you used to hold them and look at them for hours when you were younger. Do you still?

I know I always pushed away what you could do. I was scared. Mom and Dad always believed you. They knew there were other things in this world. Magic in this world. I'm sorry if I hurt you because you have a piece of it. For the longest time, I didn't want to believe. If I believed in the magic, then it was real.

Someday, we'll be able to see each other again. I don't know how or when, but I know it's true.

I'm so sorry Victoria.
I love you.
Eliza

Vee was shaking, tears welling up enough to obscure her vision, threatening to fall from her eyes as she finished reading. She had regretted the last time they spoke and had been silently mourning the relationship that they could have had if Frank had not been in her sister's life. But it gave her a small bit of comfort knowing that Eliza mourned that too, that she had loved her. The little hole in her soul that had formed when she'd lost Eliza and didn't have any closure wasn't full but had closed a bit.

With a shaky breath, she pulled Eliza's letter away, putting it behind the page beneath, but this wasn't a page; it was its own sealed, white envelope. Not a modern envelope though, even though it was the size of a standard sheet of paper. This was folded carefully and sealed with crimson wax. The paper was also thick

stationery, but it was rough and textured against Vee's fingers. She looked closer at it and saw small leaves and flowers that had been pressed into the pulp that made up the paper.

"Smells like … Fae … and Witch," Shane whispered, still behind her. Why he hadn't noticed the smell before, with it having been sitting in his bedroom for months, he didn't know, but it also wasn't surprising. Magic could mask many things, such as smell. Fiona had to have Fae origins; her last name certainly indicated that. The Witch smell, however…

Vee pulled away from Shane, the sudden urge to sit becoming overwhelming as she held the envelope delicately in her fingers. This may be exactly what they needed to find her. Or if not find Fiona herself, maybe just find out more about her. It was thrilling and daunting at the same time. She made her way over to the bed, sitting on Shane's side, which was closer to the open part of the room. He stayed where he was, watching her.

Her fingers brushed over the seal, and she felt the thrum of magic. But this didn't pulse in her mind; the most she could feel it in her fingertips as they made contact with the hardened wax. The seal impressed within the wax was strangely familiar, like she had seen it before. The Triskelion, or the Celtic spiral, sat in the center, another circle encasing it, which Vee, oddly, just *knew* represented the moon. It seemed simple, yet powerful.

Beautiful.

She hesitated to break it, but knew she had to in order to see what was within. The magic surrounding the paper now seemed to whisper to her that she wouldn't be able to open it by any other means. She also knew *she* was the only one who could open it. The seal would break for no one else.

She glanced up at Shane, feeling his desire to be near her, but his hesitation was there also, not wanting to crowd her. They needed to discuss what the Sha had said and needed to make plans to leave, but this moment seemed so much more important than all of that now.

Taking one more shaky breath, she pulled the seal from the paper, breaking it, and letting the magic pour from within and settle around her. It wasn't unpleasant, but it was strange. As if a missing piece of her was settling into place. She felt somehow more whole, and it confused her.

Vee unfolded the pages, her eyes settling over the handwritten words. These letters, though artfully written, were not the smooth, feminine curl of Eliza's, but pointed and sharp, much like Vee's own writing, but clearly more practiced.

Mo Leanbh Álainn,

> *It is with great sadness I leave you here. My heart aches just knowing I will not hold you in my arms again, or not like you are now. You delight me in a way that I never imagined in my long life that I would ever be or could ever be.*
>
> *There is darkness in this world. Darkness that I wish to keep you from, since you, like me,*

will never quite belong to any one group. There are few places for those of us who walk in more than one world. Being what we are makes them fear us. Fear leads to battle. I don't want you to have to fight every day of your life. I want you to have joy. I want you to feel loved and unencumbered, at least for as long as you can.

These people I give you to, my most treasured thing, are good. They understand the world better than most humans. They do not shy away from the magic that surrounds us. The magic that's within you. I trust, as long as they live, they will do well by you, and that is the only reason I can place you in their arms and walk away.

You are more important to this world, magical and otherwise, and for that, you deserve this small peace I can gift you. With me or with your father, you would never find those small pleasures that you will, no doubt, take solace in by the time you read this letter.

I gift you three small tokens. Talismans.

One to help you find your path.

One to help you see.

One to unleash your strength.

Your father gave me one of these, and I pass it on to you.

You are the bright, white moon to the darkness, my daughter.

I love you.
F.O.

Vee stared at the page, rereading the words written by Fiona's own hand several times before she could bring herself to tear her eyes from it. This letter was vague, which was unfortunate. She wanted more of an explanation from the words on the page than they were going to give her. Vee had the impression that her adoptive parents, Sarah and Graham, were supposed to have filled her in on some other information, either before or after she read this, but they were long dead. She still didn't know how they'd died; Eliza had kept that from her too.

The way her mother had talked about them made it seem like they were a bit more than human themselves, which could have been why Vee thought they were her real parents. The added mystery of *why them* was curious, but not entirely necessary to what she needed to know. At some point, she would look into their past and find out why Fiona had trusted them to keep her safe.

Shane had moved closer to the bed while she read the letter. For a moment, after she had broken the seal, he was nearly immobilized by the magic that poured from the page. Not threatening magic. It didn't feel

or smell like specifically Fae or Witch magic either, but unique and yet still different than the feel of Vee's magic when she wielded it. As he made his way closer, the magic having slowly retreated, he could feel it still, the energy pulsing around her.

"What was that?" he asked, leaning his hip against the footboard, trying to remain calm for her benefit. Even if he logically understood, based on the feeling of the magic, that there was no threat, his wolf senses were still on alert. He didn't like not having full control of himself, even if only for a moment.

"A letter from Fiona to me," Vee said, tearing her eyes from the page to look over at him. "It doesn't give us much of anything," she murmured, holding it out for him to take. His fingers grasped the page gently, expecting it to somehow repel him, but he held it easily enough. His eyes moved over the page quickly, trying to take it in. No, there wasn't much to go on, but he furrowed his brow as he read the end.

"Talismans?"

"I *think* I know what she's talking about," Vee said, standing quickly and moving around the bed to her nightstand. On it, she had placed the three trinkets she had kept since childhood. No matter where she moved, she had always kept them with her. In fact, they were the first things she'd thought to grab when her apartment became unlivable last March, and she'd moved in with Shane.

One was a very simple key, the one she had thought of earlier in her shop. It reminded her of medieval keys, skeleton iron keys. The barrel was long and rounded, with the teeth on only the very end opposite the bow.

But this wasn't made of iron; it was silver. The only marking on it was at the bow, another Triskelion was etched carefully there. She had always held it for comfort, but she realized, as she touched the cool metal, it held a hum of magic she had always dismissed before. It was small, barely a vibration, but it was there. Perhaps she hadn't ever really had the words to describe the way it felt before. Only recently had she become accustomed to how magic felt physically, not just how it appeared to her eyes or how she perceived it in her head.

Another was a small simple carving out of bone; it was the head of a wolf. It had never occurred to her until that moment, looking down at this beautiful bone carving, that she had any connection to Werewolves, but here in her hand, she had a wolf head given to her by her birth parents. She didn't particularly like the idea of destiny or fate, much preferring to believe that she had control over the way her life played out. But looking down at this made her shiver a little involuntarily.

Was she meant to be with Shane?

She turned to look at him for a moment. He was still leaning against the bed frame, eyes rereading the words, just as she had, trying to decipher if there was anything that was missing, anything that would give them more of a clue.

There were certainly moments when she felt as if they were meant for each other. The way they seemed to be drawn immediately to one another had been, just months ago, enough to make her want to push any feelings she had for him away. And she thought of the

words he had used a few times to describe what she was to him.

True Mates.

She hadn't gotten around to asking him about that yet, and now certainly wasn't the time.

Vee looked at the third object, or talisman she supposed. This had always been her favorite item of the three. It was about the size of her palm, a pale green crystal, polished to have a delightfully smooth surface. It was a perfect circle, domed on both sides, giving a magnifying effect when you looked through it and encased on the narrow side in a band of copper. As a child, she would spend hours looking through it. The cracks and irregularities within the crystal would sometimes change the world around her. Vee had always thought it was her imagination, but now...

She picked it up, letting the weight of it settle in her hand for a moment before she moved to stand next to Shane once more.

"These," she said to him, in response to his question just a moment ago. "I think these are the talismans. I've had them for as long as I can remember."

Shane looked over at her outstretched hands—the key and the wolf head in one hand, the circular crystal in the other. Although he knew she had set them on her nightstand almost as soon as she'd moved into his house, he had never felt an urge to look at them. Odd, considering he had thoroughly enjoyed helping her find places for her things around his home, seeing what little possessions she had that made up *her*. It had secretly delighted him to watch her try to make his home hers and have the evidence that she lived there with him scattered about. But with these objects, it was as if he didn't even notice them, despite them having clear significance to her.

"Dad?" came Patrick's voice from below, easily carrying up the stairs and through the bedroom door to their sensitive ears. "There's a Vampire on our lawn." Patrick's voice, though quiet, remained grounded, despite the cold trickle of anxiety and anger Vee could feel from him. Vee and Shane's eyes met briefly before they both rushed down the stairs, Vee stuffing her items into the pockets of her jeans.

Patrick stood at the front door, looking out the narrow windows that flanked it. There, standing in the grass of the front lawn, was a man. He was not outrageously tall but taller than Shane, Vee could tell from that distance. He was thin, perhaps built like a runner, his suit clearly tailored so well it fit like a glove. His hair was blond, though Vee couldn't tell what shade in the darkness outside. Sharp European features shaped his face, and his nose was long. His eyes were glowing, only slightly, but they were staring with a predatory gaze. A familiar shiver trickled onto her head. This was a Vampire from the house she had been working at earlier that day.

Shane opened the door but didn't cross the threshold. The hot air of the summer night wafting in as he did so.

"What do you want, Vampire?" Shane asked, his voice low and deadly.

CHAPTER 4

"Only to talk, of course," the Vampire said grinning, though his eyes were raptorial as he looked past Shane to where Vee stood in the hall. "My name is—"

"Lazare Duflanc. Yes, I know who you are," Shane interrupted. Vee noticed his hand gripping the door began making the wood creak beneath his fingers. "Why are you here?" he growled.

"I wanted to make the acquaintance of my locksmith. I was indisposed when she was by earlier. My Holly told me she didn't pay for the services rendered, and I wanted to correct that. I'm not in the business of leaving a debt unpaid," Lazare said, slowly taking a few steps closer to the house, his arms outstretched as if to show he was no threat, even though they all knew how dangerous this was. His English was very good, but there was the odd emphasis on certain sounds that were very distinctly French.

Vee stepped closer to the door, standing beside Shane. He let out a low rumble from his chest as she did so, warning her through their bond to move no closer.

"This is neither the time nor place, Vampire," Shane said, trying to keep his voice level.

"I do apologize, *Monsieur* Keenan. But there's hardly a better time for me to become acquainted with the newest member of our community. I am rather limited in when I can get out," Lazare said, as his mouth widened into a sinister grin.

"We will settle the bill once I've installed the repaired lock tomorrow morning. Please leave," Vee told him firmly, trying to ignore the way his gaze made her spine tingle. She didn't have to raise her voice; she knew he could hear her just fine from where she stood.

Shane stiffened beside her. He hadn't wanted her to speak to him. Knowing that *this* was the Vampire she had as a client that day only proved to make his intensity that much stronger, the wood door under his fingers creaked angrily.

"As you wish, Vee. I trust your work is as good as your reputation says it is," Lazare said smoothly, before smiling somehow even more broadly and turning his attention to Shane for just a moment. His smile dimmed as his eyes met Shane's, giving a challenging glower and moving inhumanly quickly out of sight.

The three of them just stood there for a moment: Shane and Vee still at the door, Patrick at the window. The evening outside was quiet, as only the sounds of

the cars on busier streets some blocks over could be heard. Shane, very slowly, closed the door a bit more precisely than he normally would and turned to them.

"How long was he here?" Shane asked Patrick, not meeting Vee's eyes. His voice was quiet and calm. Dangerous. She could feel his anger but wasn't exactly sure who it was directed toward.

"I only just noticed when I called for you," Patrick told him, his body on edge.

Shane's phone rang from his pocket.

"Thomas, did you see?"

"Was that Duflanc?" Thomas asked, a rumble in his throat. Thomas, Shane's second, lived across the street, so it wasn't unexpected for him to have noticed something, especially when two pack members were suddenly on alert.

"It was. Vee is fixing a lock for him," Shane said, finally turning his golden eyes to hers. The look he gave her made her spine stiffen. He was mad at *her*. She raised her eyebrows at that revelation.

He had been mad at her before, of course. She was stubborn, and they tended to butt heads about things on a regular basis, especially when it came to her safety and independence. But the white-hot rage he felt and the way his golden eyes glinted, as they locked with hers, made her whole body react with her own anger and a fleeting moment of fear.

"How did he find her there?" Thomas asked. Valid question. Vee also wondered that, but her enflamed anger over Shane's rage toward her kept her mouth closed tight.

"I think he must have scented her … followed her from his house to our home, since she stopped here for lunch."

Vee's eyes widened at the realization. Yes, of course. Why didn't she think of that when she came home?

Well, for one thing, despite being careful to not be detected for most of her life, she hadn't fully grasped the implications of being ousted—to being part of the preternatural community. Her scent had never been an issue before. She didn't smell like any preternatural, just a little spicier than human, as Shane had described to her. Now that it was known she was also something Other, she would need to be much more vigilant. They knew who she was, not what she was, and they were all eager to find out exactly what she could do.

"Tomorrow, Vee will need protection. She has to go back to reinstall the lock, apparently. And we'll need to call the others for a meeting tomorrow evening," Shane said, but his eyes darted to Patrick, who immediately took out his phone.

"I'll take the first half of the alphabet," Patrick murmured, knowing Thomas would hear him.

"I'll get Markus to take over the art installation, so Tommy can go with Vee," Thomas said. Vee rolled her eyes. She liked Markus just fine as a guard; she was just more comfortable with Tommy, since they were friends. She hated having Tommy's schedule rearranged constantly for her protection.

"Time to move … we've been here too long anyway, but we can't afford the Duflanc Nest being aware of this location. The pack magic that protected us is now,

clearly, broken." Thomas made a quick, affirming grunt to Shane over the phone before abruptly hanging up.

Without another word or glance, Shane headed back up the stairs. Patrick was busy texting and went toward the kitchen, leaving Vee standing in the middle of the hall alone. She understood Shane's anger, but she had made a mistake, and an honest one at that. Considering, up until recently, she had never had to think about these sorts of problems, she expected a bit more grace, not a wave of fury from Shane.

She was about to just ignore him and let him calm down on his own, but she felt something strange. Their bond closed down to nearly a dribble, she realized, only giving her ability a hint of his emotions and not from their connection.

Her own fury swelled.

How dare he close her off?

She stalked up the stairs, turning into his office, and slamming the door closed behind her. Patrick didn't need to hear them fight, and the soundproofing on the room would keep most of it from traveling to him.

"You can be angry at me all you want, but I didn't intend for this, and you know it," she hissed, eyes turning amber as she glared at him. His eyes didn't meet hers, but she could see the golden glow of them as he looked at the computer screen. His jaw tightened as did his fist that rested against the desk. "Well?" she prompted, after the seconds went by and he said nothing.

"Intended or not, you exposed this location," Shane said through gritted teeth.

He was struggling to not snap at her. He didn't want to be angry, but she'd thoughtlessly risked not only herself but the pack by leading a trail right to their home. This had been his home, the pack's home, for nearly twenty years, and though they tended to move around the city every so often, he had wanted to stay there a little longer. Mostly for her comfort. Moving the pack headquarters took planning, and now they had to do it quickly. Had she just been more careful...

But it could have easily happened anyway. Had Duflanc wanted to, he could have traced her from the shop home as well. His anger wasn't just brought on by her naivety, but with the concern that somehow the protective pack magic had been broken. Her scent had been like a tether that allowed Duflanc to penetrate it, and he didn't understand why.

He had known he could shut down the bond with Vee for some time, but never had the need or desire to do so. The magic of the bond worked similarly to the pack bonds that allowed him to communicate between his wolves without words, to know when one of them was in danger or in need of help, but it was stronger with her. He wasn't sure if it was because of a mate bond or if it had something to do with her magic, but it left more questions in its wake, like everything surrounding her.

He had clamped down on the bond to protect her from him. His wolf had very nearly taken over, as knowing their protection was broken brought every instinct to the surface. He wanted to hunt what threatened them, and he wanted to shield those under his

protection, none of which he could reasonably do now. It was wearing on his control.

And he didn't want to scare Vee and didn't want her to run from him. She had run from problems before. He was very aware that at any moment, this could all become too much for her to handle and she could try to disappear.

"You didn't intend for this…" he started gruffly. "My anger is mostly out of frustration. There is no way to predict anything when it comes to you," he said, finally looking up to meet her burning eyes with his own.

"So you're angry that I complicate your life, Shane?" Vee asked, her lips tightening into an angry line. Unpredictable may as well have meant complicated in her mind. He had definitely complicated *her* life, but she wasn't flying into a rage about it. She wasn't shutting him out, either.

"No, I'm angry that I don't know enough—*we* don't know enough—to protect you and our pack. Everything is pointing to it. The universe, the magics, are making it quite clear to us that we must figure out your past, what you can do, before we can…" He struggled for the words he wanted to say. Shane stood up while he was talking, and now they were facing each other with only the desk between them.

Vee's fists clenched, her short nails digging into her palms. The little voice of safety, the one that had kept her alive and alone for so many years inside her told her to go, to run from him, run from this. It had all been too much. The past year had been the taste of the life she would have in this world. Blood, death, and fear.

CHAPTER 4

Him shutting her out, saying she was a *frustration* and a *complication* made the old her want to run.

But she wasn't that Vee anymore. Though she had no idea exactly what her powers were, her mother said she had importance in this world. She couldn't hold onto the humanity she had clung to for so many years because it was a lie. She was no more human than the Werewolf who stood across the desk from her.

And beyond that, she didn't *want* to run from Shane. For all that she had told herself before about needing to be alone, Shane was hers. He had fought for her, would have died for her, and she for him. This man, though flawed and quick to temper, heavy-handed and overprotective, was exactly who she needed. Who she *wanted*. She wouldn't run from him.

Instead, she looked back at him with determination.

"You can't shut me out, Shane Kennan. Even to protect me. You are *mine*. My problems, your problems, they are *ours*. Never do it again," she growled, her voice menacing as she glared at him.

Shane's eyebrows shot up. She had never said he was *hers*, never said the word "mine" to describe him before. He had certainly felt intense possessiveness for her; it was impossible for a Were not to, especially when bonded, but he didn't know if it went both ways when mated with someone who wasn't a Were. She surprised him with the possessive growl that had come from her lips as she said the words, with the way she clearly tamped down her instinct to run away from the situation so she could stay and fight him. To fight for what was hers. It ignited his desire for her ferociously.

53

He blew the bond wide open, watching her for just a moment as she grappled with the overwhelming *need* he suddenly had for her. Her pupils dilated slightly as she took it in. Then he moved quickly, coming around the desk and pulling her against him.

"Say it again," he growled into her ear. She shivered at the contact, pressing herself closer.

"You are *mine*," she whispered back, letting her fingers slide up the sides of his neck to thread in his hair.

"Mine," he growled, lifting her up so their lips could meet without him bending. Their kiss was feverish, filled with an intense need to feel one another. To stake their claim.

Shane turned back to the desk, taking one hand from where he held her to push everything off in one sweeping motion, before he set her on the desk. His eyes were hungry as he looked at her lying against the dark mahogany. She scrambled to unzip her pants, toeing off her shoes as she did so, but Shane was too impatient. As soon as her fastenings were undone, he pulled them roughly from her hips. He leaned over her, one hand braced beside her head on the desk, the other slowly trailing up her leg as his lips and teeth found her collarbone.

Her skin was lovely, beautifully olive, smooth, and delicate, as it lay over her lean muscles. He loved to touch her skin and admire her body. She was beautiful; her features never really hinting exactly where her roots were from. She could have belonged anywhere, beautiful enough to be with anyone, but here she was, beneath him. She had declared him as hers.

Thankfully, his wolf hadn't completely taken over; otherwise, her shirt would have been torn away, and he knew this was one of her favorites. Instead, he let his fingers dance once they found their home between her legs. Vee gasped, her fingers digging into his shoulders as he touched her, hard but delicately enough to make sure he wasn't hurting her. She put her heel up on the desk, unable to stop her hips from moving with his fingers.

"I want you," she whispered in a moan. Shane's low growl at her words vibrated against her. He could feel the pull of her fingers as she desperately tried to bring his face up to hers. A kiss would send him over the edge. He would not be able to resist if his lips touched hers. So instead, he easily pulled away from her hands, his face traveling, lips brushing over her favorite T-shirt, which he would have much preferred was her skin, to her exposed stomach where it had ridden up.

She shook and gasped as his mouth joined his fingers. He was kneeling now before her, that reverent feeling she often felt from him punctuated by the way he was now positioned. One of her hands grasped his hair while another clutched the edge of the desk for dear life. Only since she had been with Shane did she feel pleasure this way. It began to build, and ecstasy burst from her, but not as powerful as when they joined.

"I want *you*," she said again, when he stood between her legs and looked down at her. She sat up, her eyes never leaving his as she unfastened his pants and pushed them past his hips.

His golden eyes burned hungrily as he met hers. Once his pants were no longer in the way, he bent

down to her, touching her lips with his once again. Any semblance of control he had was gone in an instant. He lowered her back down onto the desk, hands grasping at her hips as he effortlessly joined them together.

"*Mine*," he grunted, as he moved over her, lips hovering over hers.

"Mine," she moaned as a response, back arching and nails raking over his shoulders.

They let the bond take them, their feelings aligning, building, until they finally hit that impossible peak, holding it there for as long as they possibly could.

They both shook against one another for a few minutes until Vee started giggling unexpectedly beneath him on the desk.

"What's so funny?" he murmured, pulling his head up from the crook of her neck to look at her.

"Your office is in shambles," she said, meeting his eyes with amusement dancing behind hers.

"Fights with you often get messy," he said seriously, though after a moment he grinned, pulling them both up off the desk. The room *was* quite a mess now: his paperwork and various items on his desk littering the floor, even his computer monitor had been knocked into his desk chair. Hopefully it didn't take much damage. They both looked quite the sight as well, half clothed and rumpled from their hasty lovemaking.

Vee snatched her pants from the floor, happy he hadn't torn them—her clothes being destroyed wasn't an uncommon occurrence—as Shane pulled his pants back up. Patrick was still somewhere in the house. Hopefully the soundproofing in the office had done its job, but even if it had, they would still smell distinctly of what they had just been up to. She had to steel herself from the embarrassment she felt. Werewolves were not as preoccupied with shame when it came to things like sex and nudity. Those were human things that didn't apply to the instincts of their inner beast, and though she was not a Were, she lived amongst them.

Once they were both redressed, they went back down the stairs together to see what progress Patrick had made informing the pack of the meeting. He was still in the kitchen, phone wedged between his ear and his shoulder as he got the leftovers out of the fridge.

"Yep, pack meeting tomorrow," Patrick said, his voice giving away his clear irritation.

"My wife's family is having a dinner," John Meyers said with venom in his voice. His human wife's family did not know her husband and sons' true nature; therefore, having to abruptly cancel dinner plans was a bit of a sore subject.

"Sorry, John, but it's necessary. Vampire got through the pack protection, and Dad is going to have to go see the Sha. You want to miss out on the details or be part of the plan?"

"Fine," John snapped before hanging up.

"I thought you were taking the first half of the alphabet," Shane said amused, but the satisfaction in his voice was unmistakable. Patrick took after his father. He was a force to be reckoned with, and though he was young, his own dominance within the pack was not something to be ignored.

"Thomas texted me he had only gotten through two names when Cora had a meltdown about moving," Patrick said grimacing.

Cora, Thomas's wife, had put a great deal of herself into her house design. Vee had always admired how clean and put-together it was, as if it was taken directly from a home-and-garden magazine. Moving and having to start all over again would make her a frantic mess. Moving quickly, with little time for careful consideration, was not something Cora would be able to deal with well. Shane cringed at the thought of the fight that was undoubtedly playing out across the street.

"I don't envy him," Shane murmured, turning his attention to the containers of leftovers. His originally soured stomach was feeling much more ready for food now that he and Vee had thoroughly disorganized his office.

"So, what's the plan for tomorrow?" Patrick asked, not looking up from his phone as he replied to a few text messages that had come in, presumably from other pack members who he had chosen to text instead of call.

"I need to set George on the task of looking around at homes for sale and putting ours on the market. Once we've got that started, I suppose Vee and I will need to head to Sha territory," Shane said, nuking the container of steak and roasted vegetables from two nights ago, despite the stone rolling back into his stomach at the mention of the Sha.

They rotated who was making dinner. Vee usually made pasta or something with rice, while Shane made things like steak. He was a much better cook. Her practice with cooking had been for one, and she didn't really care too much about whether it was especially elaborate or not when she had just been feeding herself. A few days a week no one cooked, and they all cleaned out the leftovers in the refrigerator instead. Apparently, this was going to be one of those nights.

"I'll have to button a few things up with the shop before we go," Vee murmured, feeling that anxiety kicking in again. She wasn't good with change, and there had already been lots of changes to her life. The idea of having to move again, after finally feeling *slightly* settled, was enough to make her physically cringe.

Shane felt her anxiety through the bond and slid over to where she leaned against the counter, pressing his arm against hers.

"At least we'll all be moving this time," Shane said sweetly, kissing her hair as he wrapped his arm around her.

"You won't be able to call it 'Shane's or Patrick's house' anymore; it will be *ours*," Patrick said, looking over at them with a grin. Vee narrowed her eyes at Patrick but couldn't help the smile that spread over her face. She honestly hadn't thought of it that way until he said it. Perhaps she wouldn't mind moving again.

CHAPTER 5

Durran stood in the great dark room of the Elder Watchers, appearing before them in their androgynous true form. Their eyes unable to help the faint red glow from the anxiety they felt. It was unlike the Elders to call upon a Watcher during their guard, and Durran had already come to them once during their time with Vee as their ward to ask for help. What they had gotten in return was the reminder that Durran's orders had been to not only protect Vee, but also to find out what she was. And now they were expecting results.

The silence of the room was punctuated with the intense eyes of the seven Elders before Durran. Their faces showing nothing but vague interest as they looked the younger Watcher over. Mical stood tall at the center, letting the silence draw out for another excruciating moment or two before they folded their hands together before them.

"Durran, it has been six months in the mortal realm since we last spoke. What have you discovered about your ward?" Mical asked, their voice echoing oddly around the darkened hall. Durran sucked in a breath.

"We haven't learned much. It seems Victoria is somehow connected to the Morrigan, though she does not smell or feel of Fae or any other known creature," Durran started, voice quiet, knowing this information gleaned very little for the Elders.

"The Morrigan..." Mical repeated, their normally ineffectual voice now low and dangerous. Their eyes shone with unprecedented anger. Durran wasn't sure what the specific offense was between the Elders and the Morrigan, though they had always assumed it was about power.

The Elders were powerful. They could see just enough into the future to know when a being held importance, whether that be for the good or the bad. The stories told that the first Watchers were brought into existence because of the need to protect those fated. But the Morrigan ... they could truly *see*.

Durran had, years ago during the Great Wars, known that was a bit of a sore subject. At the time, the Elders and Morrigan had worked together to restore balance, but something had shifted between them. It was about that time that the Elders had retreated into the realm and only sent their younger ones out to continue the task of protecting.

"We plan to leave the city and seek out her mother at some of the last known places she used her aliases.

There are no leads on Victoria's father, but we are hopeful that once her mother is located, we will fully understand what she is," Durran continued, as if the energy of the room had not grown far more intense.

"You are certain of this connection to the Morrigan, Durran?" Uric asked, their voice more hesitant and quiet than Durran had ever heard it.

"Her mother's name was Fiona O'Morrigan," Durran supplied, seeing the wave of shock and horror move over the other Elders' faces. Mical seemed to become increasingly more infuriated.

"Where are you heading?" Galieb asked, eyes more focused on Mical's stiff form instead of Durran.

"Most of Fiona's known aliases have died out. I haven't yet decided where the best place to start would be. The three of us, myself, Victoria and her mate, will decide on a plan together, but I think, ultimately, we should head to Colorado. It seems Fiona spent quite a lot of time there before Victoria was born," Durran said, watching the way the other Elders eyed Mical more nervously. It was unlike the Elders to show much more than indifference. Mical was radiating rage, despite their cool exterior, their eyes glowed violently red.

"Good. Go there. Return to us once you have discovered more. The connection to the Morrigan is … well, this has made this situation more interesting," Rapha said quietly. Durran nodded, eyes moving over the Elders one last time before turning to leave the hall.

CHAPTER 5

Vee woke before Shane, as she usually did. His hand was limply resting on her hip, but he wasn't pressed to her. Quietly, she slipped out of the bed, snatching her clothes from the day before off the floor, and padded to the bathroom. She needed to be clean to tackle the day ahead of her. It was going to start off rather normal, opening the shop, finishing up the Vampire's house call, but it was going to end with packing for the trip, planning, and a pack meeting. Not exactly Vee's idea of a good time.

She got in the shower, her mind racing. She tried to close her end of the bond a little so Shane wouldn't be roused by her emotions fluctuating. Her anxiety about the day wasn't productive, but she just had to get through it. She finished showering and brushed her teeth before wandering into the walk-in closet to grab clean underwear and a shirt. The walk-in closet was probably her favorite part of the house. It had built-in drawers that Shane had evidently never really used. She hadn't wanted him to clear out his clothes from the dressers to make room for hers, so she'd opted to put her smaller items in the closet instead. The arrangement was perfect and allowed her to completely dress without having to go out to the bedroom. Very useful at times like this when she was trying to avoid waking him.

As she pulled her jeans on from the day before, she felt the weight of the items in her pockets. She had forgotten she'd put them there the night before, immediately being distracted by Lazare Duflanc showing up on the front lawn. She wasn't usually one to wear jewelry, but when she had first moved back to Kansas

City, she used to keep the key and the bone wolf on a leather cord around her neck. At some point the cord had broken, probably in the last few years, and she had simply placed them on the nightstand with the round crystal instead of replacing it.

Perhaps her life would not have become so upended if she had simply kept wearing them.

She went to set them on one of the shelves when, suddenly, the idea of leaving them at home for the day made the hair on her arms rise uncomfortably. She somehow *knew* she needed to keep them with her for now. She needed them close again. Vee had remembered when she came home to Kansas City, that the comfort of wearing them on her neck had been a sort of security blanket. Now she realized it wasn't just comfort. The hum of the magic against her skin felt protective.

She rifled around in her clothes for a piece of string, even a drawstring off one of her sweatpants, would do to hang them around her neck for the day. She was fairly certain she had a chain or something back at the shop that she would be able to use more permanently once she got there; she had plenty of odds and ends stashed in her inventory room.

Shane came in the bathroom as she was digging through the bottom drawer where she tended to haphazardly shove her sweats. He paused in the doorway to the closet, leaning against the frame and watching her with a questioning expression.

"Packing already?" he asked, causing her to look up at him.

"I feel like I need to wear these today," she murmured, opening her hand to show the key and the wolf, while she continued to dig with her other hand.

"And you're digging in your sweatpants drawer, because…?"

"I thought I might have a drawstring I could use to put them on really fast," she admitted, stopping as she said the words. She was being ridiculous and knew it. But she was trying to listen to the odd feelings, the instincts, the *knowing* she tended to get more often now. They usually meant something and she was done ignoring them, since trying to pretend they didn't hold significance got her in more trouble than not. If her body reacted that way to just the thought of leaving them behind today, she figured she would rather play it safe and keep them with her. "I'm just being crazy. I'll keep them in my pocket," she said, standing and stuffing them back where they had been.

"I have a chain," Shane said, moving to the back of the closet where another set of built-in drawers were. Vee had let those be, since they had various ties, belts, and watches carefully placed in there. He opened his watch drawer and pulled a box out from the back. The box was narrow and red, clearly a gift box. Vee had no idea how long the box had been in there. In fact, her stomach churned, feeling like maybe that box had belonged to Patricia, Shane's late wife.

"I can't use that," Vee said abruptly, as Shane turned around with it in hand.

"Why?" he asked, brow furrowed as he stepped closer. He hadn't even shown her what was inside. Why would she refuse a simple chain? She had closed her

side of the bond down, not in a malicious way but just so there was a small amount of her emotions as an undercurrent, instead of being something he could fully grasp at and understand. She usually did that when she was trying not to wake him in the morning, but he felt it shrink a bit more as her eyes focused on the red box in his hands.

"If that's..." Vee swallowed. She didn't want to refuse him, but she couldn't wear something that Patricia had worn. Shane thought for a moment after Vee lapsed into silence, his face softening when he realized the most likely culprit behind her reservations.

"Patricia's?" Shane asked. There were only a few things Vee seemed to shrink away from, and one of them was the memory of Patricia. He knew how careful she was about that particular topic, not wanting to remove or replace the only other woman who had held his heart before. They had gotten into quite a fight when he wanted to move Patricia's photo from his bedside table to his office. Vee had insisted it should stay where it was.

She looked away from the box and up into his brown eyes. He was smiling lightly, though she could feel a bit of sadness there at the thought of her.

"It wasn't hers. I got this for me, actually. When we get married, I won't be able to change with a wedding ring on. Thomas suggested keeping it at my neck instead," he told her, popping the box open and pulling out the golden chain.

Silver was supposed to lessen a Werewolf's powers, essentially becoming little better than a human, so it made sense that Shane's chain would be made of gold.

CHAPTER 5

The gold rather complemented Vee's skin as he placed it in her hand. She pulled the key and the wolf from her pocket once again, slipping them on the chain, before she brushed her hair over her shoulder, so the clasp wouldn't catch in it, and put it around her neck.

"Thank you," she whispered, looking at him from the mirror she was standing in front of. A smile touched his lips, but his eyes were hungry as they looked at her.

There she was, not even flinching when he mentioned them getting married. Last night, she had yelled at him and told him he was *hers*. And now she was, without hesitation, donning the chain he had planned to wear his wedding ring on, simply because he offered it to her. She, who fought so hard for her solitary life, continued to surprise him as she accepted him. And the mention of Patricia never seemed to scare her away either. It made her uneasy, but from what he caught from their bond, she loved him and Patrick and didn't want to take anything away, including Patricia's memory.

"You're beautiful," he said back quietly, unable to resist stepping up behind her and watching them in the mirror, as his lips came down to brush over the exposed skin on her neck. Heat rose to her cheeks. She still didn't think herself very pretty, with her large, almond-shaped eyes, partially hidden behind the dark curtain of her bangs. Her high cheekbones that came down to a small, pointed chin made her face look almost childish in her opinion, something that hadn't helped the overprotectiveness of her mate and Watcher. But she couldn't deny the way Shane looked at her, as if she were the most beautiful woman on the planet.

"We have too much to do today, Shane," she reminded him, not averting her eyes from the pull of his in the mirror.

"I won't make you late," he said, as his arm snaked around her and under her shirt.

Vee was packing her bag with supplies she might need for the lock reinstallation. She wasn't sure what would happen while she was there. Having Duflanc come to Shane's house the night before had been jarring and dangerous. She had come across Vampires a few times before in the city, but they never seemed to be drawn to her, always managing to skirt their attention. Her knowledge of Vampires was also very limited. Her little group of preternaturals that she'd spent the later part of her teenage years with didn't have much knowledge of them, choosing mostly to share what they knew of their own kind, Witch and Were.

And out of all her Vampire encounters, she had never come across someone as powerful as Duflanc seemed last night. It wasn't just the feeling specific to Vampires she felt from him; there was a wash of power as their eyes had met. A thrum of energy, dominance, that sparked in the air between him and Shane. She had meant to ask Shane what Duflanc's story was, but the night had gotten away from them.

Tommy, Lori, and Patrick all seemed to stroll in the shop at the same time. It was about 10 a.m.; the shop had been open only a few minutes, and the appointment at the Vampire nest was at eleven.

"So what's the plan for the day?" Patrick asked, after clocking him and Lori in on the tablet.

"Appointment, make signs for adjusted hours while I'm gone, and then close down early for the meeting," Vee said, the words coming out mildly pointed, since it was a mantra she had been going over in her head all day.

"Then you and Dad are leaving tonight?" Patrick asked, pulling out his own set of keys to unlock some of the display cases.

"That's what he said this morning. I feel like it's a little late to start a ten-hour drive, but he insisted. I also need to call Durran," Vee said, suddenly realizing she hadn't heard from her about what happened with the Elders and needed to let her know that their adventuring to track down her mother would have to wait until she and Shane went to see the Sha. She reached into her back pocket to snag her phone.

"Shane's probably going to have you stop somewhere partway to sleep tonight. Better than showing up to the Sha dead tired," Tommy said, posting up in his usual stool by the door. Vee used to have stools dispersed evenly by each counter. Somehow Tommy had migrated to one to sit watch, and it just never seemed to move from its new home again.

[Vee: There have been some developments. Pack meeting tonight. Have to go see the Sha. Vampire issues too.]

Vee glanced up after she sent the message just as a customer came through the front door. Lori greeted them sweetly, as usual.

[Durran: Lunch?]

[Vee: In Brookside.]

Vee wouldn't have the faintest idea of what to choose, and Durran had a very particular love for restaurants, so it was better to just give a general location and let Durran decide the final destination.

A knock came from the back door, not loud enough for the human customer to hear, but Vee and the Weres heard it quite clearly. A knock on the back door could mean one of two things. Either someone with ill intent was trying to lure Vee out in broad daylight—unlikely, but always a possibility—or it was Toby Curtis, the owner of the small renovation company that consisted of a five-man crew, who brought her antique locks. Vee was the first one to make it to the inventory room, Patrick and Tommy on her heels, protective and on edge.

Vee peeked through the peep hole, and there was Toby.

"It's Toby," Vee told Tommy and Patrick, who immediately visibly relaxed. She unlocked and opened the door, easily meeting his charming smile with one of her own.

Toby was rather short for a man, not much taller than Vee. His clear blue eyes twinkled as he looked at her and his sandy blond hair was a bit shaggy at the moment, peeking out from under his baseball cap as if he hadn't had time to cut it. Summer was his busiest time, so Vee suspected he'd cut it to its usual crew cut once everything died down. She had seen a lot of him over the past few months and had acquired quite the stock of locks to refurbish and sell at this point.

"I've got another box for you. Original fixtures from a 1903 house in the neighborhood. They're pretty beat up, but I figured if anyone could make them work like they used to, it was you," Toby said, arms outstretched to hand off the box. Vee took it, eyes eagerly looking at the contents within. There was a lot of old residual paint and quite a bit of rust, but these locks were magnificent in their irregular design. Handmade.

"Oh, these are going to be so fun to clean up," she said with excitement, turning to set them on a crate just inside the door. "Thank you," she told him as she turned back. He smiled sheepishly, hand instantly going to the back of his head in a nervous gesture. She knew he liked her and had known it for a while. Not that he wasn't a good guy, but even before Shane, she just knew it was too difficult to deal with humans in any sort of relationship other than distant friendship. She had wanted to keep herself safely alone.

"You're welcome, Vee. Hey Tommy, Patrick ... how's the new kitchen?"

It had been over a year since Shane had to have his kitchen and dining room renovated. The destruction was not any pack members' fault. Downing, the Were who caused the impromptu demolition of rooms, was now dead. But Shane did not like having outsiders in his house, so letting Toby and his small crew in to help with a few things the pack members weren't adept in completing had made him a friendly human acquaintance of the pack. Although Toby only knew that they all worked for Shane, not that they were Werewolves.

"It's great. Great enough, I bet we'll get over asking price when we move," Patrick said with a grin.

"Moving? Huh … well, don't forget about us when you and your dad get your new house. You know there's always something that needs fixing," Toby said, stepping backward over the threshold.

"Oh, I'll let him know," Patrick said, waving as Toby smiled one last time and headed back down the alley.

"He can never be around you when Shane is there," Tommy said, as soon as Vee snapped the door closed.

"What? Why?" Vee asked, turning back around and pulling the new box of locks back into her arms to examine them.

"The same reason Dad barely handles Durran's presence. But Toby isn't your Watcher, and I don't think Dad knows his feelings toward you," Patrick said unhappily, following Vee back out to the showroom. The customer had already left, and Lori was finish up settling the transaction on the tablet.

"I still don't understand," Vee groaned, setting the box down at her workstation.

"His heart rate and pheromones were … well, he's in love with you," Tommy told her, going back to sit on his stool again.

"Who? Toby?" Lori asked, getting a nod from Patrick and Tommy. "Oh yeah. He's got it bad. You're smart, funny, beautiful, and independent. And you have something in common, or at least a vague something—the locks."

Vee's face crumpled in dismay. She really liked Toby. They weren't what she would call "friends" because they basically only ever saw each other when he dropped locks off to her, but they did have enough in common that they had easy conversation normally, if no one else was around. She did not like the idea that she would have to push both his rare company, and probably this additional source of income, away.

She tried to release those troublesome thoughts from her mind by pulling out her magnifiers and getting engrossed in one of the new locks.

"Vee, you'll be late. I'll get them soaking in the paint thinner," Patrick told her, hand gently resting against hers that held the lock. For a moment Vee forgot what Patrick was talking about, but then she remembered, regretfully.

"Oh. The Vampires," Vee grumbled, letting the lock slide into Patrick's fingers and pulling her glasses away. "I'm going to lunch with Durran after this appointment. I'll probably be later than normal," Vee told him, pulling her bag over her head and meeting Tommy at the door where he stood up from his stool.

"Got to share all the good news with the Watcher, eh?" Patrick asked with a grin, as he carefully pulled the locks from the box.

"And probably get some more news from her," Vee said with a sigh, leaving the shop in the hands of her *mostly* capable Were employees and heading out with Tommy to face the Vampire nest.

CHAPTER 6

"Lunch with Durran, huh?" Tommy asked, once they were on the road. They were driving to the Vampire's house in her van, and she hadn't really considered how Tommy was going to be getting back to his truck, which was parked in front of her shop.

"Crap! Well ... you can come with us?" Vee offered sheepishly, her shoulders hunching as she gripped the steering wheel. Out of all the Weres in Vee's life, Durran seemed to like Tommy the best, so it didn't seem unreasonable to invite him. She wouldn't have gone so far as to call Durran and Tommy friends, but since he was often assigned as Vee's guard, Durran and Tommy had become comfortable around each other.

"I can always eat," Tommy said grinning, his white teeth showing beautifully against his bronze skin. He looked so much like his father, except where Thomas's skin was deep ebony, Tommy's was lighter. "I'll stay far enough away so I won't intrude on your conversation, if you don't mind. I think Shane wants me to stay with you until the meeting."

"You *think* or he ordered you to stay with me until the meeting?" Vee asked, eyebrow raised but eyes still trained on the road.

"You already know the answer to that, Vee," Tommy chuckled.

Traffic was light before eleven on a Friday. A little too early for lunch. They were early arriving at the house, so Vee parked a few houses down and let out a shaky breath. This neighborhood was full of old homes, most of them were closer to eighty years old, but this one was definitely one of the original houses in this particular area, meaning it was into its hundreds. It was an "off the beaten path" street for the neighborhood, not getting as much foot or vehicle traffic since it curved and merged with another street. Normally, Vee would have considered that to be something intriguing, giving the street and the neighborhood more character; instead, she thought it made the Vampire nest nestled there much more sinister. People could go missing here, right in the center of the city, and none would be the wiser.

"I don't think it would go over well if you came in with me, so stay on the sidewalk? I'll make this reinstallation as quick as I possibly can," Vee told Tommy, as her fingers nervously fiddled with the worn strap of her messenger bag.

"I'll stay far enough away to keep us out of trouble," Tommy told her, touching her shoulder comfortingly.

It was daylight, but a Werewolf entering the domain of a Vampire nest for any reason without an invitation could definitely cause conflict between them. The peace between preternaturals was a fine line, though Duflanc had already crossed it by approaching Shane's house the night before. Tommy didn't need to incite further tension by coming too close when they were resting.

They finally got out of the van, Vee hauling her various bags of supplies up to the door and Tommy finding a large oak tree to lean against, just outside of the property line. Holly pulled open the door before Vee had an opportunity to knock. She was furious, eyes pinched and nose wrinkled, which gave her youthful appearance a few more years. She still didn't seem threatening to Vee, but the hostility immediately gave Vee pause.

"You didn't call. This better be quick," Holly hissed, as she stepped aside to let Vee enter.

"That's the plan," Vee told her seriously, shivering involuntarily as she felt the icy chill of the Vampire minds once again. The last time she had been here, the minds were still, despite the way they made her brain tingle. This time, however, she felt a flicker of alertness, like there was a Vampire who was fighting to remain awake. From the little Vee knew about Vampires, there was no way for them to remain awake once the sun rose. They were dead to the world until morning. Feeling one of them struggle to stay alert made Vee's anxiety increase a fair amount. At least the entry was well lit from the open door.

"You got me in trouble yesterday. Of course there's something *special* about you. Just fix it and get out of my sight. The sooner you leave, the sooner his attention comes back to me," Holly spat, crossing her arms and leaning against the wall a few feet from the door. Her pout was reminiscent of a child's, eyes narrow and shoulders stiff.

Vee smiled tightly, setting her bags on the ground and getting to work removing the temporary fixture she had put in place the day prior. It hadn't been the greatest fit, so she didn't have to work too hard to get it out. She pulled the box that held the original lock out of her bag, then carefully removed it and placed it in its hollow home to see how it would fit back in there, just in case she had to add some filler or adjust something. Holly sighed as Vee pulled the refurbished lock back out and began adding quick-dry wood filler to a few places. They wouldn't dry fast enough for a screw to take purchase, but they would keep the lock steady and in place.

"Can you just screw it in so you can go?" Holly hissed.

"Does your *master* want it done fast, or does he want it done right?" Vee asked, not looking away from what she was doing. The woman scoffed, pushing herself from the wall and storming out of the entry, much to Vee's pleasure.

She glanced at Tommy, who still stood within her eyesight, as she felt a second mind stir from below. Two Vampires awake in the day? She willed the filler to dry faster, placing the lock back in and carefully screwing it into place. She didn't want to pull too hard on it; it would still take a few hours for the filler to

fully dry and set before vigorous movement was recommended, but it was sturdy and lined up properly when she tested it.

"Finished," Vee said loudly, so Holly's human ears would be able to hear her. Having superior hearing herself, as well as regularly being surrounded by Weres, made her forget sometimes that she needed to be louder for the humans around her. Cora often complained that everyone was mumbling.

Vee tossed her tools and supplies back in her bags and stood to wait for the angry intended to return to her. The consciousness of the multiple Vampires made her want to run for it. She was very nearly at the point of snatching her bags and running out, payment or no, when Holly stumbled back into the entry. A check was clutched in one trembling hand, as she looked at Vee with glazed-over eyes.

"Holly? Are you okay?" Vee said, hesitating to approach her. Holly's thin frame shook and moved oddly before it settled in place a few feet from Vee, head awkwardly angled as if she was struggling to keep it up. She sucked in a breath that seemed to rattle in her chest, making chills run up Vee's back.

"I don't have long, but you should stay far away from here, Victoria Malone." The words came from Holly's lips, but the voice was not her own. Although the voice was strange coming from her mouth, it was still barely a whisper so that only Vee could hear the words, even to others in the house. Vee could slowly see small, red, smoky tendrils of magic coming from Holly's eyes and mouth. She was entranced.

"I'm planning on it," Vee whispered back, frozen at the door.

"Lazare Duflanc wants you. He wants to taste your blood—special blood—and make you *his*," said the voice.

"Who are you?" she asked.

"You have many enemies you don't know, but you also have allies who hide. Your blood carries power, danger, and protection."

"You didn't answer my question," Vee responded stubbornly. The cryptic, vague messages were getting tired.

"I cannot here. But the madness has already started to consume him. *Stay away*," it said, before Vee watched Holly's body seize up and then deflate, like something had taken inhabitance within her and then very suddenly left. The magic snaking through Holly's eyes and mouth seemed to disappear with the presence, and Vee stood there watching as Holly's eyes returned to their normal state. She caught herself on the doorframe, blinking a few times before they settled back on Vee.

"I should probably eat something. I forget sometimes," she told Vee, clearly thinking she had a dizzy spell or briefly lost consciousness. She seemed to have no idea the conversation that had just occurred.

"Believe it or not, I completely understand," Vee said, stepping forward to take the check so Holly could remain where she stood, with the wall keeping her steady. "Thank you. Don't call on me again," Vee said firmly, slinging her bags over her shoulders.

"I hope I don't have to," Holly murmured, her emotions a mix of exhaustion, confusion, guilt, and the briefest remnant of jealousy.

Vee snapped the door shut behind her, hurriedly heading straight to Tommy, who was no longer leisurely leaning against the tree but pacing at the end of the front walk.

"What the hell was that? I smelled magic and saw you tense," he hissed as she approached.

"In the car," was all she said in response, moving immediately past him to head to her van. They got in; Vee's breath was ragged, and Tommy's eyes glowed blue. She turned the car on and pulled away from the curb before either of them made a noise.

"I think someone took over her mind," she said quietly, not trusting her voice not to shake.

"I heard some old Vampires can do that, but … it's day," Tommy said, gesturing to the clear blue sky above them, frustration and confusion joining with her own.

"She was like a puppet. Her body was wrong," Vee murmured, pulling up into one of the few parking spots available in the Brookside shopping plaza. A few minutes longer and she wouldn't have found one.

The Brookside shops had been modeled to look like a quaint, old Germanic village. Small and expensive storefronts boasted boutiques and eateries to entice the higher-end clientele that lived in the area. There were also two grocery stores within two blocks of one another. One standard, and the other called a "market" that was supposed to be better quality products, though from what Vee had seen, most of them were the same; they just charged more for them.

Vee liked the little area aesthetically, but the traffic and the people made her cringe. She spent a lot more time here, now that she lived with Shane, but she much preferred the Midtown people she saw at her shop.

"I didn't hear what it said," Tommy confided, turning to watch Vee as she shakily turned off the van.

"They said, 'You also have allies who hide.' What is that supposed to mean?" Vee asked. Tommy shook his head. Vee's phone sounded from its spot in her bag. She pulled it out and looked at the message there.

[Durran: Jalapeños.]

That was all the text from Durran said, indicating the staple restaurant in the neighborhood. Mexican food was often Durran's go-to, so it wasn't a surprise.

"Let's go chat with Durran. Maybe she will make some sense of it," Vee said, climbing out of the van and heading to the back door of the restaurant.

Tommy seemed too big in the small back hallway of the restaurant as they made their way toward the front. He had to duck to get under the archway that led to the dining room. Durran stood at the host station, eyebrows raising as Vee and Tommy strolled over to her.

"It seems I was mistaken, it will be three today," Durran murmured to the host, who seemed bored more than anything.

"The booth should fit three," she said, snatching menus and waving unseeingly at them to follow her. There was very little privacy in this particular restaurant, but something about the place made it seem like no one was really paying attention to anyone else.

Vee slid into the booth and Tommy squeezed in beside her, only once the host was setting the menus down in front of them did she realize how large, both in height and bulk of muscle, Tommy was. Her eyebrows shot up in surprise as he somehow managed to push the table away from their side of the booth enough for him to not feel so closed in. A booth for six probably would have been better, but no one said anything. The host just stared for a moment, with mouth wide open, before she turned abruptly and walked away, leaving Durran to slide into the other side. Thankfully, Durran was quite thin.

"Tommy," Durran said, with a nod in his direction.

"Durran," Tommy said with a grin, picking up the menu to look over the options.

"I'm assuming a protection detail has to do with Vampires?" Durran asked, also picking up the menu as if she were deciding what she wanted, even though Vee was fully aware Durran had already selected what she would eat as soon as she'd made the decision to come here.

"Yep," Tommy said, letting the "p" pop as he said it.

"Apparently, a big, bad Vampire followed my scent and broke the pack protection to come to Shane's house last night," Vee said, glancing at Tommy.

"Just by following your scent?" Durran asked, bringing Vee's attention back to her.

"Apparently," Vee repeated dryly.

"Interesting," Durran murmured, brow furrowed as the server came by with waters and chips and salsa.

"Do you all need a few more minutes?" she asked perkily. She actually *felt* that odd enthusiasm, which was a bit refreshing to Vee. Most servers put on a facade that Vee could see right through, but this woman was genuinely happy to be serving them. Perhaps it was because they were her first customers of the day.

"Just a few, thank you," Durran said, smiling lightly.

"So what did the Elders have to say?" Vee asked, once the server was well-enough away. Durran's mouth downturned, feelings growing tainted with uncertainty.

"There's something in the past between the Elders and the Morrigan. It's a concern, but we have more pressing ones. They seemed pacified by our plans to go searching," Durran told her. Vee felt the familiar pit in her stomach. The way Durran said there was something between the Elders and the Morrigan in the past made Vee want to be sick. As of right now, they were protecting her by assigning Durran as her Watcher but that was always subject to change.

"The searching might have to wait a little longer. The Sha called on Shane and Vee," Tommy said, clearly unable to hold up his previous promise to give them privacy. It was hard to stay out of a conversation when he was squished in the booth right next to them.

"Ah, yes ... that complication," Durran said, letting amusement touch her face.

"Shane and I are required to see them. We're heading out tonight after the pack meeting," Vee told her, her mind suddenly filling with all the things she still needed to complete before they left.

"Where are the Sha?" Durran asked.

"Colorado. Well ... that's the closest doorway," Tommy said, eyes still on the menu.

"Doorway?" Vee asked, watching his face, which seemed unfazed.

"Hard to explain, and I've never seen it. I think my dad has," Tommy told her, turning to look at her dumbfounded face. Vee wasn't sure what that meant. She had assumed they were in Colorado because there was plenty of wilderness and a few parts where humans never strayed. Tommy made it sound like it wasn't exactly located where she had imagined it was.

"So what's the pack meeting about?" Durran asked, setting the menu on the end of the table.

"All of this, I imagine, and that we have to move," Vee said, hunching a little more.

"The Vampire thing," Tommy offered to clarify, when Durran's expression abruptly changed at the mention of moving.

"Ah." Durran was still nodding in understanding as their server returned. They ordered: Tommy got two entrees, Durran's eyes sparkled as she ordered the flautas meal, and Vee went with the enchiladas over the fajitas she had originally wanted, since the table space was going to be limited. The menus got taken away, and Vee finally felt like she could reach the chips and salsa on the table that Tommy had been hoarding.

"I was going to suggest we start our search in Colorado, since Breckenridge is the last place I tracked her. It was thirty years ago, but that's her last known, except for Ireland when you were born, as far as I could find," Durran said, continuing the conversation as Vee began devouring chips.

"The Sha won't let a Watcher in," Tommy warned, eyeing Durran warily.

"I can ask around and do some investigating while Vee and Shane are with the Sha," Durran grumbled, glaring slightly at the Were across from her. It wasn't so much that Tommy had confirmed she wouldn't be allowed there that bothered her; it was more that she wouldn't be with Vee when she was put in a particularly threatening environment. Shane was a powerful Werewolf, but he would be no match for the full power and numbers of the Sha. Whatever protection Vee had, be it with the bond between her and Shane or her Watcher, she would essentially be vulnerable and alone before some of the oldest and most powerful creatures.

"I don't think they'd kill me, Durran. Shane may not be a Sha, but I don't think they'd want any trouble from him either," Vee said quietly, having felt her emotions.

"The Elders might consider you a threat because of your connection to the Morrigan. I could see it all over their faces. They rarely show emotions, but that information struck a nerve, Vee. Who knows how the Sha will react to you," Durran hissed quietly, leaning closer to the two of them.

"Shane wouldn't take Vee if he felt she was truly in danger," Tommy told them both when Vee stiffened beside him.

"No. I suppose he wouldn't," Durran ground out through clenched teeth. There were still moments when the reminder that Vee was Shane's tugged on Durran's heart. She knew how strong their bond was, having felt it both times it had been put in place. Shane loved Vee, that much Durran couldn't deny. She just had to trust he would protect her.

CHAPTER 7

Patrick had called his dad the moment Vee's van started up, and Vee and Tommy were safely out of hearing range down the street, heading to the appointment with the Vampires. They hadn't really gotten an opportunity to discuss how their birthday surprise for Vee was dashed as soon as that Vampire showed up in their front yard. Shane had enlisted Patrick and Lori to help him transform the unused attic space into a workshop for her. The final plans were supposed to take place while Vee and Shane went searching for answers about her mother, since her birthday was only a month away. Of course, now they would have to move, so there was no point.

"What are we supposed to do about her birthday now?" Patrick asked instead of a hello over the phone, as if Shane had been thinking the same thing.

"We're getting a whole new house. She'll be able to make it more her own, and we can build her a workshop there too," Shane said, seamlessly falling into the train of thought that had apparently been going through his son's head. Patrick could hear his father's fingers moving rapidly across the keyboard.

"Has George had any luck?" Patrick asked. George was their pack realtor. He had been a member of quite a few packs before he settled in Kansas City. He was not extraordinarily dominant, and sometimes that could mean trouble in a wolf pack. With Shane's leadership, George seemed right at home and had for quite a few years. He may not have been a dominant Werewolf, but he certainly dominated the real estate scene.

"It's not easy finding enough houses in the same general area. Some of the pack might be able to stay where they are. I'm going to have to consult the Sha about how to avoid this in the future," Shane murmured.

"Mom's pretty broken up about leaving our house, but Dad caved," Lori said grinning from the other side of the room. No phone call was really private around Weres. Patrick smiled at the little, wicked glint in her eye. She was recalling how the argument last night in their kitchen, after Thomas had gotten off the phone with the second pack member he called, ended with him promising Cora she could design a dream house. "She had him practically begging for shiplap by the time I went to bed."

Patrick cringed. Lori laughed.

"Thankfully, I don't think Vee cares as much as Cora," Shane said, his voice oozing with sympathy

for his second-in-command. "She and Tommy just left, then?"

"A few minutes ago, and then she's going to lunch with Durran to fill her in," Patrick said, pulling on some gloves to see how well the paint thinner was stripping the old locks.

"Yes, she texted me about that. Did she say what she planned on doing after that?" he asked.

"Pretty much just getting the shop set for her being away and heading home. She likes to close a little earlier on Fridays anyway," Patrick told him, as Lori came over with a handful of fresh towels and the toothbrushes Vee used to carefully brush off any stubborn spots. The paint came off the one he grabbed with barely a swipe of his gloved thumb.

"To avoid the Friday bar crowd," Shane said knowingly. "Patrick, I know I have Tommy with her, but just stay there until she actually starts heading home, please?"

"We rode with Tommy, so I'll ride home with her," Patrick assured him before they hung up.

Vee and Tommy got back to the shop after 1 p.m.; the restaurant had picked up business as they were eating and their happy server became immediately overwhelmed, which meant it took a while for them to settle their bill. Vee had to remind herself the whole ride back that Patrick and Lori were there and nothing bad was going to happen because she was a little late returning. After all, she was about to leave for some unknown period of time. Being away from the shop an extra hour during lunch was not going to kill her.

When they arrived, Patrick was finishing cleaning paint thinner off the locks he had started soaking when they left, and Lori was on the computer uploading photos of the most recent custom locks Vee made. Those two had been slowly, but diligently, working on building her a website to sell her pieces, with very little involvement from her. That was for the better, because she would have given up on it the moment she had to try to do anything that took more than an hour away from her work.

"No house calls while you were gone," Patrick told her before she could ask.

"Good," she grumbled, tossing her bag under the counter.

"The paint on these came right off. I was going to put them in the next solution to eat the rust, but I figured you'd want to look at them first," he said, stepping aside for her to look them over. He had been trying to learn things to help her every now and then. Over the last few months, Vee had decided to teach him the proper way instead of having him try to do it himself. One antique lock had been sacrificed that way. She couldn't be mad at him for trying, but she shuddered at the way it had corroded beyond repair overnight.

"These don't look too bad, actually," she said, turning one over in her hands. The rust was mild, and these were in some of the best shape she had ever seen come from one of Toby's projects. "You go ahead and finish these. When I get back, I'll let you help me get them in working order," she said, looking up in time to see his eyes light up. It reminded her of the way she used to feel when her mentor had let her try something new.

Just thinking about him made her eyes sting a little. He had been an old, grumpy man that owned his own shop, like she did. She had originally planned on opening her own shop when he retired, helping him through his last few years after she had become certified under his tutelage. She had still been working a few days a week at a restaurant to make ends meet and got a call from the hardware store where they bought things to keep in stock.

He had died at the hardware store. A heart attack, they thought. He had no family, no will, no one but her who cared what happened to him. His property and money went to the state, and she had to scrape together what little she had to make her shop a reality.

Vee took in a shaky breath, returning her focus to Patrick. Was that lonesome life what Vee had really wanted for herself not long ago? No one to miss her when she was gone?

Vee gave Patrick a quick side hug, him returning it a little extra tight.

She turned her attention to making some signs for the reduced hours. Honestly, her hours could always be reduced, given how she only seemed to get business midday, with the occasional person thinking she should be open well into the night.

"What are you going to do while we're gone?" Vee asked Lori, as she snagged a piece of paper from the printer.

"Finish your new website. It's almost there; I'll just wait until you're back to launch it!" Lori told her excitedly. Additional income sounded nice, but Vee still wasn't sure how she would manage running the business on top of creating enough inventory to keep up with online orders.

"You'll have to help me keep up with it. I have no idea how I'm going to stay on top of everything when you and Patrick go back to school," Vee said, as she uncapped the massive permanent marker in her hand and bent down to start making her signs.

"Oh, I will. I'm also making social media accounts for the shop too," Lori said, as she disgustedly pulled the marker from Vee's hand. "I'll just type some signs out, shall I?" she said in response to Vee's questioning expression.

"I hate social media," Vee groaned.

"But you'll get more business," Lori said firmly, leaving no room for Vee to argue.

Vee sighed, leaving Lori to the task of printing out more professional-looking signs and went back to the front to help Patrick with the repairs and finish the last few hours of the day in relative normalcy until she said goodbye to her little shop. Not for the last time, of course, but she had no idea how long it would be before they were back.

Shane had buttoned up the last of his clients' needs for the weekend and started to peruse the list of houses George had sent over. There were quite a few; the market was up, and people were ready to sell. The pack members that were in this particular neighborhood were

going to have to move, but some of the others spread a bit more around the city would be fine. Thomas and Emily, one of their relatively newer pack members, had gone to all of them to be certain their protections were still in place earlier that morning and found they were intact. That saved some of the headache.

He liked a few of the houses on the list, but he knew they were all much more exuberant than Vee would like. She had a hard enough time getting used to living in his current house. Part of her relative comfort, he assumed, was because she had spent most of a year coming there off and on to check pack members' kids to see if they'd turn when they came of age before the claim and the bond were in place between them.

His cellphone rang, giving him a much-needed excuse to ignore the list—it would be better for him and Vee to look at them together, anyway—and see who was calling.

Lieb. The Shawnee pack leader's name illuminated on his phone. His eyes narrowed in suspicion.

"Lieb," Shane answered.

"I hear you'll be passing through my territory," he said, his voice giving off a little smugness. It was traditional to at least warn another pack leader when a Were was passing through the territory, which is exactly what Shane had done. Lieb and his second had both gotten the text message from Shane that detailed their planned trajectory through the state of Kansas.

"As I said earlier," Shane confirmed.

"Going to see the Sha?"

There was little other reason for Shane to be going through that particular state. He only ever ventured across the state line that hugged close to the city he called home when there was a particularly good restaurant or store to go to on the other side. There really wasn't much beyond Wichita. Shane did not like being in other pack territories. Having the stake on territory and proximity to the whole pack gave an advantage to that leader—a dominance that unsettled Shane's wolf, even though he was much more powerful than the average leader.

"Yes, they requested our presence."

"Maybe it's better you got to keep your little empath to yourself. I wouldn't want to be in your shoes," Lieb snickered. Shane held back a growl.

Six months prior, Lieb had all but demanded a meeting to see Vee. His intention had been to ... *share* her, until Shane staked his claim. Though grotesque as Lieb's views were on women, and his abrasive, often abusive behavior toward his pack—which was not abnormal for a pack leader—it was a relief when the pack that had been working with Gwen's coven and the Watcher Cormac had not been Shane's closest neighbors as he had initially suspected, but instead the St. Louis pack that he shared some of the state of Missouri with. Pack territories didn't always line up with state lines.

"Did you call just to tell me that?" Shane asked dryly. There was a brief but heavy silence on the other end.

"Your Vee..." He paused, as though trying to figure out exactly what to say. "She knew your youngest one, the girl, was a wolf before any of you did, right?"

Shane narrowed his eyes.

"She did."

WHITE MOON

Lieb let out a breath he seemed to have been holding.

"Can she tell before the change is close?" Lieb's voice was quiet on the other end, shaking a little as he spoke. Shane had not been expecting that. Given the very quiet way Lieb spoke, Shane could tell there was some importance there that he wasn't fully aware of. Whatever it was, Lieb didn't want to reveal it to his pack.

"We'll be making a stop in Hays overnight. If you decide to join us for breakfast with whatever child it is, she may be able to tell you," Shane said, quietly enough that only Lieb would have been able to hear him if he happened to have company in an adjacent room.

"I'll see you tomorrow morning," Lieb said quickly, before he hung up the phone.

Shane sighed. The shake in Lieb's voice had been enough to tell Shane there was something a bit more than just concern lingering in the other pack leader's head. Enough to ask for help, something many leaders tended to struggle with. It was difficult for a dominant wolf to show weakness to anyone, let alone another leader. Shown to the wrong wolf, there might be blood.

He heard Vee's van pull up outside, causing him to glance at the clock. It was about 4:30 p.m., a good hour and a half before the meeting. Shane started down the stairs as they began walking in the door.

"I'll be fine, Vee. Tommy is going to stay at the house with me. Lori and I will be occupied with the shop. I won't have time to get into any trouble," Shane heard Patrick say, his voice annoyed.

"We won't get a chance to have this talk before everyone else gets here," Vee grumbled, dropping her

94

keys haphazardly into the empty planter on the narrow table. For some reason, Shane loved that little thing. It was glazed in a bright teal with some bold geometric designs on it that didn't match anything in his house. It was perfectly out of place, perfectly Vee, and he loved it.

"I'm not going to do anything stupid, Vee. I haven't gotten into any fights or anything in —"

"Since Vee's been here," Shane said with a smile. It was strange, but true. Something about Vee living with him had grounded Patrick in a way that neither Shane nor Patrick had been expecting. The last few months of the school year had proved to be some of the calmest for them since Patrick's change.

"I just felt like it needed to be said anyway," Vee said indignantly, as she set her bag on the table next to the planter. Shane grinned at her, and her face changed from stubborn to sheepish. He liked how protective she was of his son.

"What time are you leaving?" Patrick asked, trying to hide his own sly smile by turning to his dad. Of course, Vee could feel the amusement coming from him, but she decided it was less embarrassing for them both to leave that be.

"Right after the meeting," Shane told them both, feeling how Vee had wondered that too.

"I have to pack," Vee said, her voice a little panicked, darting up the stairs.

"Are we going to eat?" Patrick asked, eyes glancing toward the kitchen, hoping one of the pack members or their human partners was in there whipping something together so he wouldn't have to.

WHITE MOON

"I placed an order for pizza first thing this morning. Takes a lot to feed the pack, but they had all day to plan," Shane murmured, feeling only *slightly* guilty about placing an order for twenty-five extra-large pizzas. He had gotten the confirmation email and phone call, so he knew it was in the works. He would be sure to tip extremely well.

Vee had burst into their bedroom and gone immediately to the closet. Her smaller duffle was sitting on a stool in the middle of the room. Nothing was packed in it yet, but based on the suitcase that was sitting on the floor beside the stool, Shane had pulled it out from the top shelf where she had shoved it when she'd finally stopped living out of her bags. She was thankful, yet again, that she could do her laundry regularly for the second time in two days and began shoving things in. It wasn't until the bag was full that she realized she probably would prefer *not* to meet the Sha wearing wrinkled T-shirts. She took it all back out and tried rolling everything into tight bundles to avoid that very embarrassing thought.

CHAPTER 8

Shane stood on the stairs. Only a few steps up from the bottom but from that vantage point, he could see every member between the front of the living room, the dining room, and the center hall where he stood. Card tables had been brought in to expand the usual dining table, so nearly everyone had a place to sit. It wasn't practical to have a table as large as the one they kept at the Pleasant Hill property at this house. The dining room just wasn't large enough for that.

Vee sat on the steps at Shane's feet. She had gotten a lot better about handling the vibrations of the whole pack in one location, but it still made her a little unsteady. Sitting was better. The plush carpet on the stairs didn't hurt either.

Everyone had quieted. They had spent the first twenty minutes eating and chatting while they waited

for the last few to arrive. Now that everyone was there, it was time for Shane to speak. Vee could feel Shane's power flow from him outward to the Weres beyond. It was a silent indication that the meeting was started, and they all quieted down to listen.

"Thank you for coming," he started.

"I'm always down for free food," Tommy said loudly, making them all chuckle lightly. Shane let a small smirk quirk up at the corner of his mouth but waited until the pack quieted again before he continued.

"As some of you know, the pack protection on the houses directly in this area has been broken. It's been a while, but those of you affected will need to move. George has compiled a list of houses for everyone who needs it with your particular necessities in mind." Shane gestured to George to pass out the folders.

"Why can't we just put it back up?" came John Meyers's voice from the dining room. Patrick glared at him across two rooms from where he sat in the living room. Vee, being more accustomed to the feel of Patrick's particular mind, could feel his irritation oozing out as he stared down the other Were.

"Lazare Duflanc has come to my home. There is no amount of pack magic that will keep him from getting through to us now. It's not safe," Shane told them, eyes beginning to lighten to his wolf's gold.

Whispers started to circulate. Shane sent out another wave of power to silence them, causing all their heads to turn back to him with a start.

"That's not all," Shane started, reaching up to rub his forehead, his nervous habit. "Unfortunately, Vee and I have been summoned by the Sha. I'm hoping this will only take a day or two. At the latest a few days, and we'll be back midweek. Thomas and Margaret will keep me posted on how things are moving along. Everyone needs to be on watch for Duflanc and his Vampires. I put the new patrol rotation on the shared drive. This is for everyone's protection."

"How did it happen? How did Duflanc get past the protection?" John interrupted again. The energy in the air shifted, and everyone stiffened. It made the hair stand up on the back of Vee's neck. She could feel Shane's anger rising as his eyes slid over to John once more.

"He tracked Vee's scent. I assume since she hasn't been fully integrated as a member of the pack, the protection did not extend to her," Shane ground out. Vee could feel the tension coming from him as he said it.

Vee looked up at Shane. He hadn't mentioned to her that she hadn't been fully integrated. She thought bonding to him had made her a member, but apparently she was wrong. It made some sense to her now though. There were bonds formed between pack members too. Shane had mentioned that he could feel them and they him, as well as everyone else in the pack, though it was easier for him to shut them out and close those bonds down for privacy. She never felt anything from the pack other than her normal abilities. They were going to have to talk about that, but now wasn't the time.

But something was off with the way Shane suddenly was so angry at John and protective of her.

"So she's done it again…" John murmured. Vee was having a hard time picking out the individual emotions, having so many people in the house, but her knowledge of body language, the way his eyes seared into her for a brief moment, told her that the contempt she was feeling mildly, over the sea of other emotions, was from him.

"Vee hasn't *done* anything," Margaret snapped, her eyes having started to glow.

"She's brought nothing but problems for us. We're lucky no one is dead … *yet*." John bit the last word out, his teeth snapping angrily.

Vee was shocked. She had never gotten the impression anyone in the pack didn't like her. She had been welcomed with open arms, as far as she knew, which had been a surprise. And with those open arms, she realized this was the second time she had felt accepted into anything, except for her little, odd group of pre-ternaturals that she had stayed with when she was a teenager. Apparently, she had been wrong about a great many things in regard to the pack.

Shane was nearly vibrating with anger beside her. She stood, placing her hands on his clenched fist until he relaxed his fingers and let her lace hers between them. His anger subsided, but only a little, with the gesture.

"We are actively working to determine who and what Vee comes from. Once we know more, we can adjust our protections accordingly. Unfortunately, the Sha have changed our plans," Shane said, eyes piercing into John's. John stared back for a moment, a challenging look, before he let his eyes drop. Shane was clearly the more dominant of the two. "We leave tonight. Go home," Shane said with finality.

The pack started to file out of the house. Margaret and Thomas stayed in their seats near Shane and Vee, watching John as he shoved through the crowd making their way out. Once most of them were gone, Vee turned to Shane.

"Looks like we have plenty to talk about on our long drive," she grumbled, feeling his internal flinch.

"I don't know what John's problem is. Vee even looked into his youngest," Tommy said, his face a scowl as he still stared at the door. That was probably why John's reaction felt so shocking to Vee. One of the last pack member's children she had gotten the impression of was John's youngest son. Perhaps the fact that the child was *not* going to be a Were had tipped the scales of his favor.

"There are many things bothering John. The first of which is that I became the leader of this pack after O'Neil and not him," Shane offered, coming down off the stairs and moving to start folding chairs up.

"You killed O'Neil; of course you would become leader," Thomas grumbled, following Shane's example as Patrick and Lori started clearing paper plates and cans of soda that had been left behind on the tables.

"So he's jealous?" Vee asked, as she pushed the trashcan closer to the pile that was threatening to spill out of Lori's hands.

"Of a multitude of things," Margaret told her quietly, though all the other Weres in the room could clearly hear her.

They cleaned up in silence after that, the front rooms back to looking as they usually did in very little time. Soon after, they said their goodbyes, Margaret hopping in her SUV while Thomas and Lori waved before they walked across the street to their home. Tommy was going to stay at the house with Patrick while Vee and Shane were gone, so he snagged his bag from his truck bed and hurried back inside.

"We'll let you know when we get to Hays," Shane told them, as he pulled Patrick in for a hug.

"I'll keep an eye on him," Tommy assured them as he ruffled Patrick's hair. Patrick shot him a searing look at the gesture, but Vee felt the bubble of affection toward Tommy within him. Packs were family, and Tommy was more like an older brother to Patrick than his real brother, Ethan, was.

Earlier in the day, Emily had brought one of the Jeeps from the warehouse full of pack vehicles. Vee supposed it made sense that they'd need something better suited for rough terrain; they were heading to Colorado, after all. They had already put their bags in the back before the pack meeting started, so they just simply had to head out.

Vee climbed into the unfamiliar vehicle with a little trepidation. The day had been mostly normal—except for the Vampire speaking through a human in broad daylight—but work and a pack meeting were standard fare for her at this point. It had allowed her a distraction, so she didn't feel like anything monumental was actually happening. Now that she was sitting in the Jeep and Shane was starting the car, it was real. They were going to see the Sha.

"John Meyer tried to form a bond with his human wife," Shane said out of nowhere, once they were on the road. Vee's head snapped over to look at him; that was quite a revelation.

"It didn't work?" she asked, brow raised. She had no idea the ins and outs of mating bonds, despite having one herself.

"No. Which was not a surprise. She's fully human. Not an ounce of magic in that woman, and he somehow thought he could bond to her," Shane scoffed, his hands gripping the steering wheel. "Claims can and do happen all the time. That magic works just fine with a human, but the bond cannot form with them. Even if he *had* managed it…" He trailed off, his lips forming a grim line. "The toll her eventual death would take on him…" Shane shuddered a bit at the thought. The idea of feeling Vee die was enough to make him sick. A slow, painful human death? Complete agony.

There were many Weres who had human spouses. Shane himself, had had a human wife. While he didn't have to go through the pain of watching Patricia age before death, there were a few members of the pack who had ailing spouses while the Weres themselves remained untouched by age. John was an old Were who had already had several human wives before his current wife, Susan. Until her, all of John's kids had also been human, so it wasn't just the agony of watching his wife age and die, but he also had watched many of his children go as well. None of them had wanted to try to change and be like him.

"We don't know how long I'll live," Vee said quietly, more as an echo to the feeling from Shane. They had no idea about her lifespan, but Shane hoped, given what her mother's letter had said about having a long life, it would not be the short, brutal one of a human.

"We don't know enough yet," Shane said, glancing over at her, having felt her anxiety grow.

They were quiet for a few more minutes while they both got over the horrible possibility of her aging and dying while Shane stayed looking just as he always did. Vee let out a breath and then turned to Shane again, recalling the other thing from the meeting she hadn't known.

"I'm not pack, huh?" she asked. Shane's foot pressed a bit more on the accelerator.

"No."

"I thought our bond…"

"Pack magic is a separate thing. I don't know if you *can* be brought in," Shane admitted, the feeling of protectiveness for her only increasing, hanging in the air.

"Because I'm not a Were," Vee said, understanding though feeling a little like she had been lied to.

"Yes. We could try, but…" Shane trailed off. Thinking of doing the ritual to bring her into the pack made him cringe. It was animalistic and grotesque. Blood magic. He hadn't wanted to bring it up to her unless he knew for certain it was something that would work. He didn't want to disgust her. Being a Werewolf meant he was a monster who dealt in blood and death. He didn't want her to see that side of him any more than she already did.

"It would protect the pack, wouldn't it?" she asked, feeling his fear and disgust. She knew how he felt about himself, about what he was, though she disagreed. He was beautiful in his wolf form; it fit with him just as any other part of his personality. She also knew she could handle a lot more than he thought she could.

CHAPTER 8

"It would help," he murmured.

"We should try," she said with finality, turning her gaze back to the road before them.

Shane glanced at her, taking in her soft profile and the mild furrow in her brow she got when she was determined. She had the protective fire of a wolf tucked in her small and fragile frame. He never failed to be amazed by that. She had allowed so much change in her life, given herself over to this new life with less trepidation than he had expected. He would go to the ends of the earth to protect her, to fight beside her. Why did he continue to hide things from her for fear of her running away? She continued to prove time and time again that she wasn't running.

"You have said before that I'm your True Mate. What does that mean?" Vee asked suddenly, breaking the silence and bringing Shane's anxiety back full force.

Shane hadn't been expecting that question. He hadn't been avoiding talking to her about it, exactly; it just never seemed to come up. How to explain that to her?

"It's hard to explain," he admitted, moving around a big rig that was going too slow in front of them.

"Can you try?" Vee asked, turning her body in the seat to look at him more fully.

He adjusted in his seat a bit, trying to decide how to start.

"When I first realized your scent was something my instincts told me I should take notice of, I went half crazy. I *had* to find you, had to see you. Just a day before you saved Lori, I had figured out your scent was everywhere. You had been in my house and other pack members' houses. Your scent lingered long after you weren't around. At first, I thought the pull to find you was because you might be a threat to us. Someone who knew too much about us to be left without at least a confrontation. But when I met you that night, I knew it wasn't that.

"You were no threat. There was no reason for me to feel this unconscious and unquenchable urge to be near you. I had barely known you, and yet, when the threat of you being killed became a concern, I couldn't stand it. I had to protect you at all costs. It only got worse as I got to know you. Those months from when I met you until the claim were agonizing. If I could have justified seeing you every day, I would have.

"You had become like a drug. An addiction I couldn't shake, but I didn't want to shake it either. It became less about the instinctual pull and more about *you* as time went on. So interesting, and stubborn, and fiery, and beautiful. I knew once the claim was in place, even before the bond, that I was supposed to be yours. It was powerful in a way that I had never experienced. I had only heard of it happening long ago for others.

"I can't confirm it; there's no way to test it, but I just *know*," Shane concluded, his voice so quiet as he finished speaking that if Vee had human hearing, she wouldn't have caught it.

She took in his story. Some of it she knew, just from being bonded to him. She had also felt that inexplainable pull to him; in fact, she still did. How many times had they passed each other by in the years before they had met and never knew? Had her sometimes unexplainable and overwhelming depression and loneliness over that time stemmed from moments when she very nearly met him by coincidence?

Vee reached over and put her hand on his leg, causing him to glance at her.

"True Mates," she said, seeming to roll that around in her mind for a moment. She looked back at him, at the handsome sharp features of his face. The way his jaw clenched down as he waited for her response. "I like the sound of that," she murmured quietly, letting her love for him flow through the bond.

CHAPTER 9

They pulled up to the hotel. It was right off the highway, so they didn't see much of the city before they pulled in. That was fine by Vee, since it was getting close to midnight by that time, and she was ready to fall into whatever bed they would be sleeping in. She wasn't used to driving so long, and the day had already been strange. The streets were nearly deserted at the time; most people were home or already asleep within the hotel, meaning there weren't many minds to make their presence known. However when she stepped from the Jeep, she felt an odd throbbing that reminded her of the Fae woman, Nessa, somewhere nearby.

For a moment, she whipped around looking for the source of the feeling. It was near, but not so close she could see her. Or maybe she was just tired. The feeling disappeared after a moment. It was extremely unlikely the old Fae had followed them to Hayes, Kansas. Most likely the feeling was due to exhaustion, or it was another Fae. It wasn't unreasonable for a Fae to be out here. They were just like everyone else, travelling and living in various places. Perhaps the Fae she sensed was just one of similar origin to Nessa.

Shane gave her an odd look as she came around to the back of the Jeep. "What is it?" he asked, pulling the bags out and waving her off as she reached for hers.

"I think I'm just tired. Thought I felt a mind I recognized," she said, deciding not to fight him about getting her bag for her. He assessed her expression and through the bond for any touches of anxiety. It wasn't unheard of for Vee to downplay her own instincts. There was something there, a tension, but nothing overwhelming.

They made their way inside the hotel to the front desk. Shane talked to the person at the reception desk while Vee slumped against the counter, trying very hard to not put her head down as Shane talked to the flirtatious receptionist. Vee was an early riser, and late nights were a struggle. Though she hated the woman for flirting with her mate, she didn't have the energy to do anything more than shoot daggers at her with her eyes.

Once Shane had the keys in hand, they made their way to the second floor and found their room. It was a corner suite; the other doors seemed a far enough distance that Vee got the impression this was going to be a large hotel room. Not that she had stayed in many hotels, but she could tell right away, before Shane even

scanned their keycard, that this was going to be well above her status.

The door opened, and she took it in. A living room, complete with coffee table and flat-screen television was the first thing she noted. There was a set of double doors that opened into a bedroom that could have rivaled the one at Shane's house, and another large door that opened to a massive bathroom with a tub for two and a shower stall. She slowly turned her gaze to Shane, her mouth having dropped open.

"I thought we were only staying here one night," Vee said incredulously, unsure of where to put her duffle, which she had snatched from the ground as he talked to the receptionist. He, of course, looked like he belonged in such a place, still in his suit pants and button-down from work while she was in her usual jeans and T-shirt.

"We are, but I have no idea what to expect when we get there. I thought we could enjoy what little luxury Hays could offer us while we were here," Shane said, grinning at her dumbfounded expression as he closed the door and snatched her bag from her hand.

"Just a little luxury, huh?" she grumbled, letting him take it and following him to the bedroom.

"This isn't a Hyatt," he told her, his tone dismissive. Well, she hadn't stayed in a Hyatt either.

Moments ago, she had been dead on her feet, but the surge of discomfort brought on by being out of place woke her up a little. She knew she needed to calm down. She had to get over this predisposition to hating nice things. The only reason she reacted this way was because she didn't feel like she deserved it.

CHAPTER 9

Shane deserved it, and he was hers ... so she deserved it too, right?

"You do deserve it," Shane said, his voice husky as he came up behind her and wrapped his arms around her waist. She hadn't realized she had been projecting so much into the bond, but it made sense. She *was* tired, but not too tired to resist the tendrils of arousal that Shane was sending her to fuel her own.

"How early do we need to be up in the morning?" Vee asked, as Shane's lips came down on her neck.

"We don't need to worry about it right now," he murmured, his hands traveling to undo her jeans as he pressed against her back. Vee let her fingers slide into his dark locks, holding his head where it lay in the crook of her neck. She let out a sigh of pleasure as he began pushing her pants past her hips.

Vee released her hold on his hair so she could face him, stepping out of her pants that were pooled at her feet. He was still fully dressed, but she made quick work of all the little buttons on his shirt, roughly tugging on it and taking a moment to smooth her hands over his defined chest. He shivered at her touch, which never ceased to amaze her. This man, this beautiful man, wanted *her*.

She leaned forward, eyes locked on his, as she placed her own lips to the skin of his chest. Her hands travelled to undo his belt and pants, mimicking his slow, deliberate movements to push them past his hips. He let his arms drop so his shirt could fall to the floor behind him, and then picked her up in such a quick movement it had her squealing in surprise and delight.

 WHITE MOON

He placed her on the bed, taking just a moment to soak in the joy and desire on her face, before he leaned forward to kiss her. She still had that damn shirt and bra on, obstructing his ability to touch her skin unfettered. Vee felt his mild frustration and urged him with her body to let her roll them over. Now on top of him, but a little higher up his waist, she pulled her shirt over her head, looking him deep in the eyes as she reached behind her to unlatch her bra. She turned her eyes away to watch as she tossed it away.

Shane sat up abruptly, making her squeal with surprise. His hands were running from her hips up her back, splaying his fingers widely as if he wanted to try and touch every inch of skin he could. Her dark hair cascaded over the tops of his hands, as his palms and fingers clutched. He marveled a little at how despite his own skin not being particularly pale, hers was at least a few shades darker, even without much sun exposure. The sweat on her skin that had accumulated throughout the day only brought out her scent more potently. He wanted to lick the salt from her, to taste her.

"I can see why you think we're True Mates," she said breathlessly, after she parted their kiss, his fingers having travelled between them to find their home between her legs.

"You are *my* True Mate, Vee," he murmured, pulling back only a little to watch the pleasure move over her expressions. Vee shivered at the way he said that. She knew from the day before that his reaction to her calling him hers could practically send her over the edge. She started pushing him away—no, down on the bed. His fingers stilled and moved to clutch her thighs.

"And you are mine," she said back, watching as his eyes glowed more intensely, just before she leaned forward to take his lips with hers once more.

Vee woke up with Shane setting coffee on her side of the bed and kissing her hair. She usually woke before he did, so he didn't get to dote on her in this way often. She liked it and from the way his side of the bond hummed with love as he did so, he liked it too. Smiling, she sat up and picked up the mug. It took two sips before she realized he was already showered and dressed, and there she was still naked as the day she was born, drinking coffee in an unfamiliar bed.

"You're already way ahead of me, I see," she murmured, as she watched him pick up the dirty clothes they had discarded haphazardly around the room and put them in his suitcase.

"I couldn't wake you," he said, throwing a smile her way. What he didn't say was that he couldn't bear waking her when she looked so peaceful and happy, especially since he was never the first one awake. Normal mornings, she would have already snuck out of their bed, showered, and be drinking coffee in the kitchen before he got up at home. Vee could feel the undercurrent of his thoughts. Maybe she would sleep in a little later on Sundays, if he liked it so much.

She was about to ask what the plan was when she realized, with all the chaos of the pack meeting and

moving, she had never discussed what she had talked about with Durran, let alone told Shane that Durran was also going to be in Colorado when they arrived.

"I forgot to tell you about Durran," Vee said very suddenly, making Shane pause and look at her.

"I forgot to ask," he offered with a shrug.

"She's meeting us in Breckenridge. Apparently, that's the last place anyone could track down where Fiona was. At least until I was born, I guess. Durran is going to poke around and see what she can find out while we're with the Sha. The idea that we were going out and actively looking for clues was the only thing that seemed to keep the Elders ... civil," she told him. Originally, she had thought to say happy, but she was under the distinct impression that the Elders weren't often described as "happy" at all.

"Good that we'll also have some backup nearby," Shane said, letting a bit of his concern wash over to her.

"You think we'll need backup?" Vee asked in a small voice.

"I would rather anticipate any possibility. I know at least one Sha who would have no problem with you." He thought of Aho, the mostly silent Sha who had pulled him aside the night Downing died by Shane's hands. Aho had all but said he knew *something* about Vee, but he would stay silent about it. "... but there are more Sha than they like to let on, and they are all far more powerful than any Were I've ever come across." Vee swallowed a little dryly and nodded at his words.

"How much time do I have before we head out?" Vee asked, swinging her legs over the side of the bed and setting her coffee back on the bedside table. She knew there was another four- to five-hour drive ahead of them before they made it to Breckenridge. Shane hesitated a moment, making her look back over at him.

"We have to go have breakfast with Lieb," Shane told her regretfully.

"Lieb? Why on earth would we have breakfast with Lieb? And isn't this a little far from his normal domain, anyway?" Vee asked, her face pinched at the memory of the aggressive man she had met right before Shane had claimed her. In fact, *he* had been the reason for the first claim, since he was so volatile, Shane didn't want to leave Vee unprotected, in case Lieb came trying to steal her.

Shane sighed, moving to lean against the wall across from her.

"He called yesterday. He needs you to look at a child. I don't know what the context is, or why it's so important, but he was genuinely concerned," Shane told her. She could feel the empathy he felt for the other pack leader, hear the truth in his words as he described the way Lieb sounded. She still narrowed her eyes suspiciously.

"A child."

"A child," Shane confirmed with a nod.

If there was a child involved, she would have a hard time saying no, but the idea of helping Lieb at all put a sour taste in her mouth. She liked having the bond with Shane. She loved Shane, but their relationship could have gone much differently, more subtly and slowly had Lieb not forced them into the claim in the first place.

"Fine," she snarled, standing up and padding out through the bedroom door to the bathroom. If she was going to have to deal with Lieb and the Sha in the same day, she certainly wasn't going to do it smelling of day-old sweat and sex.

After they checked out of the hotel, they headed a little further south from the highway into one of those strange strips of town where there were strip malls and car dealerships littered on each side of the busy road. They pulled up to a rare stand-alone building on a corner that's sign boasted itself as a pancake house (not the famous one), but the sign below it had a catfish special listed in mismatched letters.

Vee glanced at Shane, but he gave off no qualms through their bond, her ability, or his face, so she allowed herself the small bit of glee in knowing she was probably going to eat some of the greasiest, bad-for-you food that you could only find in a mom-and-pop place like this, and absolutely love it. Lieb be damned; she was going to have one hell of a breakfast.

They entered the quaint establishment, and she could instantly feel the buzz of Lieb. She remembered his specific vibration. One tends to when the Were in question was quite threatening, to say the least. Shane and Vee seemed to have noticed him at the same time, so they merely strode over to the table he had gotten for them, a booth in the furthest corner of the room. He, of course, positioned himself so he had the best vantage point and escape route.

CHAPTER 9

Beside him sat a small girl, maybe five or six. Her hair tumbled over her shoulders in soft waves of black against her dark skin, and her eyes were the same green as the man who sat beside her. She didn't look up at them as they approached; the emotions she gave off were less anxious and more boredom. Lieb hadn't informed the little girl of why they were there.

Vee slid into the booth first. Shane would not have been able to stand being trapped against the wall. Once Shane was seated beside her, she looked between Lieb and the girl for a beat, trying not to show the amusement on her face as Lieb's discomfort grew.

"Your daughter, then?" Vee asked, looking down at the little girl and smiling warmly. She didn't want the girl to be scared and hoped the male counterparts would follow suit. The girl still seemed unperturbed.

"Yes. Her mother is human." That explained the uncertainty of whether she had inherited the trait or not.

"Mama didn't want me anymore," the little girl said quietly, a small wash of sadness pouring over her.

"It's not about you," he whispered down to the girl, his large hand cupping her head as he pressed a kiss to her hair. He turned back to Vee and Shane. "She doesn't want anything to do with me, not after…" Lieb trailed off, swallowing his words. He almost let too much slip out. Vee's curiosity had been piqued by that of course, seeing Lieb laced with regret. The server came by with waters and mugs for Vee and Shane without being asked, keeping Vee from prodding about his unspoken words.

"I'll give you a bit more time, since you've got joiners," the older woman said with a voice so raspy,

117

Vee assumed she was a two-pack-a-day smoker since before she could legally buy them. Usually, restaurant servers had an air of phoniness to them that bothered Vee, but this woman had clearly worked here for years; the restaurant had become part of her identity, and she both loved it and took pride in what she did. Nothing phony about her words, or the casual way she said them, before she turned and walked away from their table.

"So you are worried about...?" Shane offered once the woman was well enough away. Vee picked up the coffee carafe that sat next to Lieb's mug and poured some in her cup. There wasn't much left. They had either waited quite a while, or Lieb had been nervously drinking the coffee before they arrived. By the way the little girl didn't seem too bored yet, Vee had to assume it was the latter.

"I need to know..." He let out a breath, glancing at the little girl once more and running his hand over his bald head. "I need to know if she's going to be like me," Lieb said, eyes pleadingly focusing on Vee for a moment before they slid down to look at the little girl, who was shyly coloring on the placemat before her.

"If I tell you, will you tell me why this is so important that you know right now?" Vee asked. There was more here than just simple curiosity. Lieb wouldn't have driven out to Hays to meet them, with no other pack members around, if this was just for curiosity's sake. He stiffened and shot a look back at Vee before he smoothed his hand over his bald head again nervously.

"I made a rule some years ago, about my wolves and the children they bore with humans. I can't follow my own rule if her mother is gone, and she isn't going

CHAPTER 9

to be one of us," Lieb said, sorrow encasing him like a thick fog.

"What rule?" Shane growled, his voice low, but Vee could tell he was trying to tamp down his anger for the benefit of the girl in front of them. Shane did not like mistreatment of anyone in a pack, which included the humans that paired with the Weres. Vee knew other pack leaders didn't operate the way Shane did, but the idea a *rule* had been created ... a rule that would cause this leader to question himself when he was faced with the same predicament made both Shane and Vee's skin crawl. What had Lieb done?

"When I made it, I had no idea ... I-I love her too much..." Lieb whispered desperately, eyes glistening. Vee glanced at the little girl, who had stopped her coloring to look up at her father. Her bright green eyes echoing the sympathy she felt for him. Her tiny hand reached up to the table and held his.

"Whatever rule you have in place that would make you fear her safety should be removed," Vee said, gesturing to their clasped hands. Lieb swallowed and nodded.

The server came back, and they all stiffly ordered food. The menu was standard breakfast options. Vee ordered French toast and O'Brien potatoes, while Shane got a giant pancake and a full order of biscuits and gravy. She didn't catch what Lieb and the girl ordered, but mostly it was because, despite the seriousness of their conversation, she was extremely excited for her food.

"What I'm gathering is that you told her mother what you are, she freaked out and left. Whatever rule you've put in place in your pack might be *harmful* to her—" Vee tilted her head pointedly at the girl, "—if she doesn't turn out to be like you, and you have yourself stuck in a pretty unfortunate situation," Vee said confidently, eyes boring into the Were across the table. He flinched and nodded.

"Will you just tell me?" he hissed out in a whisper. Shane growled quietly at him as a warning, but Vee placed her hand on Shane's to reassure him. Lieb wasn't going to attack Vee here with his daughter beside him and a room full of humans to witness. He was lashing out because of his own frustration and fear.

Vee had known the moment they'd approached the table. She felt like she would have known even if she didn't feel it in her mind, just based on how much of Lieb's traits had been passed to the girl already.

"She will be like you," Vee told him, the certainty unquestionable in her voice. Lieb let out a breath, wrapping one arm around the girl and squeezing her into his side.

"Daddy, you're squishing me!" she said, though she hugged him back.

"Remember that feeling you had before I told you and realize whatever rule you've made, the other parents in your pack feel the same," Vee said, her tone more than her words telling him she expected him to change that. Who knows how many families he tore apart, how much heartbreak he may have wrought with whatever this rule was?

"I will," Lieb said honestly with a solemn nod.

CHAPTER 10

Full and unscathed, they parted from Lieb and Halima—they had finally been told her name after the food was served—to start the remainder of their trek to Colorado. That little meal seemed to have started a more cordial relationship between the two pack leaders. Shane was very different in the way he took care of his pack in comparison to most. His Weres were a family with him the head, there to not only keep them in line but to protect them in whatever way they needed. Most packs were more like a mob, living to benefit the leader more than the whole.

Perhaps this meal, and the potential consequences of his rule had Halima not been a Were, would be enough for Lieb to change the way he cared for his pack. It would be good for Shane and Lieb to be on better terms as well. Their pack territories were right

against each other, with only the thin state line between them. Vee often found it frustrating that she had to be careful about house calls on the Kansas side, which was only blocks away from her shop, because of the territory issue.

Shane had pulled out his laptop on one of the stops for gas and leg-stretching, and insisted Vee look at all the houses George had sent him the day before once they were back on the road. The houses were all still located within the city, despite suburbs potentially offering more space and privacy. The need to stay in the city was both because of her job and because the Westport Pack needed to be in the helm of the pack territory. But houses that would be practical for the pack were a bit *more* than Vee was comfortable with.

The pack had grown in the twenty years since Shane had bought the house on Morningside Drive, and though he had thought to stay there a bit longer, it was no longer practical when the whole pack needed to gather. All the houses on the list were far larger than the one they currently lived in.

"Shane, how do any of you expect me to agree to one of these houses? Just seeing the price tag is enough to make my brain turn foggy," Vee grumbled, closing a tab for a house that was listed at $2.5 million. Every last one of these had been even larger and more expensive than Shane's current house. Some of them had ridiculously ornate fixtures plated in gold that made her cringe.

"I want you to have the final say," Shane told her, though he had been chuckling lightly each time she made a pained groan.

"They're all so…"

"Huge? You've said that a few times now," he said, his eyes glittering with humor as he glanced at her. She clicked the next link after glaring at his smirking profile.

This house was beautiful with a stone-and-stucco exterior, set back a little on the property to give more privacy from neighbors passing by. It was also on a cul-de-sac, preventing random traffic. The interior pictures showed the simple elegant style of traditional older homes, as well as the flair of some wood inlays from the twenties when it was built.

It was updated, but not overly modern, to take away from the expert craftsmanship that had been in place when it was made. Large rooms, where Vee could imagine pack gatherings taking place, were on the first floor, with quite a few well-sized bedrooms upstairs. There was even a designated office space that would be perfect for Shane.

She looked at the pictures of the backyard, which was more like a park. There was a large stone patio with a pool, but beyond that, a huge area with equal amounts trees and open space that seemed completely closed off to the other properties surrounding it. It would be perfect for wolves to run around in if they needed to, without the worry of neighbors seeing or hearing anything abnormal. While this house was huge, and its price tag outrageous, she could see it. She could imagine the pack there; she could imagine living there.

She scrolled back up to see the address. Sunset Hills … off Ward Parkway. She stiffened mildly. The idea of living in that extravagant neighborhood instantly made her want to reject it, but her eyes lingered over the pictures of the house again. Something about that house felt right, even while looking at impersonal pictures. She wondered how she'd feel when she stepped inside.

Vee glanced at Shane, who turned and raised an eyebrow at her.

"That's the least amount of sound you've made since you started looking at these," he commented cautiously.

"This one is okay," she murmured, bookmarking the tab.

"Which one?" he asked, trying and failing to mask the excitement in his voice.

"You're driving. You can look at it later," she said, closing the laptop. She didn't need to see any others; that one was it.

"George can get an offer in if we let him know. We don't want to lose it," Shane said, his voice strained. Vee had never had to deal with purchasing a house and didn't know how quickly they could go off the market. She felt his excited and slightly panicked energy and found it unnecessary. Shane found her dismissiveness exasperating.

"You can see it at the next stop," she said, looking at him like he'd lost his mind when he checked the road sign they came up on a moment later that indicated a rest stop and moved quickly over to the right lane to take the exit.

"Real estate goes quickly, Vee. If there's one you like, we have to jump on it," Shane told her, as he parked awkwardly across more than one space and turned his whole torso to her.

"I don't understand the fuss," she grumbled, pulling out the laptop again and handing it over to him. He quickly pulled up the browser and looked at the tab she had kept up of the house. His mouth turned up as he looked it over. They, at least, agreed on house style.

"This is perfect, isn't it?" Shane said, eyes flicking to lock with hers.

"Lots of space. Inside and out," she told him, nodding as she fought the smile on her face from showing. Her attempts to hide how she really felt didn't matter, though, because he could feel her happiness and excitement through the bond. He pulled out his phone and quickly texted George the address, with instructions on things he needed listed in the contract.

[George: I can't wait to tell Thomas I won the bet.]

Shane laughed at George's text, making Vee narrow her eyes and try to lean over to see what was so funny.

"What?" Vee asked.

"Apparently, bets were placed," said Shane, amused as Vee's face went pouty, and she slumped back in her seat. He couldn't resist as he leaned over and caught her pouted lips with his own. She had just chosen their new home and continued to choose him.

They parted breathless a few moments later, the seatbelts and console between them inhibiting them from going much further.

"We should probably keep going," Vee whispered.

"We should," Shane rasped out, having a hard time turning back to the steering wheel. It was broad daylight, the rest stop was by no means empty, and they

were nearly to Denver. It was only about an hour more once they passed through there to Breckenridge. Vee put her window down to disburse the scents of them that were most likely only going to make Shane's control more difficult, as he pulled the car out of the terrible parking job he'd done and got them back on the highway with ease.

The drive passed rather uneventfully. The house situation being settled left Vee without that distraction, so now other thoughts started to invade. She was trying very hard to not worry about what was going to happen when they arrived to see the Sha. Would they be hostile? What would they do to her when she had no answers for them about what she was? Everyone was demanding she tell them, but even *she* had no idea.

With nothing but the endless road ahead of them to distract herself from her racing thoughts, she snagged Shane's phone from the mount on the dash and started going through it to find some music. It was a little baffling that they had managed to talk most of the car ride, both the evening previous and this day, instead of needing to fill the awkward silence with music. She had never been much of a talker, but she found conversing with Shane to be easy. Easier now that they were honest about their feelings.

In fact, they hadn't really talked about music at all, which she found both odd and intriguing. How had she agreed to marry this man when she didn't even know his taste in music?

"You don't have any music on here," she said, realizing he had no applications for music of any kind.

"No...?" he said, a little confused about her statement.

"I just realized I have no idea what kind of music you like," she said as an answer, her tone frustrated as she locked the phone again and set it back where it had been. He laughed at her frustration and took a moment to glance at the perturbed look on her face.

"I don't listen to much music anymore. It's hard for me to not be aware of my surroundings. And a lot of the music from my youth ... well, it isn't the best quality, so I find it irritating. Werewolf problems, I suppose," he told her, tapping the ear closest to her. He didn't often talk about his past, but when he did, Vee could feel the pangs of sadness there.

She supposed she knew the basics of the important parts: his forced breeding that produced Ethan, his oldest son; Ethan's mother's subsequent death during a war with another pack; Shane becoming the pack leader when the Sha came to take out the former leader, O'Neil, who had become crazed and threatened the whole of the preternatural community with his irrational behavior. All of which ultimately led to Shane's promotion to leader. And of course, his marriage to Patricia, which ended with the birth of Patrick and her death.

But she didn't know about his childhood or his family before he was changed into a Werewolf. That bothered her almost as much as not knowing what his favorite music was.

"Tell me about before you were changed," Vee said, watching his face as it contracted slightly. It pained him to talk about it, but she wanted to know. He knew

all about her life. She suspected he even knew what her favorite song was, given she played music often enough in her shop for him to have an idea of the type of music that appealed to her. The only thing she didn't think he knew was also a mystery to her, and they were searching for that together.

"There's not much to tell," Shane told her, his voice a little flat. She didn't want to push him. He was the pusher in the relationship, heavy-handed and sometimes overbearing, but that wasn't her. She knew that if she could control and use their bond well enough, she'd be able to delve into his mind herself, knowing that their connection gave them insight into everything within each other, if they knew how to look. It did feel rather intrusive to do such a thing, to sift through his memories and thoughts. Even if she was allowed and had access to it, she still didn't particularly love the idea.

Someday he'd tell her. She could live with waiting.

"I'd like to know, whenever you want to tell me," she murmured, sending reassurance to him as she touched his leg. He let one hand drop from the steering wheel to grasp hers. They sat quietly just driving down the highway in silence for a few minutes, Shane's thumb running over the top of her hand. She suspected he would be rubbing his forehead if his hand was free.

"I wasn't *changed* in the traditional sense ... I was born a Were but just didn't know it," he said, breaking the silence suddenly. That made sense. He didn't have any scars to indicate he had been attacked, like several of the others did, but he was also old enough, and she knew those sorts of scars faded with time.

"I thought—"

"Yes … my parents were human. Or the people I knew as my parents were human. I think my father was actually mine, but back then, children out of wedlock were kept as quiet as possible. I was the oldest of my siblings and looked like a spitting image of him. No one ever suspected a thing, and I was never told."

Vee let that information settle in her for a moment. His mother's identity was just as much a mystery to him as hers was, if not more so. At least she had a name.

"So, they didn't know you would change?" she asked, eyes wide as she thought of Lori's change—of how horribly that could have gone if Vee hadn't intervened.

"No, they didn't." He paused, shifting a bit uncomfortably as he processed the memory. "I was fifteen, my brothers were all twelve and under. We were camping at the Ozarks, my dad and my brothers. I had been feeling strange, picking fights with them over silly things. Just before the sun set, I had stormed off into the woods around our camp. I'm glad I did … not for who I found there, but that I didn't kill my family," he murmured, holding her hand a little tighter.

"Who did you find?"

"Duncan O'Neil," Shane growled out through clenched teeth. Vee suddenly saw a flash of moonlit woods, a huge wolf standing on a downed tree, eyes glowing orange and malicious. "He would have attacked me if it hadn't been for his second at the time."

"What did your father do when you told him?"

Shane smiled briefly and let out a breath.

"He told me he always knew I was magic. He had been saving money for me to go to college and gave it to me, then he handed me over to the pack, to O'Neil

… and I left. I didn't talk to my father again. I didn't see my brothers until Dad died."

The quiet settled in the car again, Vee still holding Shane's hand in a vice grip. It was a different time, sure, but he'd had no one of his own, no family anymore. It was as if he *had* been attacked and changed for as much preparation he'd had to deal with it. Just like many Weres who were changed that way, he'd had to leave his family behind.

"My favorite song when I was that age was 'How High The Moon.' Seems a little coincidental now," he said, breaking the silence.

"Which version?" Vee asked, eyes lighting up a little. She liked a very wide variety of music and often fell into slumps where she only listened to certain genres for a stretch of time, often doing a little research into parts she found particularly interesting. Jazz had been one she dove deep into, and it was especially easy with how important the jazz scene had been in Kansas City.

"I always preferred Ella Fitzgerald's version over Mary Ford. Ella's voice was far superior, and she recorded it first," Shane told her.

"Jazz, then," Vee said, ticking an imaginary box in the air with her finger.

"Hm?"

"Music you like," Vee said confidently. His eyes sparkled as a smile spread over his face.

"Yes, I do like jazz."

Vee and Shane pulled up into a hotel that was right off the highway and right beside a river. It had the cliché charm of a log cabin on the exterior. She supposed that's what a lot of people expected when they came visiting Colorado. Durran had texted her the name and address for the hotel she would be staying at while there. It had dual purposes, one as a place to meet Durran before they headed to see the Sha, and two for a place to park the Jeep. Apparently, they weren't going to need the car where they were going.

Vee got out, stretching and breathing in the air. It was much cooler here than it was in Kansas City. Being nearly 1 p.m., it had only gotten up to the mid-seventies in temperature, but it felt positively delightful in comparison to the humid ninety-degree sauna they had left behind at home. Durran appeared just across from where they parked, hopping over the small crude fencing that encased the little patio area outside her room.

"It's a little later than I thought you'd be," Durran said, as Shane pulled their bags from the back of the car.

"Had to eat breakfast and stop a few times," Vee told her with a smile.

"Just breakfast?" Durran grumbled, shooting a glare at Shane.

"The Sha will be feeding us when we arrive. I had expected to get here a little earlier as well," Shane snapped back at the obvious tone in Durran's voice. The fight for who took better care of Vee was tiresome to say the least. She rolled her eyes at them and pulled her messenger bag from the floor of the front seat to sling it over her shoulder.

"When will they be meeting us?" Vee asked to get the conversation moving away from whether she had eaten enough to the important tasks at hand.

"I let Min know already," Shane told her.

"I have only been here a few hours. I don't know how cellphone reception is there, but I will try to keep you informed as I come across information," Durran said, as Shane reached out to place the keys in Durran's outstretched hand.

"You keep strange company, Young Black Wolf," came a voice from the trees adjacent to the parking lot. Everyone whipped their heads over to see Min stepping out.

Vee had never met a Sha before, but she had felt them. Their vibrations in her head were about as intense as a Were who was on the precipice of a change. It made her feel lightheaded for a moment, but she didn't let the weakness show.

Min was fairly average in height and lean-muscled. His skin was the color of teak and his hair blue black, braided in two that came down over his shoulders. His face didn't give any specifically discernible Native American features, other than his coloring. She wouldn't be able to pin him to a certain region or tribe. The more she took in his face, the more confused she got, since some of his features reminded her of native people from other parts of the world.

"Min," Shane said, nodding his head respectfully.

"Watchers aren't permitted to come with you," Min said, eyeing Durran. The tension in the air kicked up at that, Durran stiffening at the way Min's eyes began to glow.

"She is staying behind. This is Durran. She's Vee's Watcher," Shane told him, not wanting to give all the reasons for Durran's presence away but needing him to understand the Watcher was not a threat. Min's eyes turned to Vee then. She felt the weight of his gaze, as if he were trying to pull her apart and see what was on the inside.

"Interesting," Min commented.

CHAPTER 11

With barely a goodbye to Durran, Vee and Shane left the parking lot and followed Min back into the woods where he had appeared from. At first, Vee found it a little strange that the entrance to the place where the Sha stayed was smack dab in the middle of a city, even if there was a mountain and wilderness right up against it. But they broke through the tree line on the other side to reveal another parking lot.

Min approached an ATV that could seat four with harnesses and two more on another bench seat facing backward. Min took the bags Shane had unloaded from the Jeep and strapped them on the bench, securing them with bungee cords. Somehow the idea of this man, a powerful Sha, driving an ATV around Breckenridge seemed odd to Vee, but then even preternaturals had to do normal, mundane things every now and then. Fae did laundry at laundromats, Werewolves went shopping for groceries—just the day before, she had put a lock in for a Vampire nest.

They all got in: Shane in front with Min, Vee taking the back seat directly behind Shane. She strapped her harness on with fumbling fingers before Min took off, driving quickly and rather recklessly, in Vee's opinion, off onto the street and further into town. As they passed through Main Street, Vee was enthralled with the colors, interesting storefronts, and historic buildings. It was magical. If they weren't headed to see the Sha, she would have liked to poke around and sightsee.

They passed by the Quicksilver SuperChair, a lift to take skiers up the slope, and started toward the wooded area beyond. She was surprised none of the humans around seemed to notice the ATV as they passed. Either they were used to it, or there was some magic keeping their eyes away. Werewolves had magic like that, to keep humans from noticing or fully comprehending what was right in front of them. It had been that sort of magic that kept Kansas City from falling into chaos after Downing had run all around it, half-changed into a wolf, the summer before. They still had to be careful, though. There were some humans who could see the truth, but that didn't seem to be a concern for Min as he raced through the streets, dodging cars and people with swift jerks on the steering wheel.

The terrain became rough once they got off the road. They were not traveling on any path that was well marked for normal tourists and hikers. Several spots between trees, the vehicle seemed to barely squeeze through.

After what seemed like ages, Vee's hunger that she hadn't noticed when they first arrived was finally ramping up. Min began to slow the ATV until they reached two great Douglas fir trunks. They each had to be six feet wide and went so high, Vee could have craned her neck and still wouldn't have seen the top. Once stopped, Min got out, silently indicating Shane and Vee should follow suit. She unbuckled her harness and stepped out onto the dry pine needles carpeting the ground, staring at the space between the two trees. There was an odd shimmer and warp in the air there, the bits of light from the evergreen canopy reflecting off of it.

"We can drive through it, but I thought you'd like to sense it first, so it's not so disorienting," Min told them, nodding as Shane began approaching it.

To Shane's senses, he could feel the power radiating from the space between the trees and smell the Sha magic at work there. It confused him as to why there would be a ward set between these two massive trees, with seemingly nothing of interest behind them, and the ward did not stretch beyond it. But to Vee, she could see the shimmer of somewhere entirely different hiding behind the veil of magic. It reminded her of the way the Fae glamor shimmered and shifted over their true skin. She knew no one else seemed to see magic the way she did. Vee realized that when she had tried to explain to Shane how magic seemed to seep from his mouth when he had claimed her. He had told her he could only feel and smell magic.

"It's the doorway," Vee murmured, stepping a bit closer to view the snippets of the unfamiliar land on the other side. Tommy's words at lunch the day before made so much more sense now that she was standing in front of it.

"Yes," Min said, tone curious as he watched her approach it. The way her body moved cautiously, but curiously, forward intrigued him. How she knew it was a doorway was beyond him. Sha could only sense magic, like Weres, but she had not proven to be any sort of shapeshifter.

The little bit the Sha had dug up on her told them basically nothing. She was a locksmith from Kansas City, nearly thirty, and only recently got tangled up in preternatural affairs. She had hidden in plain sight from them all for years. Her appearance was meek: small, thin, but clearly strong for her slenderness. Her hair was dark brown and straight, not ugly but nothing special. She didn't seem to possess anything particularly extraordinary, either in appearance, or from what he could sense about her abilities, except for her astonishing emerald-green eyes. To him, she was not more intriguing than any human he had ever come across.

Min's eyes glowed as his thoughts drifted to what could be so special about her. How could this small, unassuming creature be such a draw? But his beast seemed to disagree with him, rebelling at his general hostility toward her. He was internally battling between intrigue, disdain, and the need to protect. Protect her from who? Himself?

Shane had begun to watch Vee as she got closer to the space between the trees as well, but his instincts told him danger was a hairsbreadth away from her. At first his eyes scanned the surrounding trees, then he

turned them to Min, to see if he had also sensed the same feeling. Min was glaring at Vee, his eyes glowing. Shane couldn't tell exactly what strong emotion Vee's curiosity over the gateway would have brought on to make Min look at her that way. With the distance between them and the breeze sending his scent the other direction, Shane had no idea what was truly going on in Min's head, but he knew he didn't like it. He let a quiet growl escape his throat, causing Min's gaze to snap from Vee to him instead.

Shane had known it was dangerous to bring Vee here, for her to be surrounded by the Sha. He had known it was very possible some of them would wish her ill will, especially because she was a crossbreed of more than one preternatural. He didn't, however, expect Min to have been one of the Sha he would have to keep an eye on. Shane had considered Min a friend for years, being their pack's Sha liaison. Shane would have to be even more vigilant about Vee's safety for however long they stayed there.

"Let's keep going," Min said abruptly, just as Vee was reaching her hand out to touch one of the trees. She folded her fingers into her fist instead, though her eyes lingered a moment longer. It was beautiful to her sight, and she was continually learning more about the way she experienced magic around her, which intrigued her.

They all got back in the ATV, and Min moved his gaze over them for a moment, his expression unreadable, but Vee felt his curiosity and slight amusement. She could also feel Shane's possessiveness and anxiety for her ramp up. Something had set Shane off in those woods, though she hadn't been privy to what it was. She watched him. Seeing the tightness in his jaw and feeling the waves of emotion from him set her on edge, as Min started pulling forward between the trees and through the veil.

As the magic glided over her skin, Vee felt oddly comforted by it. It was pulsing, as if it were a living thing, but it wasn't repellent to her, almost like it had its own mind and was welcoming her. The shadows of the forest behind them changed, the sun seeming warmer above the new canopy over their heads than it was a moment ago. The trees were different too, some evergreens but also more tropical plants. Types of plants that didn't seem like they would be able to cohabitate together were side by side. The air was a bit heavier, like they had both come down in altitude and added some moisture.

There were animals everywhere. She could hear them rustling in the trees, while many different bird sounds could be heard from above. It was like everything beautiful about all the different wooded lands from all over the world had joined together in a strange harmony. They were certainly not in Colorado anymore. They might not have been anywhere on earth for all she knew. After twenty minutes, all of which seemed to pass by in a blink while she took in the strange and beautiful place around her, they reached the edge of the forest and broke through the trees.

Before them was a large open swath of land. A town was in the center, and she could see beyond it in the distance much more land and mountains. The open space between the trees and the town was more like a large pasture, Vee realized. There were fences in some areas with small barns close to the tree line. She couldn't quite tell what kinds of animals were there from that distance, as Min drove on a path straight to the town. Once they got just outside of it, he pulled into a small shelter that housed a few other ATVs and turned it off, gesturing for them to follow him. No one grabbed their bags, but Vee was somehow certain they would be brought to wherever they would be staying.

Shane turned to her, reaching out his hand to take hers once she was fully out of the vehicle. He needed the contact, the feel of her skin, to keep him from losing his control. The way Min had looked at her was not only violent, but hungry he decided. He had to protect her here. She was vulnerable and breakable, and he had brought her here amongst powerful preternaturals. Shane didn't even know what they wanted from this visit, what they wanted from her.

And perhaps it wasn't even Vee's powers that set Min off. Perhaps it was simply *her*. She was beautiful, unusual, and intriguing. The Sha number was also stagnant; not many new ones being born, especially after so many had been killed in the Great Wars. If Min was looking at Vee as if she were a potential new mate, he would need to think again. Vee was *his*.

Vee's fingers effortlessly sliding between his, and the comfort of her touch helped him settle a little. His wolf acknowledged she was really only safe if she was right beside him. Her hand in his let him breathe a little more, both because the feel of her warm skin on his let him know she was with him and safe, and that she chose him. They were True Mates. Even if his suspicions were correct about Min, or Durran, or any other person who may pine for Vee, she chose him.

Subtly, Shane could tell Vee was also concerned, on alert to the danger in some small way, but also very intrigued by the strangeness of this place they had come to. She was far less used to looking out for danger, having successfully hidden herself for years. She didn't have to watch for it as much as other preternaturals. He would, as usual, be on alert for the both of them as long as they were there.

As they walked, Vee noticed the buildings that were an odd combination of ancient-looking and more modern. Small stone-and-clay structures dotted amongst more contemporary storefronts. Most of the buildings housed handmade items, and there were multiple places that had various grocery items. One had dairy products, cheeses and milks of all varieties; another was purely dedicated to spices and herbs, and smelled amazing as they passed by. Right beside it, oddly, there was a small electronic repair shop.

They walked on the smooth stone walking street—no cars or ATVs to be found anywhere around. There were people, many of whom looked very much like Min, but some that seemed to have lighter or darker skin than his. They all had black hair and dark eyes. Everyone continued with their tasks, but Vee could feel the stares in their direction. They were definitely being watched.

For once, Shane seemed more out of place than she did in his slacks and button-down. He hadn't gone with a blazer, mostly because it was uncomfortable to drive in for long periods of time. They saw everyone

in the small market wearing jeans and flannels; a few women had beautiful, colorful skirts on but still casual. Vee was in her usual jeans and T-shirt.

That morning at the hotel, she had wondered if she should have dressed up more for meeting the Sha, but she had only really packed one nice outfit—the only one she owned—and she didn't want to sit in it all day. Now that she looked around and noticed Min's attire for that matter—a worn pair of jeans and a loose T-shirt—she didn't feel so bad about not having changed once they'd arrived in Breckenridge.

"We don't often call people to come here. Not anymore. They are all curious about newcomers," Min told them, as he locked eyes with a woman who had been staring so intently at Shane, her body frozen in the middle of placing an apple from her basket onto the front display of a produce shop. She turned her eyes away once she noticed Min's gaze toward her, a faint bit of red coloring her cheeks before she resumed stocking.

"These are only storefronts," Vee said aloud, wondering where all these people lived. She hadn't seen any homes when they approached; it was just the one walking street with shops on either side and beyond them, the pastures and barns.

"We build our own homes when we grow of age to leave our parents. We build them wherever calls to us. Our center is here where we all gather," Min told her, gesturing around to indicate the whole of the path they had walked. "It wasn't always that way. This center had started as everything to us, with only a select few making their homes away from the group, but times changed."

CHAPTER 11

They came to the end of the wide path to stand before a large building. The entrance looked like it had been built first, the original version of whatever this great structure was having begun as a simple stone-and-clay building. Deep but precise symbols were carved into the frame of the doorway, looking barely touched by time. The massive stone slabs of the addition melded off the small clay structure, as if they were meant to be together. It towered over them, enormous columns that boasted ornate and colorfully painted designs loomed like the fir trees had. The art style of the designs were geometric, sharp lines and patterns that were so precise they would have been difficult to paint by hand. They did not seem to come from any particular culture, but many. Though the colors were still vibrant and beautiful, Vee knew they were very ancient.

"Where will we be staying?" Shane asked, looking up at the structure before them, his cautiousness easily flowing into Vee as he squeezed her hand. It made him even more uneasy, seeing the building towering over them. Perhaps not maliciously, but everything in his body was feeling malevolent intent at the moment. With each passing moment, it increased within him, telling him to flee or fight. He wanted a moment away from prying eyes to settle, needing to ground himself a little before he dealt with the Sha in their entirety. Vee had seen him and felt him with a wide range of emotions plenty of times, but the way he was practically vibrating as he fought to keep his cool, and the way he clutched her hand, told her this was more than just anxiety.

"We will have a meal here in a few hours; you are to stay with Aho. He insisted," Min said, a slight edge to his voice, as if Aho wanting them to stay with him had been a source of contention amongst the other Sha.

As though Min's mention of Aho's name had summoned him, the Sha came walking around the side of the building. He wasn't smiling, but his eyes sparkled a little as he approached.

"An honor, Aho," Shane said, bowing his head to the man.

Vee looked at Aho, taking in his appearance. He was striking, with his snow-white hair in contrast to his teak skin. He was not large, quite short really in comparison to men of modern times. Had it not been for his hair and the wisdom that hid in his dark eyes, she might have placed him in his early twenties. He looked very much like Min, she realized; the implacable features on Min's face were mirrored on Aho's face. She couldn't be sure, but she had the distinct feeling Min was Aho's son. Although it could have been the other way around, as they looked the same age.

"Come," Aho said, gesturing for Shane and Vee to follow him. They nodded in thanks to Min and followed Aho away from the town center, through a wide grass path between fenced pastures toward the tree line again, but this time in the direction of the mountains beyond.

There was a small dirt path that they came upon once they hit the trees, clearly made from years of foot travel over the same area. Vee noticed Aho was barefoot as they followed him and felt like she would have liked to feel the earth against the soles of her feet in this place too. She could feel the hum of energy coming from the ground, different from the feel of most magic she came across. A distinctive type of magic altogether: baser magic.

After a few more minutes, they came upon a small clearing in the woods; a pond sat in the center, water tricking from a small rocky cliff beside it. It was almost like a grotto, and there must have been a small stream that fed it from the higher ground above. A modest-sized structure lay a few yards away, being part-log cabin, part-clay. There was a porch with a swing and what looked like a little tree stump with a half-finished wood carving lying on it. Wind chimes softly sounded as they rustled slightly in the breeze. Aho gave no welcome as he walked through the front door of the house, clearly expecting them to follow him inside.

They entered, and it was not at all what Vee had expected from the exterior. Inside was quite modern. Well-cared-for hardwood floors stretched across the front room, which was both the living and dining room. There were handwoven rugs, worn with time, placed under tables to define the spaces with more intricate geometric designs on them. The furniture was well-made; some of it had clearly been handcrafted many years ago, except for the expansive and comfortable-looking sectional couch. Surprisingly, there was a flat-screen television over the stone fireplace as well as a stereo system.

"Shoes off, if you wouldn't mind," Aho murmured quietly, heading through the dining room to the kitchen.

Vee and Shane glanced at each other for a moment before toeing off their shoes and placing them by the door, where a set of well-worn cowboy boots sat on a small rug. They hesitantly walked through the dining room to the kitchen where Aho was busily grabbing sandwich fixings and setting them on the kitchen table. This table clearly saw more use than the dining room. The kitchen wasn't tiny, but it wasn't huge either. The floor was made of stone, and the countertops matched the hardwoods in the other rooms. The cabinets were painted a light gray with cast-iron pulls.

"Sit, sit," Aho told them, having turned around and saw them standing awkwardly in the wide archway. They did, settling in two seats on one side of the four-seater table, while Aho placed glasses of water in front of them. "So, Young Black Wolf, this is your Vee, hm?" he asked, after he sat across from them.

"Yes," Shane said, his voice gravelly and his intensity still heightened. Aho seemed to not notice or care, continuing to gather ingredients and place them on the table before them.

"I thought you two might be more comfortable here than with one of the others. There is some concern about how you two have become mated. What that says about Vee. And from what we've gathered from the rumors, no one knows what she is," Aho said, beginning to assemble a sandwich on his plate. His voice was calm and rather nonchalant for the words he said.

"Why would we be more comfortable here, then?" Vee asked, watching him as he carefully folded pieces of meat and cheese on one side of the bread.

"I am not hung up on things such as purity, like the others," Aho told her, eyes locking with her emerald ones for the briefest of moments. There was the faintest amount of surprise and familiarity she felt from him in that look, but it faded just as quickly as his eyes returned to sandwich assembly.

"We don't know what she is. We've been trying to find out, but as of right now, we still are unsure," Shane told him.

"But you have your suspicions, yes?" Aho asked, cutting the sandwich in half with a long sharp knife, then picking up the plate to hand it to Vee. She took it, setting the plate in front of her as he began making another.

"I know the name my mother went by, and a few places she's been, but that's all," Vee told him. He was quiet for a moment, simply constructing another sandwich, but Vee could feel his emotions fluctuating in reaction to what she said. Curiosity and intrigue were certainly the most prominent.

"Hmm … I have lived a long time. Perhaps after you eat, I can see if I can shed any light on the matter for you," he offered, finishing the second sandwich and handing it to Shane. Shane also set his in front of him but didn't eat, waiting for Aho to make his own sandwich. "Tell me, Vee. What do you do when you aren't helping your wolves?" Aho asked.

CHAPTER 12

I t had taken everything in Durran to not follow when Min led Vee and Shane away. The goodbye had been so unceremonious before they disappeared into the woods from where Min had appeared. She had watched them as long as she could, gripping the keys to Shane's Jeep in her fingers. It was still a struggle to leave Vee's safety in the hands of anyone else, let alone watch her walk into unknown land with the Sha.

The Sha's involvement and cooperation with the other preternaturals in the Great Wars had been one of the biggest reasons it had come to an end. That had also been when they closed themselves off, not allowing any of them to marry or mate with outsiders. They had been mysterious before, but since then, they had become almost as inconceivable as the Watchers were, with only the Weres that they presided over having any idea about them.

But Durran couldn't stand there in the parking lot, wondering about Vee's safety and reminiscing about the Sha's past all day. She was starting to get odd looks from the few people wandering around. So, she moved quickly back to the small patio outside her hotel room, hopping easily over the railing and through the sliding glass door. She glanced at the small notebook on the table amidst the otherwise barren room. She hadn't really needed a hotel room while she was there; Watchers generally didn't need much in the way of comforts. They did sleep, just not often, and their glamor took care of clothing.

She, having nearly always been assigned a ward and rarely spending much time in the realm, had developed quite a few human habits however. Showering was a favorite pastime as was eating out at restaurants. She kept a small studio that was very close to Vee's previous apartment simply for the shower. Otherwise, it was practically empty. A restaurant, however, was someplace she would always be willing to go to. In fact, that was where her first stop would be, a restaurant. It just so happened to be one that a Fiona Morgan—one of the aliases Vee's mother had used—worked at thirty years ago. Durran hoped there was at least one long-time employee there who would be able to tell her more about the woman.

Durran snatched the notebook and left through the proper exits to get to the parking lot once again. After staring at the Jeep that smelled of Shane and Vee, even from the outside, she decided against driving. Her

destination was within walking distance, so no reason to torture herself with … them.

She moved down to Main Street, looking over the beautiful historic buildings and feeling, for a moment, like she was back in time. She had to stop herself from shifting her glamor to a male body in front of people. The last time she had been anywhere that resembled this place, had this sort of feel, she had been in her male form. Not only could she expose herself if the wrong person happened to notice her shift, but people were more likely to open up to a woman, and she needed to use that to her advantage here.

The front of the saloon was reminiscent of the other storefronts around. The horizontal siding that adorned the front of the shop was painted a pale green and was accented with red doors and window frames. Durran walked through the door, the scent of burning wood, beer, and food wafted to her nose. She walked to the end of the bar, letting a small smile touch her lips as she passed the very old wood-burning fireplace that was gated off to one side. It looked like it was an original fixture of the building.

Most people in the saloon were locals, she noted, which made sense. Despite Breckenridge being a tourist town, this was not skiing season. She sat down with an easy view of the entrance, snagging a menu that had been discarded on the bar ledge. As she looked it over, a middle-aged woman approached after having noticed her sitting there while in mid-conversation with one of the locals. Her hair looked like it might have been vibrant red if it weren't lightened with grey hairs, her eyes carried laugh lines, and her smile was warm and genuine as she slid a coaster in front of Durran.

"Would you like something to drink while you look that over?" the woman, who was the bartender, asked. Durran smiled in return. She didn't much care for alcohol. It didn't affect Watchers the way it did humans, and though she sometimes found the taste enjoyable, it felt like a waste when there were much better things to be drinking with food. But she had walked into a saloon, after all.

"What's local that you recommend?" Durran asked, figuring she could at least appeal to local pride, instead of seemingly looking uneducated about beer selections.

"We have a really nice seasonal IPA on tap. It's got a little tropical flare to it," the bartender told her, eyes sparking as she snagged a chilled glass from a bus tub filled with ice.

"Sounds good," Durran said with a nod, watching as she poured the beer from the tap with expertise only gained from years.

Durran thanked her and the bartender moved back over to the regular patrons, giving Durran some time to look over the menu again. It was a difficult choice; while the selection wasn't extensive, everything listed sounded fantastic. And the smells coming from the kitchen didn't aid in her decision-making either. She decided to go with a lamb French dip, since she rarely ate lamb back in Kansas City unless she took Vee to eat Indian food.

The bartender came over once she noticed Durran's menu was set aside.

"Decided, have you?"

"It was hard. Everything sounds so good," Durran confided.

"You'll have to stop back in while you're visiting and try something else then," she said with a grin. "So what did you decide on for today?"

"I'll have the Lamb French Dip," Durran told her, watching her smile widen as she said so.

"A favorite. Good choice. I'll put it right in." She turned to the computer, her back facing Durran as she did so. Durran took a moment to examine her. Yes, middle-aged was right, and by her comfort and experience behind the bar, she estimated that this woman had definitely worked here for about thirty years. It would have been too easy for Durran to have stumbled upon someone who knew Fiona right away, but she knew she'd have to ask this woman, if for no other reason than to eliminate her from the unformed list of people who might have.

Durran's food was served with a wink and a smile a bit later, and she happily ate it, while trying to think of the best way to broach the subject of Vee's mother with the bartender. At some point, she heard someone refer to the woman as Janice, and she was glad to finally have a name for her. Names were powerful. They could be used for good and ill will, depending on who was wielding it. Durran had no intention of using the name for anything other than to lure Janice into answering a few questions.

Janice came over and flicked the side of the near empty glass of beer in front of Durran with an eyebrow raised, a clear gesture to draw attention to its dwindling contents.

"Want another?"

"Yes," Durran said with a nod. She finished her last bite, wiping her fingers free of the sandwich grease on her napkin just as the beer was placed down beside the other glass. "That was fantastic."

"Like I said, it's a favorite," Janice told her, pulling the empty plate away and setting it on a drink mat at the far end of the bar.

"Janice, right?" Durran asked, getting a nod and a smile from her in response. "You've worked here a long time, haven't you?" She was hoping the question wasn't too presumptuous and pushy. Thankfully, Janice took the question the way Durran had intended.

"About thirty years, give or take a couple months."

"Hmm … I wonder…" Durran murmured, furrowing her brow in mock thought. Humans were inherently curious creatures. To Durran, her hint there was something interesting just on the other side wouldn't have intrigued her, but she could tell by the glint in Janice's eye that she had caught her with that murmur.

"Wonder…?" Janice prodded, leaning forward on the bar.

"Oh … it's not very interesting really. A friend of mine was abandoned as a baby. We're here trying to track down her mom who apparently was living in this town right before she was born," Durran told her honestly. Sometimes being completely truthful was the best way to get what you wanted. Janice's head tilted slightly as she brought her thoughts back to thirty years prior.

"Do you have a name?" she asked, her eyes a little unfocused as she dove into her memories, driven by the intrigue of the mystery.

"Fiona," Durran told her, finishing off the first beer and picking up the new one. Fiona wasn't a very common name, so if this woman had known her, she would most likely recall it.

Janice's eyes flickered with remembrance as she whisked the empty glass away. Not for the first time, Durran wished she had Vee's powers. If only she could tell what that carefully controlled look on Janice's face meant.

"If it's the same girl, she left not long after I started working here. She actually trained me before she went back to her country," Janice said, glancing back at Durran with an odd expression she couldn't read.

"Her country?"

"Ireland. She had an accent, not a strong one or anything … but it was obvious where she came from. She had fallen in love with some local boy. I never met him … still don't know who it was, and I know most of the locals. Told me she had come here off and on for years before she settled in for a longer time. She honestly didn't look old enough to have come here for *years*, but it could be my memory," she told Durran.

"A local, huh?" Durran mused, looking around at the patrons. Any one of them could have been Vee's father … or not. There was too little to go on with what Janice said to be sure, but Durran found it enlightening, nonetheless. Given that Janice didn't look pointedly at anyone in there, Durran assumed it wasn't one of them.

"She did run around with some Native Americans. One came in pretty often when she worked here and was training with me. He looked so young … but his…" She trailed off, brows furrowed as she recalled the memory.

"Yes?" Durran asked, trying to keep the excitement from her eyes. She was actively resisting letting her eyes glow; it would have scared Janice. But there must have been a flash of red that came through, because the bartender recoiled a little and shook her head.

"A month later, she was gone. She gave a couple days' notice, and I never saw her again," Janice told Durran, nervously using the bar towel to wipe a spot on the counter that didn't need wiping. Durran had been too eager and let it show. She could tell Janice would have said more about the Native American man, or even perhaps Fiona herself, had she kept herself in check.

"Do you know where she stayed when she was here?" Durran asked, pulling out her wallet from her coat pocket. The sign of her departure seemed to ease the anxious bartender a bit.

"I'm pretty sure she rented a room from an older woman who lived close by. I didn't know her well enough to be sure, but I know Old Ness would bring her sometimes, so she didn't have to walk."

"Does she still live there?"

"I'm not sure … I haven't seen much of her in years. She used to pop in every now and then, now it seems like she never comes by. I'm almost always behind the bar, so I'd notice," she said with a slight smile, having relaxed back into the conversation a bit. "I can write the address down for you if you'd like."

Durran paid and thanked Janice, letting her know how much she had helped them, which seemed to warm the bartender. Janice smiled happily, her eyes wrinkling a little in the corners, and asked if her friend would stop by with Durran before they left Breckenridge. Durran certainly would want to come back for the food, if nothing else, so she thought she'd try to convince Vee to come along as soon as she re-emerged from wherever the Sha had taken her.

At that thought, Durran's bond to Vee went from growing slightly distant within the area to immediately almost gone. It was the same feeling she had when she travelled to the Elder Realm. The bond was still there, but they were a world away from one another now. She had to hold onto a lamppost for a moment to come to grips with the suddenness of the feeling.

That confirmed a suspicion that the Elders had theorized for many years about the Sha. They remained out of their purview because they had a separate realm of their own. She didn't like *that* at all. Vee was wholly outside of her protection, and she would have no way of getting to her if something disastrous happened while she was in there. And now, with the knowledge she was outside the common plane, depending on what came of Vee and Shane's visit there, Durran would have to tell the Elders.

She shook the fear for Vee from her after a moment of adjustment. There was nothing she could do right now. With a breath, she continued to the address Janice had written down for her. She stepped off Main Street and headed toward a more residential area. The houses here looked small but beautiful and historic in their own right. She came upon the address on French Street. The house was obscured by a few trees in the small, gated front yard. The cream-colored exterior shadowed by leaves made it seem more mysterious than Durran would have expected.

It had a sign attached to the front gate, which indicated it was being sold, and she could tell the house was empty of occupants and staged for showing from the one large window facing the street. She pulled out her phone to do a quick search of the property. It had been on the market for at least two years, which was shocking. This house, while not huge, was in a prime location for people wanting to move to this city. Breckenridge had become a major tourist destination and a top place for younger people to move to with all the activities they could do there, and the more liberal laws in place.

The price tag was hefty, but not outrageously outlandish for what other homes in the area were selling for. Yet somehow, based on the information that her search came up with, not one person had put in an offer. She took in a deep breath, looking back at the house, and caught a distinct scent.

This home belonged to a Fae.

The smell was fresher than Durran would have expected, as if this Fae had recently been by, which was odd, considering how long the house was on the market and that it was staged inside for selling. But the fact that it was a Fae at all who had lived here explained a few things and muddled a few others. Fiona clearly had Fae in her, given her more prominent surname used was O'Morrigan, but Fae, like other

preternaturals, didn't take very kindly to anyone who was a half-breed. If Fiona had stayed here with a Fae, she had found a rare ally, indeed.

Durran looked thoughtfully at the building for a few minutes longer. It seemed like Fiona was full of surprises, just like Vee. She supposed the most surprising part was that Fiona had managed to disappear after handing Vee over to the Malones. Vee had essentially disappeared from preternatural eyes when she'd left St. Louis all those years ago and came back to Kansas City, but that wasn't particularly difficult to do, since she had barely registered on anyone's radar at that point. If Fiona came from the Morrigans, her disappearance for thirty years without even a trace was a shocking feat.

Or maybe she was dead.

That thought sent a chill through Durran.

Vee had already lost so much. If this search ended with the knowledge that her birth mother was dead, it might send Vee over the edge.

With a reluctant sigh, Durran turned to head back into town. She would deal with that only if it came to it.

CHAPTER 13

Vee watched Aho take a bite of his sandwich and look up at her expectantly. She lifted her own, mildly confused by his question about her occupation, but didn't feel like she couldn't answer it.

"I'm a locksmith," she told him, taking her own bite of the sandwich. He nodded, taking that information in, as if that confirmed something for him. He looked like he was considering his next question, when Shane's exasperation flooded her. He already felt extremely on edge, didn't like her being interrogated, and they had yet to discover exactly why they were summoned there.

"Why were we called here, Aho?" Shane asked suddenly. Aho's face grew solemn. He set his sandwich back down on his plate and folded his hands together.

"I told you. Your mating has caused some concern. The Sha now need to know what she is," he said quietly.

He looked over Shane, who was rigid in his seat, power
from his wolf radiating out from him.

Vee would have thought being in Aho's house and
less exposed to all the other Sha would have calmed
him a little, but apparently she was wrong. Aho's
answer had not been what Shane or his wolf needed
to ease them. Nothing seemed to be capable of that
at the moment. He was struggling with control; the
skin on his hands seeming to wriggle with anticipated change just under the surface. She could feel his
internal struggle, wanting to remain calm and continue conversing with the Sha before him, but his wolf
battled within him. Usually, the two were in sync, but
right now, with Shane's golden eyes glaring at the man
across the table, Vee knew that his wolf was only a
whisper away from taking over.

Aho, careful not to look into Shane's eyes and inad-
vertently challenge him, turned his gaze to look at Vee
with burning amber eyes. "Your room is the last one at
the end of the hall. Your bags are already waiting there
for you. Take some time to rest. We will talk, then we
will head to the feast that's been planned," Aho told
them, bobbing his head in the direction of a doorway
to a hall behind him that Vee hadn't noticed before.

Shane stood from his seat abruptly, the legs of his
chair scraping noisily against the stone floor, before
grasping Vee's hand and pulling her through the
doorway and down the hall to a closed door. Vee suspected the reason Aho dismissed them like he had was
because he, like Vee, could tell Shane was on the verge
of being overtaken by his wolf. Vee managed to be the

one to catch the doorknob, opening it before Shane had a chance to break it under his grasp.

He stomped in the room, a low rumble coming from his chest, while Vee closed the door behind them, turning slowly to watch him pace.

"What do you need?" she asked quietly.

He paused, turning his golden eyes to her before crossing the few steps between them and pinning her to the door. She couldn't help the little gasp of surprise that escaped her lips at the suddenness of the action. Shane momentarily seemed to pause, breathing in through his nose to make sure he didn't smell fear from her before tightening his grip just slightly. Even in this state, he wouldn't hurt his mate.

"You. I need you, but we can't right now," he rasped out, running his nose from her collar bone to the sensitive spot behind her ear. Vee knew he meant he needed their full bond, he needed that full connection, but she also understood that they were in a strange position being in Aho's house.

"Open up," Vee murmured. He shuddered a little, overwhelmed by his own feelings, but he started to let the small wall he had built up in the bond fall away. She could feel everything he did: anxiety, protectiveness, possessiveness, anger, lust. Everything at an alarmingly high concentration. She had felt it building after they'd moved through the veil. That magic had triggered something in him, making everything he felt amplified. Vee listened and heard Aho walk through the house and close the front door. He was on the porch now, she thought.

What could she do to take away whatever was affecting him so much? She touched either side of Shane's face, looking into his burning eyes. She could feel him pressing even harder against her body, hands grasping at her roughly, as if he were trying to regain mastery of himself and fight his own impulses by only allowing himself to feel her. She felt his hips pressing into hers, and an unfamiliar object was also jabbing from her pants pocket.

For a moment, she was confused by it, but she realized it was the pale green stone.

She had put it in her pocket, since it couldn't go on the chain around her neck like the key and the wolf head. Her mind immediately went to the letter from Fiona.

To see.

Vee pulled her right hand from Shane's face, trying to assure him with her eyes she wasn't going to push him away, before she dug her hand in her pocket and retrieved it. She didn't know exactly what she was doing or what she expected to happen, but she held the stone in front of her right eye and looked at Shane through it. She could see a very thin shimmer just around his eyes.

She thought back to the moment they'd moved through the veil; something had happened between Min and Shane, something that made Shane upset and overly protective of her. She had felt the veil as they passed through almost welcoming her, but she could sense that had she not been in the right frame of mind, that magic could have done *something* to her. It was magic that had been placed there long ago, old, she knew innately. It had a mind of its own.

Vee pulled his head down to hers, pressing their foreheads together. What his wolf needed was their bond, but right now was not the time. Not when they had just arrived here in this potentially hostile domain, when they needed to be alert and aware of everything that was happening around them.

His breath was ragged as he struggled, his control slipping with each passing moment that whatever had attached itself to him at the gate writhed over his eyes and within him. There was only one other way she could think to get him out of this situation. She tried to think of calm, soothing things, pushing her thoughts toward that and what had happened to him through their bond. If he understood, maybe he could fight it, but a little push from her abilities to help stabilize him wouldn't hurt.

At first, he resisted it. He didn't like her influencing his emotions any more than she liked doing that to someone unwillingly, but he understood the need for it. Shane hadn't lost control like this for decades. The closest he had ever come, since he was newly changed, was when Vee had been attacked and even in both of those times, he had never felt so disconnected to his wolf, so at war with the other part of himself. Their desires, their objective, was usually the same.

This was wrong. This was different.

Logically, he also was very aware that they were in Sha territory, in Aho's house. He couldn't afford to lose control here. He *had* to let her influence him.

Shane let himself go in the feeling of comfort she was sending him and the sureness of her touch. He saw her thoughts on what had happened, as if they were images in his own mind, and considered how threatened he'd felt by Min just before they went through the veil. How the way Min looked at Vee had put his wolf on alert. And then as they'd passed through the doorway, how it seemed to pull at him, resisting his entrance, even feeling like it lingered there, dragging at him until they broke through the trees.

"He's not a threat. Let him go," Vee whispered, so quietly he wouldn't have been able to hear it if he wasn't pressed fully against her. Her words, the sound of her voice, and her touch, seemed to dissolve whatever was left of the magic from the doorway that was still clinging to him.

Immediately, it was like something clicked back into place between him and his wolf. He was able to think logically, and the beast understood. He relaxed slightly, leaning further into the calm Vee gave him and pressing his face into her neck.

Vee felt it leave him, passing over her with oddly intelligent interest, and then it was gone. It felt different than other magic she had encountered. Sha magic. Older and perhaps more primal. She realized it seemed to acknowledge her and embrace her instead of attack, like it had to Shane. Odd, considering he was, being a Werewolf, much more closely related to that magic than she was.

She slowly pulled back the calm she was sending Shane but kept their bond open. They both needed the additional contact. He did from his end too, and although the extremeness had gone, all the other emotions remained.

"Their magic felt your hostility to Min, it seems," she murmured, her hand now gently caressing the back of his neck, which had collected a bit of sweat from the effort he had just put forth.

"I didn't like the way he looked at you," Shane said, his voice slightly muffled against her. She let her chest shake with a silent chuckle. He pulled back only enough to look into her eyes. "I thought I'd be protecting you here ... but you," he brushed his lips against hers, "you protected me."

"You're mine," she whispered, pushing her fingers up into his hair.

"You are full of surprises," he told her with a rumble of quiet laughter, closing the distance so their lips met again. It was hard to resist her when she said those words to him, and they would have loved to take it further, but Vee pulled away, breathless, recalling there was an ancient Sha waiting on the porch outside for them and, later, a feast of some kind to attend. Shane regretfully gave her one more quick kiss, then pulled away from her. She shoved the seeing stone back into her pocket and took in the room they were in.

It was a decent-sized room, able to hold all its furniture without seeming cramped. The floors were the same hardwood as the rest of the house and were complemented nicely with the thick, wooden bed frame. There were a few shelves of books and a reading chair tucked on one side, as well as a small table that had a beautiful reading lamp beside it. The lamp shade was made with intricate stained glass, clearly done by hand. Their bags were placed on a trunk that sat at the foot of the bed.

Shane started opening his suitcase to grab another shirt, his had soaked through with sweat.

"We shouldn't keep him waiting much longer. I don't know how long we've been in here," Shane admitted, pulling on another button-up. Vee wasn't sure how he'd managed to pack those without them coming out all wrinkled. She was certain all her clothes would still be wrinkled despite her efforts the day before, though it didn't bother her as much now that she had seen the way the people here dressed.

They wandered back out of their room, glancing around to see if Aho had come back in the house but found he hadn't. It looked like he'd cleaned up the sandwiches, which disappointed Vee slightly. She had only gotten one bite, and Shane hadn't even touched his. They had only eaten breakfast that morning and though the greasy food had stuck with her for their car ride, she was now painfully hungry.

They stepped out onto the porch to find Aho on the swing, his hands carefully working on the wood-carving that had been placed on the tree stump when they'd arrived. The sun was starting to set, and Vee realized she had no idea what time it was or how long they had been there. It had barely been afternoon when they'd arrived in Breckenridge, but that seemed so long ago now.

"I'm sorry for that. I'm usually much more controlled," Shane said, trying not to show his embarrassment. Showing weakness in front of other predators could be deadly, though out of all the Sha for Shane to have that occur in front of, he was happy it was Aho.

"The Spirit of the Gate is very protective of our kind. I wasn't sure it was her until I saw your wolf in your eyes and smelled her in your anger," Aho told Shane, not looking up from his work. The admission that it was, in fact, the gate that had affected him from Aho helped ease the remaining bit of anxiety. Because though their assumption it was the gate felt rather sound, there was still a possibility something else was at play, and Shane couldn't afford to lose control of his wolf.

"Old magic can have a mind of its own," Vee parroted her own thoughts from before. Aho chuckled quietly, looking up at her.

"Or they were made with their own mind," he said, his eyes twinkling with a subtle smile on his lips. "Sit there," he told her, gesturing to the stump. She did, leaving Shane to lean against the porch post beside her.

Aho's eyes moved over her, studying her face, his hands having stilled on the wood he was carving. The intensity of his gaze grew slightly uncomfortable as she felt his intrigue, so she looked down at the carving in his hands. It was small, maybe about the size of her palm, which was not large by any means because her hands were tiny. The wood was still rough and the carving not nearly close to being finished, but Vee could make out the subtle shape of an animal of some kind. She recognized the grooves that were being dug into it to add texture. They were like many of the wood furniture that was carved inside his home.

"Tell me what you've discovered about your past," Aho said after several long minutes. Vee looked back up to meet his eyes. Unlike Min, Aho seemed gentler,

kinder. She didn't know why, but she felt like she could trust him, at least trust him as much as one could trust a Sha.

"All we know is my mother gave me over to a human family when I was about nine months old. We're not sure what type of preternatural she is, but we have a few … guesses. I have a letter she wrote me. She said, 'We walk in more than one world.' She basically disappeared after that," Vee told him, watching his face for any sign of recognition.

An intense feeling of shock washed over him for a moment, turning his eyes burning amber only briefly before it faded away. He opened his mouth to say something, but they all heard the footfalls of someone coming down the path, causing him to snap his mouth shut as they turned to see who was approaching.

Min came slowly into view, walking along the path. There was no sense of urgency in his gait as he passed the pond and stood just outside of the porch, but his eyes narrowed in suspicion at the silence that greeted his approach.

"Food is prepared," he told them.

"Good," Aho said, standing from the swing and holding out a hand to Vee. Shane stiffened, but Vee shot him a look to indicate it was okay, taking Aho's hand in assistance and standing from the stump.

Aho was still barefoot, and she realized so was Min, so she had no urge to put on her shoes once more, but Shane did, briefly ducking back inside to grab them before they made their way back through the woods on the small path.

CHAPTER 13

Vee took Shane's hand in hers, and they followed the two Sha. Something about the way Aho looked at her when she'd told him what she knew made her think he *did* know something about her past. The shock she'd felt from him, and the burn of his eyes … her intuition told her he knew far more about her past than anyone else did so far. Suddenly, a bit of exhilaration bubbled within her that this trip, originally disruptive to their search, might have been the key to discovering more than they would have with the packet alone.

They came through the tree line as the sun dipped below the horizon, the sky finally darkening into a deep purple. They could see lights and fires flickering at the town center. The smell of food wafted to their noses as they got closer. Vee's stomach made an involuntary growl. She didn't care how volatile this first meal was going to be; she was starving, and she had seriously lacked the coffee that normally kept her appetite at bay.

Once they passed between the buildings, a huge table was revealed to them. It was long, stretching down the center of the walking path for probably sixty feet, only broken up in the center where a huge fire was positioned with roasting spokes. She hadn't noticed it when they'd walked through the first time, but the stones on the path were laid out in a massive circle there, she supposed, to mark the center for this very purpose.

Many more Sha were present now than what they had seen when they'd originally walked through. Hundreds of them, at least, were sitting at tables or talking in small groups. The ease and joy that came from everyone present gave Vee an oddly cozy feeling in her chest. There were no children that Vee could see, only a few people she guessed were about Lori and Patrick's age, since they were laughing and throwing things at the fire pit, giving off an air of teenager mischievousness. There were a few people playing music, nothing specific, like they were just jamming together to warm up. Several had strange instruments she had never seen before, quite a few had drums of various shapes and sizes. People were still placing food at the center of the tables.

A woman who looked to be Vee's age came forward, having noticed when they stopped to take everything in. She was small in stature, her eyes much larger than Vee would have expected on her delicate face. She had very similar coloring to Min and Aho, as if they could have all been related. But she supposed everyone here was. Shane had told her that the Sha could only be born from each other, and as such, they did not stray from their own for mating. She wasn't sure if they were all terribly interbred and the defects were kept at bay with magic, or if most of them were simply *that old*.

"Shane! I'm so glad to see you again. How is Thomas's arm?" the woman asked, coming close to him and pressing her hand to his cheek. It was too familiar a gesture for Vee's liking, and her grip on his hand tightened.

"Thomas was back to himself fully just a few hours after you left," Shane said, giving Vee a reassuring squeeze back on her fingers.

"I suppose it was over a year ago. I was a little concerned I didn't set it properly," the woman, whose name was Yona, continued, face beaming with joy.

"Yona, this is Vee," he said, turning his gaze away from Yona to Vee, a hint of amusement there and through the bond at her possessiveness.

Yona smiled brightly, eyes large and wide as she pulled her hand from his face and touched it to Vee's cheek instead. Apparently, she was big on physically touching others. Instantly, Vee felt her excitement through the contact with her skin. There were no hidden emotions, only happiness and interest.

"Vee, you are quite the mystery, aren't you?" she said, more as a statement and less as a question. She then dropped her hand to take Vee's free one and pulled her, and subsequently Shane, over to the main table. The conversation at the table quieted with their approach as a sea of brown eyes all turned to them. There was a tense anticipation in the air. The way most of them looked at her was as if she was going to reach out and bite them. Vee's heart, which she knew they could all hear clearly, beat wildly in her chest. Between her own anxiety and the emotions that were flooding her from the Sha, her throat felt tight, and her fingers dug into Shane's hand a little harder as they moved closer.

CHAPTER 14

Yona brought them to the end of the table closest to the fire pit. There were four others already seated on the other side of the table, two women and two men. They also had oddly ambiguous features, nothing to point out exactly where they came from. But both the men had skin so dark, Vee felt like they could melt into the shadows and disappear, while the women beside them were fairer than her, despite the undertone still being olive. Their dark eyes peered at her emotionlessly as she sat.

"This is Shane Keenan of the Westport Pack and his mate, Victoria Malone," Min told them. She was taken aback only slightly at the use of her full name. Names were meaningful to preternaturals, she knew, but it never ceased to jar her slightly when she was presented formally before others. She had thought that

Min and Aho were in charge in this realm, but now that she looked across the table at the four who sat there, she wasn't so sure. If Min was introducing them to these four, it was possible he answered to them.

"These are the others on the Sha Council: Long, Hurin, Urmah, and Bao," Aho said, as if he'd read her thoughts, each giving a brief nod as he said their names. "First, we will feed our guests before you start questioning them, yes?" he continued, sitting beside Vee and pouring himself a glass of dark-colored liquid from the pitcher in front of him. It smelled sweet and mildly yeasty. Vee assumed it was some sort of beer.

"Yes," the woman named Long said, her face twisting into a knowing smirk before she gestured for everyone to continue what they had been doing. The anticipation was thick in the air. Questions sat on the tips of their tongues, but they instead resumed the meal.

Normal conversation picked up around them, and the music started up again. Vee and Shane waited for the others to start filling their plates before they did, but once she started, Vee couldn't be bothered to care how offensive her ravenous eating was. She had gone far too many hours to care. By her estimation, it had to have been about eight at night, over twelve hours since she had last eaten a real meal. The meek bite of sandwich earlier had only reminded her of how hungry she actually was.

And ravenous she was. The food was delightful, rich, and full of flavor. Meat that had been spiced and cooked perfectly on the spoke, so the skin was crisp and the flesh tender. There were fruit and vegetable dishes Vee had no exact way to describe, but they were so delicious, she couldn't even stop to ask. Even the bread was better than she had ever had, no hint of preservatives, and nutty and dark with unrefined grains.

It was only once she started slowing her eating, wiping her face with the cloth provided for her beside her plate, that she realized how uncivilized she had been behaving. Tentatively, she glanced around but was surprised no one seemed perturbed by her lack of manners. In fact, no one there was behaving as particularly formal. This felt more like a casual extended family barbecue rather than a feast with some of the most powerful preternaturals in the world.

Long's gaze seemed to lock on Vee once she had finished her food. Vee couldn't help but look back. Long's hair was pinned up on her head, jet black, from what Vee could tell, even though it was well into the night. A few silky strands of hair were falling around to frame her oval face. Vee couldn't feel hostility from her, but uncertainty prickled along the edges.

"Victoria, we've done a bit of research on you, but we didn't come up with much," Long said. Her voice was lower than Vee expected, but beautifully rich. She could have spoken in any language, and Vee would have wanted to hear it for hours.

"I don't really like attention," Vee told her honestly with a shrug.

"You have kept a very low profile from humans and preternatural alike until recently," Long affirmed.

"You go by Vee, is that right?" the man named Urmah asked. He was much taller than the others, towering over them even while still seated. His dark skin was like the midnight sky, and his hair was made into long, perfect locks that cascaded over his broad shoulders.

"That's what I prefer, yes,"

"She is interesting, mysterious, and beautiful, Shane. How did you manage to stumble across her and claim her as yours?" he asked, a smile spreading over his lips to reveal his beautiful white teeth. He had been physically intimidating before, but with his smile and the way the fire seemed to dance across his eyes and skin, he was beautiful as well. They all were.

The mention of her own beauty had Vee casting her eyes down at her empty plate. She would never have considered herself beautiful before. Not ugly, by any means, but not anything spectacular either. That perception seemed to change for her when she felt how Shane saw her through their bond. To her, she seemed plain and mousy, her only good feature being her eyes. To Shane, she was stunning. To hear someone else call her beautiful made her cheeks feel hot.

"It was just that, honestly. I stumbled across her," Shane admitted, glancing at her as he did so, a little flicker of amusement and joy flowing to her as he recalled it again.

"I wonder what it is about you that allowed you two to bond," Bao speculated from the end of the table, looking at her curiously. It was a similar expression to the one Min had given her earlier. As if Bao was trying to pull Vee apart with just her eyes. Bao's eyes were a bit more predatory than the others, but again, not necessarily hostile, just interested.

"I think…" Shane started, hesitating just slightly and brushing his thumb over the top of Vee's hand. "I believe she's my True Mate," he said quietly. The whole gathering went silent, even the musicians stopped; only the crackle of the fire remained for a beat or two.

Vee felt everyone's surprise and disbelief flood her, except for Aho, who was beside her, still leisurely sipping that dark liquid and crunching loudly on a crusty piece of bread. There was a strange sense of *knowing* in him.

"It's not possible for someone who is not a Were or Sha to be the True Mate of one of your kind. That magic stems from *us*," Hurin said to Shane, his brow furrowing as he looked at the two of them.

"But it is so," Aho said, his voice calm and casual as he brushed the crumbs from his fingers. "Don't you see it? He may not have pulled her into his pack completely yet, but their bond is far greater than a normal mating bond. It reminds me of the bond you, Bao, had with … well … when your mate lived."

Bao sucked in a ragged breath at the mention of her dead mate, turning her head away from them to stare at the fire. Bao was feeling a despair so deep that it made Vee clutch to Shane's hand for dear life. She had never known such a feeling … except when their bond had been ripped from her body. Vee used every ounce of self-control to keep herself from crying out at both her memory of that pain and Bao's.

"Unnecessary, Aho," Yona hissed beside him, reaching across the table to hold Bao's hand. Vee found it strange Bao's mate's name wasn't said, but it was probably better, given the reaction. Sudden warmth flooded Vee, radiating from fingers entwined with Shane's. He was silently comforting her through their bond, almost immediately making it easier for her to breathe.

"You managed to make a bond with her, but haven't tried to bring her into your pack?" Min asked, his voice carrying curiosity, which was more emotion than Vee had heard from his tone the entire time she had been around him. She could tell his question was meant to not only satisfy that inquisitiveness, but also to distract from Bao, giving her a minute to collect herself in front of the others. Shane stiffened at the question, trying to close down their bond a bit so Vee couldn't feel the reason why, but she lashed out, sending her irritation through to him.

Never again.

He glanced down at her, taking in the pinched look around her eyes, and sighed.

"Not being a Were, the ritual might be too gruesome for her," Shane told them, his anxiety over her potential fear and disgust washing over her. A little wave of understanding went through the group. This piqued her interest. Gruesome, huh?

"I don't even know what the ritual is. Maybe I can make that determination for myself," Vee said back in a clipped tone, gaining grins from nearly every Sha in view.

"Perhaps tomorrow we can all remedy your ignorance, Vee. Being protective of your mate only benefits her if you don't keep her from things she should know," Urmah said, tipping his cup toward Vee, but his eyes were on Shane. Vee liked the idea of understanding Weres a bit better. She had been surrounded by them, working and then living with them, for over a year;

however her understanding of them had not grown as much as she would have expected. She still felt like she knew little more than what she'd learned as a teenager when she lived with Jack, Bea, and Talia.

"But tonight, you'll enjoy," Yona said, standing and reaching between Aho and Vee to grab her hand, pulling her toward the musicians by the big fire at the center. They had started playing an actual number that seemed well-known to the Sha, since people were surrounding them and the fire, singing along with the melody and starting to clear a space in front of where the band was playing. It wasn't a tune Vee was familiar with, but it was lively, and others had started dancing happily.

Shane reluctantly let her hand fall from his grasp and watched her for a moment as she awkwardly swayed to the rhythm of the drums, while Yona tried to get her to move her body more.

"I *do* see it," Bao murmured, causing Shane to turn back to the Sha across the table. Her eyes were narrowed as she looked at him. "How did you manage that?" Her voice was wistful as she said it, full of yearning, Shane supposed, from the memory of her True Mate. The thought of living on if Vee were to die was unbearable. The hollowness in Bao's eyes reflected that sentiment.

"She's a lot more than she seems. A lot more than she knows," Aho said, watching Vee, who was getting a little more comfortable dancing with Yona. She was at least moving to the rhythm of the music, which was an improvement over her stiff, uncomfortable feet shuffling around like she had been doing moments before.

She laughed as she tried to imitate a few steps Yona was teaching her and stumbled a little.

"Full of surprises," Shane murmured with a nod, turning back to watch her as well.

The feast died down, the exuberant dancing giving way over time to smaller, quieter conversation. Everyone helped to clear the empty dishes from the tables, setting them in large washing troughs where several Sha were busy scrubbing. Everything was a team effort. They all worked together, even the ones in charge. Vee and Shane had just finished talking to one of the musicians about their instrument when Aho let out a short cry, getting everyone's attention.

"Time for our guests to rest from their travels," he said, once he had everyone's attention. They all seemed to nod, several of them approaching to press their hands to their shoulders in farewell before they followed Aho back through the buildings to the gated path toward the woods ahead. The lack of light pollution made the moon and stars seem so much brighter as they walked, casting the woods in softer shadows than Vee would have expected.

Aho passed through the front door of his house, again without ceremony. He turned once they were inside, and Shane was pulling his shoes from his feet.

"My room is there," he said, pointing to the first door in the hallway. "The next is the bathroom. I need to run," he said shortly, turning and nodding to them, before going straight back out the front door. It was

abrupt, and Vee found herself staring after him for a beat. It was strange, but then again, everything about this was strange.

Aho had seemed deep in thought for the last several hours of the evening. She had turned to catch him looking at her, not that many of the other Sha weren't openly staring at her as well, but his eyes held a sense of longing, excitement, and mild dread. This run, which is what all shapeshifting creatures seemed to call a shift into their beast, was being used to help him collect his thoughts. She couldn't change into anything, but she imagined running in animal form helped him focus. Shane had sometimes done that, but it was hard to run in the city as a wolf. He would have a much easier time in the wide swath of land behind the new house.

She went into the bathroom, while Shane headed to the room they were in before. The bathroom was quite normal, almost shockingly so. It had white tiles that smoothed over the floor and halfway up the walls. The shower and tub were one, like her apartment had been, but she suspected it drained much better than her apartment shower ever did. She washed her face and looked at herself in the mirror for a moment.

This was still scary, she had to remind herself. Even though the Sha had been welcoming and kind so far, there could always be ulterior motives. She had to remind herself that these were dangerous and mysterious preternaturals. While they ruled over Weres, they were in no way obligated to *her*.

But that didn't change how she felt strangely at peace in this place. The moment she'd walked through the gate, she felt the wash of serenity overcome her.

Almost like she was meant to be there. Vee glanced at her own reflection, realizing had her eyes been brown, she would have fit in well in a place like this and despite having always been a city girl, the harmony of the nature here called to her. The comradery of the people of the Sha felt natural.

Then she caught sight of those emerald-green eyes and shook her head, smiling ruefully at herself. No, she didn't fit in anywhere. This place was no different.

She wandered back to the bedroom where Shane was. He stood, striding over to her before he kissed the top of her head, a pair of sweatpants clutched in his hand before he passed her to go to the bathroom himself. She rummaged through her own bag, disdainfully realizing she had neglected to pack anything to sleep in. Shane had pulled out a worn T-shirt of his own and set it on the bed for himself. Well, that was going to have to do.

She had just put the shirt over her head when Shane came back into the room. He froze in the doorway as he watched his shirt fall over her, overly large for her small frame and stopping just below mid-thigh. He never wanted to see her in anything other than his shirts again.

He snapped the door shut without turning his eyes away, making Vee turn to him with the heat of his gaze.

"I somehow forgot to pack anything to sleep in," Vee said sheepishly, pulling her hair out from under the collar. He took the few steps to her quickly and pulled her against him, bending to run his nose against her neck. She smelled like her ... and him.

"I'm glad," he said against her skin. She shivered under his touch.

The day had been so strange. They were out of their element, unsure of how much, if any danger they were in, but here touching each other, they felt at home. Shane pulled away from her neck to touch his lips to hers. It was soft, asking if she was comfortable rather than demanding. She returned the kiss a bit more aggressively. They had held it together earlier when he had nearly lost control, but they were alone here for the time being, even if it wasn't their house. Aho's mind was nowhere nearby.

Shane took the invitation, fingers gliding up her legs with gentle pressure and under the hem of *his* shirt. Their kiss intensified, breathing ragged as his hands gripped at her rump. Vee was running her fingers over his chest, her fingernails digging in as he effortlessly tore her underwear away. She shook slightly as Shane's lips travelled away from hers to her neck again, gently pushing her hips onto the bed. She began trying to pull the shirt up, but he caught her wrist.

"Leave it on," he growled, kissing her again and using his weight to lie her back against the mattress.

His hands, strong and long, moved up her thighs once again, fanning out as he reached her hips.

"I wanted to give you more," he rasped out, pulling away from her to take the sight of her in, sprawled on the bed, dark hair fanning around her head, her legs parted, shirt rumpled, and face flushed as she gazed up at him. Her eyes burned amber as they stared up at him, breath coming in uneven pants. "But I can't wait," he said in a growl, pushing his sweatpants off his hips and pulling her roughly by her legs until she was on the edge of the bed. She didn't want him to wait. She didn't need more right then. She needed him.

She stared into his eyes as he stood there in all his beautiful, naked glory. His eyes were molten orbs of lava, only for her. He lifted her off the bed, holding her easily in his arms as he kissed her again, turning to press her back to the wall.

"It took so much effort not to do this earlier," he hissed out as they finally connected. She moaned and gripped his shoulders, her legs wrapping around his waist as he began moving. Nothing about this was slow or patient. This place was surely magic, and feelings were heightened here as they joined. She didn't want it to end, but she wanted it faster, harder. Vee was certain she'd hurt him, her nails digging into his flesh, urging him to keep going. He readily obliged, his pace quickening so much that her feet unhooked and her back arched.

As they came down from their high, Vee still pinned to the wall with Shane's head buried in her neck again, Vee felt the exhaustion of the day settling into them. Shane lifted his head, his eyes back to their normal warm brown. With one more soft kiss, he carried her to the bed, curled around her, and they both fell soundly to sleep.

CHAPTER 15

The darkness moved over Breckenridge swiftly once it hit 8 p.m. Durran had texted Vee updates about what she'd found in her daytime searching, but having been away from the hotel so long, her phone died while she had been searching for more information about the house. She decided to follow the faint scent of the Fae, since it had been relatively fresh at the empty house. What she would do when she came across this Fae, she wasn't sure, but she did have a name, and that could prove to be useful when dealing with Fae.

Durran hoped that if this person had been an ally for Fiona that they would be for Vee too. Though logically, she knew any additional preternatural involvement in Vee's life was bound to be trouble. Vee needed allies, not more enemies.

CHAPTER 15

It was odd that the scent had been so fresh and in sync with their arrival to Colorado. Strange that this house had been sitting for so long without anyone wanting to purchase it. She wondered if it was Fae magic keeping the humans away, or if there was some other, sinister reason the house remained empty.

Finally rounding a corner, following the scent, Durran stopped as she was met with another distinct smell. She was back at the parking lot for the hotel. The scent in the air was not what she was expecting. There, standing beside the Jeep, was a Vampire. His blond hair was slicked back, long fingers hesitating as they moved close to the passenger door where Vee had exited. His pointed nose clearly scenting the air, scenting for Vee.

Breckenridge was not a good place for Vampires. Though it snowed there, human-shaped predators didn't often do well in places where the humans stayed cooped up in their homes most nights. Durran's eyes glowed red in the darkness, watching this creature as it hungrily took in what he could glean from her scent there.

"Duflanc. what are you doing away from your nest?" Durran asked darkly, causing the Vampire's head to snap up and look at her. She didn't make a habit of letting other preternaturals know who she was, but night creatures tended to notice her more often. She had come across Duflanc a time or two over the years but had managed to keep Vee far from any topic of conversation they may have had.

"What are *you* doing here, Durran?" Duflanc asked, his confused expression turning smug as the pieces clicked together in his mind.

"I am a Watcher. I move around. You tend to stay with your flock. Why have you left them?" Durran continued, trying to keep the subject of conversation on Duflanc's intentions.

"Your ward ... it's this woman, Vee, isn't it?" Duflanc asked, pressing his hand to the door of the Jeep and inhaling sharply. "She's marvelous. Her smell ... I don't know how I didn't notice it before."

"She is not your concern. You should return to Kansas City," Durran warned, her height growing slightly as she stood across from him.

"I haven't had blood like hers in so long. It's my favorite, those mixed bloods. Their power so untapped..."

"Vee holds no power that you are privy to, Lazare," Durran said coldly.

"Nor you, even if you *are* her Watcher. Mated to the pack leader. How very *interesting* she continues to be."

"Her power is only for her. You need to leave," Durran growled. No, Vee's power *was* only for her. Even Shane knew better than to try to use her for it. And what Vee's power was, was still so much a mystery. She hadn't yet repeated what happened in Pleasant Hill, but there was something hiding within Durran's ward. Some kind of magic was lying dormant there.

"Just tell me where she is. I wouldn't kill her," Duflanc said, his eyes glowing with the intensity of a shark who smelled blood.

"You wouldn't be able to get to her now, even if you tried. Go home," Durran hissed, eyes noticing the humans in her peripheral vision. They hadn't taken notice yet, but if Duflanc escalated things, they certainly would.

"I *need* her blood, Durran. Need it to go on," Duflanc said quietly, closing his eyes as he scented the air once again. His voice was odd as he said those words, shaky and breathy. Hollow with unquenchable yearning.

"She will not give her blood to you, Vampire," came another voice, startling Durran more than she would have liked to admit. The woman who stepped from the shadows was hunched and frail. Her skin was heavily wrinkled and her hair a mess of short, white curls, but she moved like someone who was quite a bit younger. She stepped closer between Durran and the Vampire, her face full of authority.

Durran could smell her as she came nearer. Fae.

This was Ness, the woman she had been searching for. The scent had led her straight here, hadn't it? But now as she looked at her, Durran realized she had seen this old woman before. The scent had been familiar, but not enough for Durran to catch on right away. This Fae had been the one who Vee had encountered at the laundromat over a year ago. The revelation that this woman had been right under their noses this whole time would have sent Durran into a frenzy of frustration, had there not been a genuine threat before them.

"Fae," Duflanc hissed, ripping his hand from the car. His eyes burned with fury as he looked at the Watcher and the Fae before him.

"She cannot be sullied by the likes of you," Ness nearly spat, upper lip curled in disgust. Duflanc's hands curled into fists, his whole body tensing as if he were going to attack, but the sounds of the humans nearby cut through the darkened parking lot, causing them all to still. This was too exposed for a fight.

"*Ce n'est pas fini,*" Duflanc hissed before he ran from the parking lot, his speed so fast, he seemed to have disappeared.

Durran and the Fae named Ness were silent and still for a moment, waiting to be certain the Vampire was truly gone. She turned to Durran, her brilliant blue eyes looking at her with little change in the hatred that had been previously directed toward Duflanc. Durran bowed her head slightly as a greeting toward the woman but did not drop her eyes.

"I take it you are Ness?" Durran asked, slowly taking a step closer. Though Ness's body looked frail, it moved with grace and power as she also took a step forward as well.

"That is what I go by here and other places. You are the Watcher for the girl named Vee," Ness said, her voice not hiding behind the shaky notes of the old woman's glamor anymore. It sounded odd, as most Fae did, like a low bell was ringing at the end of each word.

"I am," Durran confirmed with a nod.

"*She* didn't come here seeking."

"She came for another reason," Durran said, gesturing to the empty Jeep that Duflanc had defiled with his touch.

"She knows too much and not enough," Ness said as she sighed, letting the tension of the previous minutes leave her.

"You were her mother's ally, were you not?" Durran asked, taking another step forward.

"Stop there, Watcher. I helped her because of those I serve. Do not tempt me to harm you. She will need you for the times to come," Ness said coldly, causing

Durran to settle where she stood, planting her feet and crossing her arms instead of taking another step.

"And you are here to help Vee?"

"I told her I would, and she comes here without a moment to spare. She's seeking truth, while others seek what's inside of her. They cannot have it."

"What is it?" Durran asked, brow furrowed as she tried to parse through the Fae's cryptic words. Clearly, the attack from Gwen months ago had been just a taste of what was to come if Ness mentioned more wanting to take from Vee. Duflanc was on the list, but his intentions were rather clear. Ness's head titled slightly as she looked upon Durran with interest.

"I am not told everything, only what I need to know to follow those I serve," Ness confessed, seeming to wilt a bit. "You, Watcher … you are not a threat to her as of now. But your kind…" Ness grimaced at the implied mention of the Elders. There was hatred and fear in her eyes.

Durran wanted to know what had happened between the Morrigan and the Elders. What had caused this rift between them, when their purposes were so similar? She did not want to make a deal with a Fae, but she wanted information. Information held power; it had to be equal.

"I will tell you something you wish to know, if you tell me what happened between the Morrigan and the Elder Watchers," Durran offered. There was other information she should be asking about, but Vee's fate could be tied to how the Elders reacted to her relation to the Fae.

A strange eagerness came over the face of the woman. Durran had seen it before, when she was trying to get Vee's name that day in the laundromat.

Hunger.

Fae craved bargains.

"Are you not old enough, Watcher, to know the tale?" she asked, her tone a bit condescending as she looked Durran over.

"I'm old, but we are not told tales that aren't deemed necessary for our duty," Durran told her. Watchers were not raised like children of any other creature, human or preternatural. They were raised to know their duty, their path, their ward's path, and nothing more. Stories of old were not shared unless it was vital to their mission.

Ness smiled grimly at her, taking in a breath.

"I would love to make such a deal with you, but you are still needed by Vee, and because of that, I must wait," Ness said, her teeth chattering a bit with the effort to keep herself in check.

"Wait for what?"

"I cannot answer that right now. I must wait, and you must wait. Wait for Vee to return from the Sha. Wait for her true path to unfold. Wait for the final thread to show itself and to see what fate truly befalls us all." She shuddered a little as she said it, looking up at the night sky for a moment. "We had all been exactly as we were supposed to be until Fiona. One small creature made such a difference, but then she made another. They both are outside of the purview. They belong nowhere and everywhere, and therefore their fates are always uncertain," Ness said finally, eyes turning back to Durran.

For one brief moment, Durran could see the true form of the woman. Her skin dark, face heart-shaped with eyes as large as Durran's palm. She was beautiful and frightening. "You'll see me again, Watcher," she said, before she strolled back the way she came, leaving Durran standing in the middle of the parking lot a bit shaken.

CHAPTER 16

Vee woke to the sun hitting her face at an unfamiliar angle. Shane's arms were still wrapped around her, so she nestled in a little, enjoying the comfort of his weight against her. It didn't matter where she was— Shane was with her. But she felt that unfamiliar and intense buzz of Aho's presence near, and she remembered, very suddenly, where they were.

She wasn't sure how she managed to slip out from under Shane's arms, but she did, stopping briefly to admire his relaxed body against the bed, his face still serene with sleep. She would have preferred to take a shower before seeing Aho, since she was certain she still smelled of their activities before bed the night previous, but somehow, she thought Aho would probably care less about that than the pack back home would. She wasn't sure if it was because he appeared more laid-back in general, or if it was because he seemed like he was born in a time and with people where sex was viewed as just as natural as the trees growing.

She pulled on her jeans from the day before, but left Shane's shirt on, tucking it a bit into the front of her pants so it didn't hang down quite so much. She quietly left the room, giving Shane one more glance before she closed the door behind her.

Coffee was ready and sitting on the counter in the kitchen with mugs. Vee poured herself a cup, hesitating a moment before she opened the refrigerator to inspect for milk. There was a small glass bottle sitting just inside. She imagined it had to have been very, *very* local milk. It seemed like few things here were brought in from outside. As she suspected, the rich, creamy milk had no label as she picked it up, and it clung thickly to the glass as she poured it.

She had slowly gotten accustomed to not sweetening her coffee since she'd moved in with Shane. Not that he didn't have plenty of sweeteners and sugars available, but she had unconsciously found herself backing off from it, so she made no attempt to dig around for anything else to add from this kitchen, even though the curiosity of what a Sha would keep in their cupboards tickled her a bit.

Aho had not made an appearance while she rummaged through his kitchen, so she wandered out to the living room, feeling for where his presence was, which seemed to be the porch again. The front door was open, letting in the cool morning breeze. She stepped out and looked over at the porch swing where she assumed he'd be. Not surprisingly, there he was; however, instead of the flannel and jeans he was wearing the day before, he was in only a pair of worn sweatpants.

She noticed he had a leather cord around his neck with a simple white circle attached to it. That and his white hair hanging against his chest made the richness of his skin stand out even more. His head turned to her as she came to stand and lean against the porch post just as Shane had the day before.

"Forgive me for leaving you both after we returned. I needed to think, and you both needed your time together," he said quietly, eyes sparking with a knowing smile.

"We did. Thank you for that," she said, feeling a bit strange about thanking him for giving them time alone in his house, but as she suspected, he seemed unfazed. He nodded, looking back down at the woodcarving he was still working on.

"Your mother's name ... you said you knew it," he murmured. It was an implied question, and he was waiting for a response, but she simply nodded. "I might know her, but I wouldn't want to give you false hope. Her name?" he asked blatantly this time.

Vee felt an odd notion from him. A strange protectiveness and eager anticipation. She furrowed her brow at him and took a sip of the coffee, watching his face, which was still firmly planted on his evolving creation.

"Fiona O'Morrigan," Vee said, watching his eyebrows shoot up on his forehead and his hands still. His expression changing surprised her the most. He didn't seem to be one who was easily shocked. He appeared to be one of the most controlled people she had ever come across, but she had clearly taken him aback.

"Hmm," he grumbled, his head nodding. "I had a feeling when I met you … but I couldn't be sure." If he had been expecting it, she didn't understand his surprise. That was genuine. Had he been thinking he was mistaken, then?

He stood, setting his carving back down on the stump, snatching his own mug of coffee from the floor, and moving quickly past her off the porch toward the pond. She followed him, eyeing him and weighing his emotions. He hiked up his pant legs and sat on a large, flat rock on the edge of the water, which had room enough for both of them, and settled his feet inside the water. She stood there for a moment, not sure if she should join him on the natural bench or not, but he finally turned his eyes toward her and beckoned for her to come.

She set her mug down, beginning the difficult task of rolling up her jeans. It had been much easier for him. Other than how wonderful last night's reaction from Shane had been to her misstep in packing, she really wished she were wearing her own sweatpants or pajama bottoms at the moment. Once finally accomplished, if not a little awkwardly, she moved to sit beside him, sliding her own feet into the warm water.

"I chose this place when I came of age. It had already been my place, with the pond here. My place to be alone when I was a boy," he started quietly, moving his feet around in the water and scattering the fish that had started swarming. "I built a small house, just enough for me. Long before there was anything but a fire to keep warm at night. I've lived many human lifetimes," he said, glancing at her for a moment with a smile.

"I figured," she said back, trying not to grin. His smile widened.

"Do I seem old to you?"

"Clearly not in looks … although the hair is a little jarring," she told him honestly. White hair on a man who looked like he should be no older than her was odd, to say the least.

"It wasn't always that way," he said, one corner of his mouth turning up in a way that reminded her of her own sly smile she would give Shane on rare occasions. "I married a woman," he said before he paused, as if the air in his lungs stopped suddenly. Vee looked at him intently, expecting him to tell her his wife's name, but he met her eyes and shook his head. "We do not say the names of the dead. It holds them here when they should be free. That is especially dangerous when you live as long as we do," he told her, turning his gaze back out toward the water that rippled when a fish came close to the surface.

That explained what happened at the feast the night before, when Bao's mate was mentioned. In the culture Vee was raised in, it was often that the names of the dead were mentioned in remembrance. As if mentioning would make them disappear. The Sha were very different than anything Vee had experienced before, but she found it more interesting than deterring.

"We were meant for one another, then. We were meant to make our son, Min. And she was meant to die to protect us all. All of us that are Other."

Vee glanced over at the house again. She could almost envision a small Min running from the porch and out into the woods. Her suspicions of Aho being

Min's father didn't comfort her or make her gloat. His story was enlightening but leaving an odd sensation in her stomach.

"All Others?" Vee whispered.

"She believed we could not live if we didn't live in harmony. She protected a Fae child, and it caused her death." He let out a strangled sigh and smiled without humor, eyes burning amber. "If she hadn't been who she was, hadn't taught me to temper my beast, I would have slaughtered everyone for her death." There were no lies in his words, and nothing burned behind her eyes. She felt the truth as well as his beast came to the surface, but only for a moment. Wild and powerful, burning just under the surface.

"I had been alone for many years. I spoke very little once she was gone. Though I believed she had been right, and that preternaturals should come to a truce, I could not bring myself to speak with anyone but my own kind. Even for my own son, I chose my words very carefully," he said, his tone changing a bit, a hint of amusement perhaps.

"Min isn't a man of many words either, I've noticed," she said, causing him to grin.

"That is true, but he has a general disdain for anything that he doesn't know everything about. He considers knowledge and respect to be superior to close bonds. The only exception being our people."

"I think he respects Shane," Vee said, trying to think back to the way they'd conversed before Shane's loss of control. Min had been Shane's Sha contact for years, she knew. Shane had told her about the chase through the city after Downing, that Min was right beside him and there was no hesitation in either of them. They could trust each other in a fight.

"He does. That took some time, though. It helps that Shane is a good man, and he leads his people by example," Aho affirmed, picking up his mug beside him and taking a sip.

"What does this have to do with my mother?" Vee decided to ask, after several beats where he merely sipped his coffee and swished his feet in the pond like a young man might have.

"I am not finished. There's a lot of memories to sort through," he said to her a little incredulously. She held up her hands and made an apologetic expression, turning to get her own mug and taking a sip. After several moments, he set the cup back down on the stone beside him and sighed. "Again, I was alone for a long time. I never took another wife, but one day, a woman walked through my bedroom door from somewhere else."

Vee's eyes widened, the surprise of his words making her mug wobble in her hands. He reached over, took the mug, and set it on the stone for her.

"I'll spare you the details, but Fiona told me she had intended to go somewhere safe—the next place she was *meant* to go—not to the home of a Sha." He chuckled, glancing at her with amusement. "Walking into the Sha realm is not supposed to be easy, nor is it safe. I kept her secret. Never told the others she had come through our gates somehow. And she kept coming here." Vee felt the flutter of something bubble within him as he thought of her mother. His eyes were distant, looking out at the pond, as if he was reliving the memory.

"It started as infrequent. She would pop into my home from a door. A whole different world would lie behind her. She started only coming every few months. But as our friendship grew ... she came more. She was stubborn, funny, hot-headed ... I fell in love with her. I didn't think I could love again, and I don't think she expected she would fall in love either."

Vee swallowed dryly, looking over at this man who had lived a thousand lifetimes, a man unchanged by time. His eyes met hers, and she saw her own amber eyes burning back at her.

"She told me she was pregnant, and that she had to leave for your safety, and I gave her this," he said, reaching out to touch the bone wolf head that hung around Vee's neck. Vee didn't hesitate as her hand reached up and touched his hand. The light touch bringing her so much more of his emotions than she had been feeling from him up to this point. A feeling of kinship, adoration, and love broke through the other feelings with the contact.

How could someone love a person they had just met?

"You're..."

"I am your father, yes," he said, curling his hand around hers without breaking the contact she had started there.

"But..." She let the tear that had been threatening to escape cascade down her cheek. He reached up and swiped it away quickly, watching her face as it changed rapidly from confused to excited, panicked to angry.

"I regret many things in this life. Not knowing who you were or where you were for so long is one of them. Though, it was better for your safety. Even here, when you were small, you wouldn't have been safe," he told her seriously.

"Have you seen her?" Vee managed to choke out. He still loved Fiona. She could feel it in the way the mere thought of her pulled at his heart. She could almost imagine him watching the doors within his home on lonely nights, waiting for her to walk back through.

"Not since she left. I have not gone searching, either."

"Why?" She furrowed her brow, not understanding how one could simply just *let* the person they loved go.

"She, like you, is not just one thing. She was Fae, I knew that, but she was also Witch. That combination is dangerous, and she kept herself moving and hidden for many years before I came across her." A shiver ran through Vee at the thought of just how dangerous it was. Gwen Tallon had sought Vee out to take her magic, and her coven had destroyed her home in search of the information about Fiona that Cormac and Frank had gathered.

"If I sought her out, I could have put her in more danger," Aho barely whispered. Vee felt that sting of regret and pain at saying those words. He would have wanted nothing more than to have left with her all those years ago.

"Shane would never let me go," Vee murmured, feeling him as he finally began to stir inside the house. It was a wonder she had been able to keep so much from him to let him sleep this long with the way this conversation had turned. Aho smiled again at that, a bit of pride seeping in.

"If it was to protect you, I suspect he would. Men like Shane are rare, and even better, he's your True Mate. There is no bond greater," he said, releasing her hand as Shane stormed out onto the front porch, eyes scouring the landscape until it settled on the two of them by the pond.

Aho stood slowly, showing there was no threat and no need to be upset, despite Vee's emotional changes. Shane approached, eyes still golden, but his body had relaxed a bit. He had at least managed to pull the sweatpants on, instead of storming out of the house naked.

"I'll start making breakfast," Aho said, hopping from the rock and heading into the house, leaving Shane to stare at Vee, who was fiddling with the items on her necklace. He waited until Aho was in the house and the door closed before he sat beside her, legs crisscrossed instead of dipped in the water so he could face her.

"He made you cry," Shane rumbled, reaching over to turn her face to him and wipe another tear that had rolled down her cheek.

"Yes, well ... you'd think I'd have a better handle on my emotions, but apparently when I'm surprised by something enough, I can't help myself," she said with a humorless chuckle. "He's my father," she whispered after a moment, looking up at him and releasing the hold on the bond to let him feel everything she felt. He let out a puff of air as he took it in, before effortlessly pulling her onto his lap. They sat there for a long while silently as Vee processed it all. Her fingers fiddled with

the little bone wolf on her necklace, and Shane simply rested his chin on her head.

She looked up at him, searching through her ability and their bond for any trepidation. She was, as usual, full of surprises, and though she knew he would never leave her, she wondered if there would be a final straw. Something that he would find too overwhelming to deal with when it came to her.

"You *are* full of surprises. But you're mine, Victoria Malone," he said, having gotten a glimpse into her thoughts from the bond. She tried not to shiver, always feeling something triggered in her when he said her full name … in a good way.

"I might turn your hair white," Vee said in mock seriousness. Shane let out a loud laugh at that, pressing his face into her hair.

"Then so be it," he told her, turning her chin so their noses touched. She closed the small distance left between them and pressed her lips to his.

CHAPTER 17

Vee and Shane had gone back into the house, show-ered, and come back into the kitchen while Aho was finishing making breakfast. Shane took the time to check their phones while Vee was dressing after her shower, which did, in fact, have service.

"No missed calls … but a lot of texts. George said we got the house. Contract is pending. He took Patrick to look at it. Patrick's text to you was that you have fantastic taste," Shane told her, smirking as she rolled her eyes.

She had to reel in the momentary excitement she felt. They *got* the house. She hadn't even seen it in person, and yet it was somehow theirs. Her attempt to bring herself away from the little jolt of joy she felt brought her back to the reason they were getting a new house in the first place.

"Any Duflanc sightings?" Vee asked, as she brushed her hair out.

"No ... I'm a little surprised," Shane confided, brow furrowed. He was certain while they were away, and the pack was in such a state of flux, the Vampire would make things more difficult. Several pack members were probably going to complain relentlessly if there wasn't any actual action.

"Anything from Durran?" Vee asked, coming to sit beside him on the bed.

"She just said she found where your mother stayed while she lived in Breckenridge. Then she said her phone was going to die, and nothing since," he murmured, handing her phone over to her. Vee looked at the short, fairly uninformative texts that were Durran's standard fare and shook her head. Two could play that game.

[Vee: I found my father.] Vee texted her, handing her phone back over to Shane where he set it on the bedside table next to his.

"That's all you're going to text her?" he asked, eyebrow raised, having glanced at the still lit screen beside him.

"She'll find out when we see her again," Vee told him with a mischievous smile. Shane shook his head at her and looked at her phone once more as it sounded with a new message.

"You have one more. No one you have saved. Maybe a customer?" Shane asked, snagging it from the table and handing it over once again.

CHAPTER 17

Vee pulled the text message up. It wasn't a local area code, but in recent years, it seemed like area codes mattered so much less than they once did, since everyone had a cell phone now. The message was short and cryptic.

[Unknown: He followed you there. Be careful.]

She furrowed her brow, looking at it over and over and having no idea what it meant. Who followed her? Maybe it was a wrong number. Vee moved around Shane and set her phone back on the table. She would have to think about it more later. They had more pressing things going on at the moment.

They came out and saw Aho had changed as well. Jeans and a flannel shirt again. He set the last plate of the spread out on the dining room table and looked up at the two of them from the archway. Vee felt like the amount of food spread out across the dining room table was a bit much for three people, but then again, she knew Werewolves could eat their body weight worth of food in one sitting, so she imagined the Sha could as well.

"Min decided he's joining us this morning," Aho said, glancing at the front door as it opened, and the aforementioned Min walked through. His face gave away nothing he was feeling, but Vee sensed his concern and frustration.

"You told me there was important news; that hardly made this my decision," Min said, as he walked to the table and sat down at a spot that Vee assumed was always his when he ate there. Aho sat beside him, leaving Vee and Shane to sit across from them. Aho started filling his plate with the various foods he had made, indicating the others should do the same.

Vee pulled some toast from the pile while Shane scooped eggs for them both onto their plates. Too many eggs for her to finish, but he always seemed to think she wasn't eating enough. She narrowed her eyes at him, and he gave her a little smirk. When she turned back, Min was watching the two of them with an odd expression. She could feel a little ... jealousy. Not out of any sort of attraction to her, but at their playful, wordless exchange.

"What is this news?" Min said, casting his eyes back at his plate once he saw Vee had noticed him looking.

"Do you remember the Fae-ish woman who lived in Breckenridge some years ago?" Aho asked. The question was clearly meant for Min, who stilled a little as he cut into a piece of sausage.

"You seemed to have a strange attraction to her. Yes, I remember," Min said, eyes popping up to look at Vee. Recognition oozed from him. Aho wasn't ever one to go into any town, not from any gate out. So when he started going into Breckenridge with regularity and drinking at a saloon of all things, Min had noticed. Min had always been the one who made appearances in Breckenridge the most often, and he would accompany his father out on those trips to the saloon on occasion. Going with him had mostly been out of curiosity. Why would his reclusive father be going into a human town?

Of course, the answer to the question had made Min worry. Fiona Morgan had been interesting and beautiful, to be sure, but the way his father spoke so freely to her when he barely spoke a word to anyone else had made him uncomfortable at the time. Enough that he'd actually cautioned his father about his friendliness with the woman. Min had no idea *how* friendly they had already become. He understood now, as he looked across the table at Vee. She definitely bore a resemblance to the woman from years ago. Her emerald eyes were the most jarringly similar feature.

"Vee is her daughter. And she's mine," Aho said, his voice so much more nonchalant about it than the weight of the information warranted. He could have been talking about how mild the weather was, instead of revealing that she and Min were siblings.

A silence fell over the room, heavy and full of emotion. Min carefully set his utensils down and inhaled through his nose. Clearly, his words all those years ago to protect his father had fallen on deaf ears, since the proof sat across from him at that very table.

"How long did you know?" he asked through gritted teeth, eyes still piercing into Vee while talking to his father.

"I wasn't sure until this morning," Aho said, taking a bite of his food. He seemed to be utterly unperturbed by this conversation, which rattled Min more.

"But you knew you had a daughter—that *I* had a sister for how long?"

"I knew Fiona was pregnant when she disappeared. I gave her a token before she left," Aho said, pointedly gesturing to the wolf on Vee's necklace. He'd had no idea if the child had even survived, let alone that the child was a girl.

"This complicates things..." Min grumbled, tearing his eyes away from Vee's face and toward the door, as if the other Sha would somehow appear there.

Min liked Shane. Shane was a good leader, a fighter, and after all his time being the liaison between the Were packs across the United States, he found Shane to be a friend, while the others were merely burden-some. He was definitely intrigued by Vee. A woman, not a Were, but interesting and magical enough to be bound to Shane had to be interesting. But now he had to decide how faithful he was to the Sha.

Did he mind that she wasn't fully Sha? Would they mind?

So many years they had been forbidden to go out-side their own, and here she was, proof that Aho had secretly done just that.

"Does it? I'm not sure ... we wanted to know what Vee is, and now we do," Aho said, that sly smirk finding its way to his lips again as he looked at Vee.

"We did not think she was Sha," Min hissed, glow-ering at Aho.

"*Part* Sha. We still don't know what she can do."

"Other than feel emotions and tell the difference between preternaturals, I don't know what all it is I can do either," Vee admitted, turning her attention to her plate again. She felt Min's conflict within him. She couldn't yet tell if he would settle on the side of casting her away or not.

Min returned his gaze to look at her speculatively. His interest increasing with each passing moment. He had been an only child, born at a time when so few other Sha had children. A boy raised alone amongst adults. There were no other children to play with or court sweetly as he grew. From what he had dug up about Vee's past, having been the one tasked with the digging, they were quite similar in that. Vee had a sister she grew up with but had also led a very lonely existence up until recently.

Odd how she had stumbled upon Shane, and they happened to be True Mates. Odd that such a loner would accept a Were like himself, who had a whole pack to care for and lead.

"I suppose that explains why you two are True Mates," he said, looking at Shane now. "There were old stories about Weres being True Mates with the Sha … but that was long before we shut that down."

"We?" Aho asked with an abrupt, humorless laugh. "You mean Bao. She was so distraught over her mate's passing, she forbade anyone from *loving* outside of their own kind," Aho practically spat, clenching his fist around his fork.

"She thought she was protecting us," Min said, but his voice was colored by his own pain. Bao's mate had been a Were-tiger and her True Mate.

"And at what cost? I could have protected her, cared for her, helped her know her own powers, but she's lived unaware for the last thirty years," Aho said, an anger in his tone that made him almost unrecognizable. The normally cool and collected Aho was showing his emotions, eyes burning.

"Not yet thirty," Vee grumbled, stabbing a piece of fruit she didn't recognize with her fork. Her attempt to lighten the mood of the room with her little comment didn't seem to faze the conversation.

"We are only dwelling on the past for information to help Vee now. There's no use arguing about how things could have been," Shane said, trying to not get pulled into the anger that Aho was feeling. The Sha's dominant power was washing over everyone in the room, putting them on edge. Vee touched Shane's leg to ground him, but even her eyes glowed amber.

"Do we tell the others?" Min asked.

The tension ramped up a little with that question. Of course they had to tell the others, but how would it be taken? Vee had gone from feeling like this would be a mostly pleasant trip to feeling that familiar stone forming in her stomach, full of the unknown.

They, as an odd foursome, were set to join the other Sha Council members at a Great Lake that had been hidden from view by the large structure at the end of the walking street and an impressive hill that Vee realized the structure had been partially built into. She was still nervous about seeing the others again. Aho and Min didn't reveal what the plans were for the day, and she only vaguely recalled what had been discussed at the dinner previously.

Yona had tried her best to keep Vee entertained and unfettered with anxiety. At the time Vee had been grateful, but now she wished she had paid more attention so she could be mentally prepared for what she was potentially facing today.

Once they got to the top of the hill, a whole new view of the landscape was revealed. A large lake sat within a basin of hills; beyond that, vast woods climbed up mountains and plateaus scattered across her view. There was a small structure not far from the shoreline, white smoke billowing from a chimney that smelled of spices and wood.

What were they going to be doing in there?

"To unlock what her spirit knows," Aho said quietly, answering the unasked question. She wasn't sure if he had read her mind or just understood the slight pause both she and Shane had made when it came into view.

"A vision quest?" Shane asked, tightening his grip on her hand and pulling her to a halt. "That takes days…"

"It's not a vision quest in the way our First People cousins know it. It's earth magic, moon magic, sun magic … bringing out her true nature. All Sha go through it. Unlocking the spirit helps us know what animal we most closely relate to, and therefore what our beast is more naturally inclined to," Min said, stopping as well and turning back to look at them.

"Both of you identify with the wolf," Vee said, having just realized. It made sense why Min was the liaison with Werewolves.

"Yes," Aho affirmed, grinning widely. "Just as Long identifies with the dragon, and Bao the tiger," he continued. Vee's eyes travelled to the lake as she thought about that. As she did so, she got the distinct impression there was something very large and serpentine swimming under its dark depths.

"It doesn't take days, or fasting, but it does take a bit of time. More for her, I imagine, since she is not accustomed to our magic," Min said, looking at Vee thoughtfully.

"But the others don't know I'm part-Sha. Why would they have me do this?" She hadn't been expecting this. She had thought a sit-down talk, perhaps a demonstration of her abilities, but not a magical quest to unlock something in her. She'd had enough revelations for one day already, but here she was about to meet her own spirit.

"Connecting to your *zi*, your soul, is not just for Sha or Weres. Every creature holds their own *zi*, and this will help you tap into it. It will help you understand better what it is you are capable of," Aho told her, his tone soft. She took a deep breath. Knowing more would be helpful, in so many ways. Vee was becoming dangerous for those around her, simply by not understanding her own magic and how it worked. She found herself hesitant but curious.

Aho and Min turned to continue their trek down the hill. Vee looked up at Shane, who still had concern flooding for her from their bond. She rubbed her thumb on the top of his hand and sent him reassurance, despite her own unease.

"I'm worried. That's all," Shane told her, taking his eyes from the two Sha walking from them and looking down at her.

"We need to know," she told him, letting the truth of those words settle him slightly. He knew it was true. They had a way to understand more about what she was capable of. It was worth it to take the opportunity, especially now that they knew she wasn't just a hint of Fae; she was also Witch and Sha. Those magics alone were powerful. But together…

Vee thought back to the last time she had thought about her soul. The soul was the keeper of the magic within. Even Vampires, though dead, had a soul that contained their magic, not the soulless creatures they were depicted as in popular culture. Just six months ago, Gwen had wanted to steal Vee's soul and, therefore, her magic. It had been excruciating, and that pain had allowed her to do more with her magic instinctually than she had ever done before—more than she could have ever fathomed before.

She was going to find out what her spirit knew, Aho had said.

Shane let her pull him to follow the other two, and they soon came upon the structure. She had been expecting a sweat lodge like she had read about and seen documentaries on, a domed structure covered in animal skins and blankets. But this was a permanent fixture. It was also domed, but it was covered in clay that had been painted with many designs depicting people and animals. The paintings were simple, but beautiful and stylized in a way that was clearly specific to the Sha, now that she had seen a small sampling of their decorations.

The door that faced them opened to reveal Urmah. He had to crouch quite low to step over the threshold and out to them, his long locks pouring over his shoulders like snakes. Once he was fully upright, he smiled warmly, his dark eyes looking down only at Vee.

"Ready or not. It's time to find out exactly what you can do."

CHAPTER 18

Vee stiffened at Urmah's words. *Ready or not ...* of course she wasn't ready for this.

The lake water sloshed suddenly, causing Vee to turn her gaze to it instead of the intimidating Sha before her, and she watched as a massive, scaled tail snaked from under the water, pointing to the sky briefly before submerging once again. Then closer to the shoreline, a human head popped out of the water. Long emerged at the shore, completely naked and breathtaking. Her blue-black hair fell over her back and shoulders, so extreme in its length that it nearly touched her feet.

She approached them, unashamed of her nakedness as all shape-shifting creatures seemed to be, and smiled, her eyes still faintly glowing from her dragon form.

"You act as though *you* were ready to meet your spirit, Urmah," she said with a smirk, once she was close to him.

"No one is ready," he confessed with a grin, shrugging his shoulders unapologetically at Vee.

"Are the others here?" Aho asked, looking bored at the exchange.

"Hurin, Yona, and Bao are getting it ready," Urmah said with a nod.

"Let's go in, then," Min said, gesturing for everyone to go inside.

Vee followed behind Aho, who took the lead. She glanced at the door for a moment before stepping inside. It was wood, with designs reminiscent of the ones she saw on the columns of the temple. With no other explanation for what the structure had been, Vee had decided it was a temple. She never seemed to see anyone going in or out of it, but it was clearly the oldest structure there; the large columns and lovingly placed designs over it showed how much these people revered it. The designs on the door were oddly geometric and beautiful, but this was far more intricate with clear symbols that reminded Vee of cuneiform or runes, carved within it that throbbed with magic. The magic felt protective, but more, it gave her the feeling it was to protect those on the outside from whatever happened within.

That tingly feeling, as if a wall of magic was flowing over her, encased her as she stepped over the threshold. The interior was ... well, she hadn't been sure what to expect as she walked through, but it certainly wasn't this. The floor was soft green moss, her bare feet stepping onto it and feeling it gently give under her weight. Vines and ivy hung from the ceiling, which was, from what she could tell, a living thing. Branches twisted and twined up the walls from various grounded trunks, all evenly spread to make up the circular room. At the center was a pit of stone. Two large fires shaped like semicircles flanked an open center. Clay exhaust chutes took the heavily scented smoke up and out, only leaving the air spiced with fragrance and warmth instead of being overwhelming to their lungs.

Long was pulling on a silk robe she had snagged once she made her way past the fires to the other side of the dome, where the three other Sha waited. Bao and Yona were humming and chanting in a language Vee couldn't quite place. It sounded old and guttural but was complimentary and beautiful coming out of their mouths, even if it made the hair on her arms rise uncomfortably.

Hurin stood before the two chanting women. He was dressed in nothing but a white cloth around his waist, clasped together with an intricate piece of metal. His dark skin glowed as he stood there, his beautiful face exuding the seriousness of what was about to begin. He walked through the opening between the fires, straight toward Vee. He wasn't nearly as tall as Urmah, but he was still huge in comparison to her, his body built more like a linebacker, broad and domineering.

Vee hadn't realized she had stopped so close to the center of the room, but she didn't let the instinctual flinch show at his abrupt approach.

"Drink," he said, holding out a bowl that looked small in his hands but huge in her held-out hands as she let him place it gently there. She was vaguely aware of Shane, as Aho and Min wordlessly ushered him to a spot in the moss to sit. She looked down at the liquid. It was opaque, like a black tea. Bits of whatever herbs they had steeped in the hot water were still floating here and there, and some had clearly settled at the bottom of the pale dish. Now that she had it in her hands, she realized the bowl felt like the bone of her wolf pendant. What had a bone big enough to make this bowl?

She suddenly realized…

She was about to drink out of a carefully carved and polished skull.

Whose skull was used for these rituals?

Who had died to make this magic possible?

She had no idea how old it was. It could have been millennia.

The steam swirling from the odd tea was laced with spirals of magic. She took in a deep inhale through her nose, smelling those potent spices and wishing she had Shane's nose so she could better distinguish scents, but she knew this brew was magic … she didn't need to smell it. She could see it swirling and dancing gently with the steam.

Vee glanced up at Hurin's face one more time, his emotions somewhere between anticipation and curiosity. How would this affect her? Would it be the same or different from others they put through this?

She put the rim of the bone bowl to her lips, tilting slowly. She let the liquid come into her mouth as just a sip at first. It was not the worst thing she had ever tasted, but it certainly had an earthy flavor hidden

under the rich spice. Odd but not disgusting, as she had imagined. She drank a bigger gulp, pulling the bowl from her lips for a moment.

"All of it," Hurin urged, gently pressing on the bowl to indicate she should continue.

As she did, she could feel the magic blossoming within her, spreading from her stomach out to the rest of her body. It was warm and inviting, but also invasive in its pursuit through her. With her final sip, she became aware that the domed structure around her no longer felt real. Her eyes and the weight in her hands disappearing told her Hurin was taking the bowl from her, but his movements were odd, almost like she could see him in slow motion as he turned away from her and walked back through the space between fires.

Bao appeared before her a moment later. Vee hadn't noticed her approach from where she had been sitting and chanting. She was just suddenly there, still chanting, though the sounds seemed distorted now. Vee could see the familiar tendrils of magic snaking from her lips, like they did when others spoke magic, but now, with Vee's vision being so strange, it looked much more solid, as if Bao was eating a live squid and somehow still speaking.

She couldn't help the flinch this time as Bao touched her, brushing her bangs to the side as she placed a single finger on her forehead. The spot where she touched felt wet once she pulled her hand away, and Bao repeated this touch on Vee's wrists, hands, and feet. Then she reached back up and touched the suprasternal notch, the little divot between the collar bones at the base of her throat.

Vee looked down at her wrists and saw what Bao had left behind. Each touch had been a bit more than what Vee had felt, it seemed, leaving odd symbols like the protective ones on the door, but these were not for protection. Vee knew, without fully understanding their meaning, that they were for evocation.

Suddenly she was surrounded by Sha. Urmah, Bao, Long, Aho, Yona, and Hurin all encircled her. Bao's chanting was now accompanied by theirs and ushered her from where she stood to the center of the dome. Her feet touched the cool stone surface, which she now noticed also had symbols, though they were iridescent, glowing and flickering as if they were alive beneath her feet.

Vee looked at the room around her, the fire looked more like elementals; humanoid figures made of flame were dancing and writhing with the rhythm of the chanting, instead of the normal flames they had been moments before. She glanced at the vines hanging from the ceiling. They were throbbing … beating, like a heart.

The Sha that had surrounded her slowly backed away, their chanting continuing, but now she could feel the chanting within her, changing the beat of her own heart to match the vines and the dancing flames. She finally looked beyond the changing room around her, her eyes immediately meeting Shane's.

He seemed so distant from her, even though she knew he was only a few paces away. His eyes were burning golden, their bond told her his urge to protect her and letting her go through with this was battling within him. But there was no turning back now, she

realized, as she watched his wolf form sit around him, slightly transparent, but their eyes lined up. She could see all of Shane at the same time: the man and the wolf.

What would she see if she looked at herself?

And as she thought that, her vision tying her to the world disappeared.

Vee looked at the new and unfamiliar surroundings. She could still feel the beat of the chant, but she could no longer hear it. The quiet sounds of night were the only things that touched her ears. It was a forest, but she knew it was different from any she had ever seen before. Moss coated the tree trunks and the branches seemed to reach down to her, as if they were beckoning her to them. The moon was right above her, full and brilliant in the sky, shining blue-tinted light down on everything. Magic hummed around her like it was singing to her.

She was certain this was just in her head. It had been daylight when she entered the dome structure, and while that place was odd in its eco-harmony, the air felt wet and cool to her here in this place, much different from the warmth of the domain of the Sha.

Before her appeared a door and the hum became eerie whispers, urging her to go to it. The door was rounded at the top, elegant knots intricately woven with vines that encased and decorated its surface. There was an ornate silver handle that was held to the door, as if the vines had grown around it, but below that was a keyhole. It had no face plate; it was not a separate lock that had been placed within the door. No, it was like it had always been there.

She realized she had something in her hand, suddenly feeling the weight of it between her fingers and her palm. She looked down and saw her key. The simple metal key with the Celtic spiral on the bow was there instead of hanging off the chain around her neck. She knew the key would fit there. Oddly, she understood the key would fit any keyhole she decided it should go into. No matter the size or shape, this key would open any door. Not just in this world, but in hers as well.

And as she stared down at it, she realized it wasn't silver. Had it been silver, she would have noticed it dampening Shane's abilities. No this wasn't silver ... it was bone. What kind of bone, she had no idea. She didn't know of any creatures who had bones like metal. A bone wolf and a bone key.

Blood and Bone, Earth and Moon.

The voices intensified, begging her to unlock the door.

She stepped forward, putting the key in its home within the hole, and turned it, pulling the handle.

Before she had a moment to comprehend the door swinging open, she was being pulled through. The darkness yanking her in different directions. The whispers were louder and more intense as she fell, unsure of which way was up. One final yank, and she was aware of something smooth and hard touching her hands, and as she felt it, the same smooth hardness was under her legs as well. She was on her hands and knees, but she didn't recall having come crashing down into whatever surface it was.

And it wasn't all a dark void now. As she looked down at her hands, she saw her own reflection looking back at her. Light from an unknown source dimly lit the new space she was in, keeping her surroundings hidden from her view. Her reflection beneath her showed her eyes were amber, burning, not with anger but from an equally intense emotion.

Fear.

She wasn't one to give into her fears. To avoid them, yes, but not give in. However, in this place, she could predict nothing. There was nothing to ground her, to distract her, or to save her. Not here.

She looked down at her reflection: first the eerie glow of her own eyes catching her attention; then a smoke-like substance started trickling from her eyes, as if they would be tears, but they came as wisps of amber-colored mist instead. It flowed to a point a few feet from her, the opaque amber smoke becoming more solid as it formed together. After a few moments, though it could have been quite a while as Vee's perception of time was strange here, an amber crow stood before her.

The crow shook briefly for a moment, fanning out its feathers and snapping its beak. With each twitch and movement of its body, the amber seemed to shake off its feathers in a fine metallic dust, uncovering the black silky wings beneath. She just sat there, staring at it. That crow had come from *her*.

It cawed at her once and then turned, heading into the vast darkness before them. She stood, slowly following as it intermittently flew and stopped, looking back to make sure she was still there. The darkness was fading, or perhaps it was just more things were coming into view. The mirrored floor becoming rougher and less reflective with each new step. She barely noticed when the crow transformed into a cat. It seemed to happen from one blink of the eye to the next. This black cat reminded her of Midi, her old neighbor Una's cat, who would often greet her outside the apartment building she used to live in.

She missed Una and the cat.

The newly lit surroundings revealed a strangely sterile version of her old apartment, including her furniture that had been destroyed by the coven of Witches who had tried to kill her. All the colors were muted and lightened, and her clutter of books and odds and ends were all very neatly put away. The ceiling was missing, revealing the moonlit sky above.

"You still hold onto this place," came a voice. She got the impression the voice was not speaking English, but she could still somehow understand it perfectly. Vee turned around to see who it was, but no one else was there. She looked again at the creature that had come from her, who had guided her there, and the black Midi-like cat was gone; a huge black wolf, much like Shane's wolf but perhaps slightly smaller, was in its place. It looked at her with its own amber eyes, shining brightly.

"Who are you?" Vee asked, aware that she hadn't spoken a word in this place since she came.

"I am you. I am the part of you that you don't wish to see. The you that is hidden, even from yourself," the wolf said, though its mouth moved and it spoke, it didn't move in the way a human's mouth would have.

"I have never changed with the moon," Vee said, a little doubtfully.

"No. You needn't heed the moon's call."

"But…" she started, urging the wolf to continue.

"You walk in more than one world."

"I've heard that before," she said, her mouth forming a tight line. This was all in her head, so it made sense it would regurgitate things she already knew.

"You both belong, and do not. You bring chaos and harmony. You see truth and lies. You hold power to give and take away. Your path remains undetermined. Outside of the weave of the Fates," the wolf said, its body shimmering slightly. It transformed beautifully in a sea of amber mist into a woman.

The woman was not much taller than Vee's short stature. Her skin impossibly white and glowing, as her hair framed her in wild curls. Her hair was odd, being mostly black, with strands interwoven of vibrant red and shocking white here and there. Her eyes were glowing, huge, emerald orbs that somehow did not take away from the beauty of her face, which Vee knew was also a face to fear. Much like the glamor she could see through when she looked at other Fae, her face and body seemed to snake and shimmer, sometimes appearing youthful, and other times showing wrinkles and age. She had a silver collar around her neck that held the fabric of her dress, which cascaded down her body in soft folds of shimmering black. Bands of silver adorned both her biceps and wrists.

The Morrigan, Vee thought, but the words could be heard out loud in this place anyway.

"Daughter of Fiona. Daughter of the white wolf. One who calls the magic of the white moon. You, like the Morrigan, are blessed and cursed with the power of three." The words came from this woman's mouth, but sounded like three women were talking in unison. The effect was chilling.

"What does that mean?"

"Fae, truth. Witch, power. Sha, beast. You hold all three. You are the only creature who lives outside the web the Morrigan weaves."

"Outside of fate?"

"Fate can guide you, but not hold you like it does with others. Fate brought you to where you are now, but you have more power to change your path than you know. You, your wolf, your pack create your own fate now. You can do more than you perceive. Trust yourself. With each challenge before you, you will begin to *know*," the Morrigan said, mouth turning up in a smile that felt sinister.

"What is it that I can do?" Vee asked, feeling as if she was being pulled away, the room starting to dissolve around them.

"Keep a close eye on those who watch. The dead, the living, and those weak in power will soon uncover their eyes. They want to show truths better left hidden. One woman, one pair, one pack to defend and protect. Magical and human. Blood and bone. You must see your own truth," the Morrigan said, her voice rising as she raised her gaze to the moon above.

Vee watched as the world around her dissolved back into the black void. The beat of her heart returning to the rhythmic state from the chanting in the dome.

She could once again smell the heavily scented air and feel the minds of the others around her. She could feel Shane.

She took a deep, gasping breath and opened her eyes.

CHAPTER 19

S hane never took his eyes off her. It was almost med-
itative, as he watched her mostly still form lying
there between the fires. He had no idea how much
time had passed. The only thing he was aware of was
Vee. She held nothing back from what she was feeling
through the bond, so he let it course through him.
Her fear would have made this more difficult for him
had he not felt her determination matching it. The air
around her body seemed to warp as time went on. Her
hands twitched and chest heaved with the rhythm of
the Sha's chants.

Min sat beside him watching as well, tension radiating off him. Shane knew it was nervousness over the
unknown. It felt like an eternity, waiting for her to pull
through the magic and come back to him, but as he

sat watching, her emotions surged, and with that, the magic pulsing around her … he watched her *change*.

At first, he wasn't sure of what he was seeing. He thought perhaps he had imagined a black crow lying where Vee's body once was, but no, it persisted. Then the crow changed into a sleeping black cat. He furrowed his brow, trying to concentrate on the animal that had taken his mate's place, when the cat grew, becoming a black wolf. The wolf opened her eyes, amber, like Vee's, staring only at him before the hair seemed to ruffle in a wave from its snout to its tail, changing the color of the wolf's fur from black to white. Shockingly white, as if it emitted its own glow.

Shane could sense the unease filling the Sha in the room, Min stiffening beside him but continuing to watch. Vee's white wolf form lay there before them for another moment, before it shifted from one breath to the next, back into Vee's human shape. Her back arched, body rising slightly from the floor before she let out a loud gasp, coming back down to the stone ground, and opening her eyes.

The chanting stopped abruptly; that was all the indication Shane needed to scramble over to her on all fours with a speed that would have rivaled his wolf form. At first, he hesitated to touch her, leaning over to look at her face as she continued to pant heavily. Her amber eyes locked with his.

"What did you see?" Bao asked, her voice quiet but now that silence had filled the room, except for the sound of Vee's breathing, it felt jarring.

CHAPTER 19

"Give her a moment," Shane hissed, not taking his eyes off Vee's. He could feel her struggling to remain calm, even with the mild comfort from his gaze.

"'One woman, one pair, one pack,'" she whispered hoarsely. She had so much to tell him, to show him, but he could tell she was struggling to be coherent.

"What did she say?" Urmah asked, turning to Long who was standing beside him. She simply shook her head, not taking her eyes from the two at the center.

The feeling in the air started to intensify, like electricity before a lightning strike. Shane could feel the power surging within her, magic that smelled and felt distinctly Vee. Fear shot through their bond, fear like she had felt while she was within her vision, but this time, she wasn't alone. She had Shane. He gently cupped her face in his hands, letting the touch sooth her and their bond solidify a little. With the touch, she could *show* him.

Her vision began coming through to him. It wasn't fluid but in pieces and fragments: the woods, her standing before a door, the key, the void. But then she had him focus on the crow, the cat, and the wolf. He watched each one, how it moved, how it looked at her.

That was a look she gave.

Those were her eyes.

The moment the wolf began to change shape into a woman, he couldn't quite see it. Nothing about the woman's features was enough to hold as an image in his mind, but he could hear the words she spoke.

One woman, one pair, one pack.

One pack.

Shane made a rash decision in that moment. He knew she didn't like decisions made for her, but the power she was building within her as she showed him her vision was becoming so thick in the air, he could taste it on his tongue. Only one way he could think to help her to not explode here. To avoid what she had done to defeat Gwen and potentially endanger them while they were still in the domain of the Sha.

He searched her eyes for a moment, hoping she could see and understand what he was about to do. He hadn't wanted to scare her or disgust her, but the magic of the pack would help center her. He intuitively knew it would help; that's what the pack did for each other. They grounded each other, strengthened each other. He lifted one hand from where he'd placed it on her face and took hers from where it lay on the floor beside her. He called just enough of his wolf forward to elongate his teeth, lifting their joined hands together to his mouth, and biting at both of their wrists until blood began to trickle down their forearms.

He pulled on his power, the power that was given to him when he was named leader of the Westport pack. The bonds, though distant, that he had with his members, opening fully and freely as they did every time they welcomed a new member.

"My blood becomes yours. My pack, your pack. Do you take it freely?" he asked, looking into her amber orbs and hoping, willing her to accept the pack and him once again. Her power continued to pulse around them, eyes glowing more than he'd ever seen them. She pulled a little on their joined hands, bringing his bloodied wrist to her mouth.

"I take it freely," she said, her voice haunting, as if she had heard this ritual a thousand times over like he had. Her lips parted, and she placed them over the wound on his arm and let his blood fill her mouth. Instinctually, he leaned forward, catching her wrist with his mouth as well. They just looked at each other, the magic within him cascading and surrounding them both, taking in her magic as well.

This was incredibly intimate. More so than any other time he had brought someone into the pack. He could feel her settling even further into him, the already astonishing strength of their bond somehow becoming deeper as she spread out through the pack bonds, making her own connections with each of them. He could feel the way they all called for her, welcoming her there, the silent howl accepting her as one of their own echoing.

Her magic spread throughout them, changing them and their bonds together in a way he wasn't expecting.

One pack.

Vee's eyes widened, her body shaking. She released her mouth from his arm and her back arched once again. Shane's hand that was still at her cheek snaked around to the back of her neck to pull her face closer to him. As he pulled her to him, her hands came up to his face, and suddenly he was no longer sitting on the floor holding Vee. He was now standing in the same forest Vee had been in when she went into her vision, but she was standing with him this time, fingers firmly laced between his.

He could feel the pack bonds getting stronger as Vee fully accepted them and they her. Slowly, as the bonds solidified within her, ghostly images of the pack started to surround them in this haunting place.

"I changed them, didn't I?" Vee asked, looking over at these vague images of each member. Patrick and Lori were grinning broadly, though their eyes, like the others, were unseeing. They weren't pulled into this place; these were just the images of them that the pack bonds created in Vee's mind.

"We all change a little when someone new joins the pack. That's just how it is," Shane told her, trying not to be overwhelmed by the strangeness of what he was experiencing.

"This is more than that, I think," she murmured, glancing over at him. "I don't really feel like I understand what I am or what I can do more than I did before this," she told him, her voice a bit shaky.

"You *changed*," he told her, watching as her face crumbled a little with confusion.

"Changed?"

"You shifted."

He watched her eyes widen, brows still drawn together as she took in what he said.

"We don't heed to the moon's call," came the voice of a white wolf that was suddenly standing before them. The same wolf Shane had seen staring back at him when Vee changed.

"I am not a Were," Vee said to the wolf.

"No. We are our own something, made from Fae, Witch, and Sha blood. Now our pack is a little something else too," the wolf said, eyes turning to look at the still wispy versions of the Werewolves.

"It will all come together in time. You needn't understand it all right now; that's not what this is for, but your pack ... you'll need them in the times to come, if you are to change the fate of our world to your will," the wolf said with a sense of finality. The forest they were in melted away, and Shane found himself once again in the domed structure, Vee on his lap with blood from both of their wounds covering them.

He could tell it had only been moments that they were away in that other place, because the Sha around them hadn't moved from where they had stood before, the tension still palpable in the air, despite Vee's power having dissipated. Everything was still and silent for a moment as Vee and Shane simply looked at each other. There was going to be a lot to unpack with what had just occurred, but they weren't certain they wanted an audience for it ... in fact, they weren't certain they wanted to even be in the Sha domain for it.

"What did you see?" Bao repeated, her question still directed at Vee.

"Perhaps Vee should clean up and rest before we question her," Min said, having stood and joined the circle of Sha around the couple at the center when Shane had moved over to her. Bao and Hurin gave Min quizzical looks at his statement but said nothing, as Shane easily stood with Vee in his arms and moved to walk her out of the dome.

"How did she change? What *is* she?" Long asked, causing Shane to pause just as he got to the door.

"She's my daughter," Aho said. He had followed right behind Shane, moving to open the door for them.

The other Sha made odd hissing noises, Bao's face twisting in fury instantly at his admission.

"Truth," Yona said, her voice shaky and eyes wide.

"How could you break our laws?" Bao spat, venom laced in her words.

"Not now," Aho growled in response, as he followed Shane and Vee out, leaving the rest of them in shock in their wake.

Durran felt the unmistakable surge of Vee's power. She had been sitting in her hotel room, researching Ness from the property information she had gotten off the house for sale. This Ness did, in fact, own a house in Kansas City as well and had for nearly seventy years. It seemed like wherever Fiona's aliases ended up, so did this Fae woman. But she was frozen in place, just as she was about to click the next link and tie yet another alias to property Nessa Seeley owned, by the feeling she got through her one-way bond with her ward.

Fear from Vee hit her like an icy fist, nearly knocking the wind from her chest. Her power rushed through the bond with a strength that Durran hadn't even felt when Vee had faced off with the Witch. She scrambled to her phone, which she had plugged in to charge but hadn't turned back on. How stupid of her not to make sure she was accessible. Even if she couldn't reach Vee where she was, she still needed to be available to her.

Waiting the precious seconds it was taking for her phone to boot up was excruciating, and what she could feel from her shallow bond only increased as the seconds ticked on. She was finally able to see what messages she had received when magic that smelled very much like Vee, and a little of Shane, washed through her, making her stiffen for a moment. Durran was somehow aware that she was feeling Vee's magic spread out through bonds that she only vaguely had a perception of, but it was also spreading through her.

The feel of Vee's magic was both hot, like humid summer air, blanketing over Durran's skin, but also icy cold, running through her veins. She could feel her own magic adapting to it. Durran's true form seemed to burst forth, pushing away the glamor of their female form, like tearing away a curtain. It took everything to resist the urge to fully extend their wings, the force of the change leaving them panting and standing almost bare in their true form, eyes burning red.

Just as suddenly as it began, the overwhelming feeling of being pulled into Vee's magic calmed, leaving Durran standing in the middle of their hotel room, shaking and sweating. They looked down at the phone in their hand, finally seeing the singular message that was sent many hours earlier that simply read, "I found my father," and a strange wave of understanding came over them. Something happened in there, whether it was because one of the Sha was Vee's father, or simply because they too, wanted to know what it was she could do, but something happened that made Vee's abilities explode from her, reaching out to touch anyone and anything that was bonded to her.

Durran briefly wondered if Shane was also having some strange reaction to this. He was far more deeply connected to Vee than Durran was.

They looked over at the mirror that hung in the wall above the unused dresser, and was shocked at their own appearance. Black wings quivering behind them, full glamor of clothes stripped away to reveal their form, their skin glowing in a strange way it never had before.

They changed back, with mild difficulty, donning their glamor once again and shifting back into their female body. There were enough connections between Ness and Fiona. Durran didn't need to research it anymore, and she knew Ness was in Kansas City. The old Fae could be tracked down. Right now, she needed to figure out where Vee was. She could feel the pull to be near her ward. She looked out at the night sky through the window. It was cloudy enough; Durran could probably get away with flying if she needed to.

She left her hotel room, slipping into the employee stairwell that travelled to the roof access door. Thankfully, no humans were traveling up at this time of night, but she heard the quiet murmuring and the stench of a few employees sneaking a cigarette a few floors below on a basement level of the stairwell. They didn't want to be caught just as much as Durran, she assumed, since they quieted briefly when the door opened with a creak and resumed their conversation when it closed. Her movements didn't make a sound to their human ears.

She made it quickly up all eight flights, using her strength to break the lock on the door so she could step out onto the small portion of the roof that was flat and look up into the sky. As it closed behind her, she smirked momentarily, thinking how upset Vee would have been with her for breaking a perfectly good lock. Vee would have spent the few more seconds to pick it, but Durran couldn't help the urgency she was feeling. She had to be near Vee … *now*.

With barely a glance at the streets below, Durran extended her wings and shot up into the clouds.

CHAPTER 20

Aho had shifted into a giant white wolf to run ahead
of Shane, who kept his pace at a fast walk to not
jostle Vee too much in his arms. She was becoming
much more coherent now that she wasn't in the dome
anymore, her vision more normal instead of seeing
everything pulsing and moving when they shouldn't
have been. She looked up at Shane's face, his eyes
glowing, jaw clenched, but his hands were still soft as
they held her close to him.

Worry. He was worried about her. He was worried about the pack. As usual, the more they learned,
the more confusing it became. She felt like she would
be fine to walk on her own, but she had a feeling he
needed to hold her more than she needed to be carried at the moment. She recognized the path they
took; they were very nearly at Aho's house, the dark

shadow of trees on the path cast by the moon's glow above them.

When did it become night?

She had entered the dome when it was still morning, late morning, but the sun had definitely been in the sky. How long had she been in that vision?

Shane slowed as they passed the pond and approached the porch of Aho's house. Vee watched as the great white wolf that was Aho shifted seamlessly back into his human form in a moment, instead of the excruciatingly long minutes it would have taken a Werewolf. She wasn't certain if it had to do with how old he was, or if it was because he was a Sha, but she remembered how quickly it had been for Long to change from the dragon that had been hiding under the surface of the lake into her human form.

Aho quickly put his pants back on that he had carried in his mouth and opened the door. Shane passed him and went through, moving to set Vee on the couch and crouch before her. The fierce gold of his eyes as he looked her over was shocking, only because she realized he was still fearful of a reaction she wasn't going to have.

"I'm okay," Vee said to the unspoken question in his eyes.

"I'm sorry," he murmured, smoothing his thumbs over the top of her hands.

"Nothing to be sorry for," she told him, watching as his shoulders seemed to relax a little.

"I didn't stop to think before I–."

"It helped. Bringing me into the pack," Vee said, her voice soft and reassuring. He relaxed even further at her words, pressing his forehead to hers.

But the moment was fleeting. A surge of rage went through the pack. For Vee, it was small, but it was there. She imagined her ties to the pack were either limited because she wasn't a Were, or she had exhausted herself. Shane's eyes, however, went distant as he felt it, his body tensing once again.

"We need to leave … we have to get back to the pack," Shane said, as they heard his phone vibrating in the bedroom where he had left it.

"Go get it," Vee told him, bobbing her head in the direction of hall. He hesitated a moment, but then pressed his lips to her hair, glancing at Aho, and walking quickly to the bedroom to get his phone.

Aho had been standing at the door since Shane entered with Vee, but now that Shane was gone, he went to sit on the coffee table across from her. He rested his elbows on his knees and clasped his hands together. His face and posture looked too youthful for what he really was, but his expression was far from lighthearted. She just sat there exactly as Shane had left her, slightly slumped and still trying to decide if everything she was feeling in that moment was true, or if it was still the effects of the Sha magic.

In Shane's arms, she had felt like she'd have been able to walk just fine, but once she had moved to the couch, the world was spinning again.

"How do you feel?" Aho asked, searching her face.

"Odd. I'm still not sure what I'm experiencing is real," she admitted ruefully, trying to sit up a little straighter.

"It does take a little time to get accustomed to your own skin again when you've journeyed to where your spirit resides," Aho told her, nodding a bit as he looked through her a little, as if he were recalling his own vision many, many years before.

"That didn't exactly explain things to me," Vee said to him, as his concern washed over her.

"No. It is for interpretation, but usually the message is clear enough to the person who experiences it."

"There was a lot to interpret, then," she grumbled, chewing lightly on the inside of her lip.

"You have never changed before today?" Aho asked after a brief pause.

"No … I wasn't even aware I had at all until Shane mentioned it. What did I change into?"

"A crow, a cat, and a wolf," Aho said, eyebrows rising on his forehead as he said it, the recollection of it bringing his surprise rolling back through him. "Most children who were born from one Sha and one human would change, but only into their Sha parent's pre-ferred form. It was how some of the first Weres were created. Their attacks on humans were far more likely to change a human into one of them than a Sha would have in an animal form. But never could a person not fully Sha carry more than one form."

"Is that why you can't have children outside of the Sha?"

"That and Bao's declaration … her pain…" He shiv-ered thinking of it. Vee nodded solemnly as she thought back to what she had changed into. The three animals that had appeared in her vision. She didn't even feel her body change. When she had been there, she was just herself as she had always been, in her human body.

"I never went through a change when I was younger. I don't even have Were abilities normally. No smell, no strength or healing … I can only *hear*," Vee said, dumbfounded that she changed at all. She listened for a moment to Shane's voice as he spoke to someone on the phone. She assumed Patrick, or perhaps Thomas.

"I don't have an answer for that," Aho admitted quietly.

Vee felt the weight of his gaze and turned hers down to her body. She was mildly astonished being covered in blood. She knew the blood exchange had happened, but she didn't think so much of it had gotten on her. She still had the metallic taste of Shane's blood in her mouth, and she could feel it on her lips and chin. The ritual that Shane had been so scared to tell her about … just a simple blood exchange. Not that she'd loved having to drink his blood, but this wasn't something so disturbing that he would need to shy away from telling her about it.

She knew enough to not be disgusted or discouraged by blood, and the scariest bond had already been formed, their mating bond. If she could deal with that, she could certainly deal with a little blood and more safety for the pack. But now that it was done, she would much rather be clean than feeling it drying and crusting to her skin. Without a word, she moved to stand, being slow and deliberate to not make her head spin again. Aho let her, watching, but choosing not to step in unless she asked. She moved to the bathroom, glancing at the end of the hall to see Shane pacing with the phone still to his ear.

She closed the door behind her, taking a moment to breathe before turning to face her reflection. She was covered in blood that had gone down her chin and neck, staining her shirt. She looked down at the arm Shane had bitten. The wounds were already closed, just a bite- shaped smattering of red marks. She assumed it was Shane's saliva that had already closed the wounds. He had healed her quickly that way once before, not long after they had met. That time, it had been an extraordinary gift to give to someone who wasn't a member of the pack. Now, she had barely noticed he had done it.

Her eyes went back to her face on the mirror. Was she different now?

She had *changed*.

She woke, and despite the comfort of having Shane before her, the panic she'd felt coming back into the real world ... well, she couldn't control how her body instinctively pulled on that feeling, threatening to do anything in its power to protect her.

From whom?

From herself?

How idiotic...

She wasn't someone who lacked control. In fact, when she had done something similar, dealing with the black Witches, that wasn't a loss of control; it had been all about *finally* using what had already been within her. She hated the idea that she could have done unknown damage to everyone in that dome, and she'd had no way of preventing it. Vee had still been under

WHITE MOON

the influence of the Sha magic, but it wasn't an excuse. When she couldn't control her powers, she didn't need to be around anyone else.

The door opened abruptly. She hadn't heard Shane's footfalls as he came down the hall, but suddenly he was there in the small bathroom with her, closing the door behind him and quickly wrapping his arms around her waist, meeting her eyes through the reflection of the mirror.

"You have me and the pack. You helped me when I lost control. I help you. Give and take," he said quietly. His touch and his words soothed her a little, letting her shoulders relax as she brought her hands up to meet his. He was also covered in blood, and his eyes had yet to turn back from his wolf's golden glow.

"I'm still quite a complication … and apparently I've changed the whole pack," she said, her voice barely a whisper.

"They will adapt, but we do need to get back to them," he said seriously, his eyes tightening a little.

"What's going on?"

"John is … well, Thomas is having a hard time helping him remain controlled," Shane murmured. Vee's guilt struck her suddenly. It was because of whatever she had done once she became part of the pack. It was odd, but she could feel the subtle trickle of power flowing out of and through Shane. He was trying to help them from afar, but it would have been much better if he was there in person.

After they both hastily washed the blood off themselves, and the odd symbols that Bao had drawn on Vee, they changed clothes and grabbed their meager belongings, heading to the front door where Aho and Min were already standing.

"I've got the ATV ready to take you just outside the tree line," Min told them, his outward appearance remaining claim but Vee could feel the anxiety boiling within him.

"The other Sha?" Shane asked, as Aho opened the door and stepped out first.

"They're outside," Vee said, having felt them as they began arriving not long after Min had. The three men stiffened slightly at her words. Min had tried to move quickly enough to avoid a confrontation with the others, but he had failed. He was just as determined to protect Vee as Shane and Aho. Apparently, he had made his decision. If the choice was between Vee or the Sha, he chose Vee.

They all went out, the others standing near the pond but blocking the path to leave.

"They need to get back to their pack," Aho said, stopping just off the porch.

"She can't leave until we know what she is," Bao hissed, body tensed, fists clenched, and head down with her back hunched, as if she were ready to attack. Long stood beside her, eyes on Vee like the others, but clearly her focus was split between her and her unstable kin.

"They don't have time for this. They already have a long journey," Min said, his anxiety turning into an instinct to fight. His voice was rough with his beast coming to the surface. Vee was momentarily taken by how quickly Min had gone from uncertain of her, to determination to protect her. Perhaps it was less that she was his sister and more his respect for Shane, but it still surprised her.

"We asked them here for a reason. We have yet to know if she's a danger," Hurin said, though he was also wary of Bao's stability, his eyes flickering over to her as if he expected her to explode.

"Let Yona see the truth. Have Vee tell us what she knows now," Urmah suggested, the massive man seeming more collected than the rest of them. Everyone turned to look at Vee expectantly. Shane's fingers tightened on hers for a moment, but they both knew it was the only way they'd get through this peacefully. No one wanted this to take that fatal step toward violence, except for Bao, who was still vibrating as if she was barely holding herself back.

Vee stepped forward, letting Shane's hand slip from her fingers, and approached the empty center between the two groups.

This was the danger of coming here. This was the moment she and Shane had feared when they first got the call for them to come. She would do whatever they asked to avoid conflict. Vee felt like she had demonstrated her willingness already but would not hesitate to show them more. They had to get back to *their* people.

Yona stepped forward and met Vee where she stood. Just the night before, she had taught Vee to dance. They had laughed and talked about music, surprising Vee with her vast knowledge of popular songs. Her wide, caring eyes looked upon her now with hesitation, instead of the warmth that Vee had seen there before.

"It will work better if I hold your hands," Yona said, holding hers out as an invitation. Vee had to keep herself from saying the silly comment she wanted to, about how her powers worked better with touch too, but this wasn't the time for that. She placed her hands in Yona's, feeling her emotions so much more clearly. She was torn between how much she liked Vee as a person and the fear that had blossomed from watching her change and feeling her power in the dome earlier.

"What are you?" Bao asked, her voice gravelly and odd. She was fighting to stay human.

"I am an empath. I only recently … today actually, found out my mother was a Fae-Witch, and my father is Aho," Vee said. She had no urge to lie, but she could feel Yona pushing her power over her anyway.

"Truth," Yona said.

"What abilities do you have?" Hurin asked this time.

"I can feel and influence others' emotions. I don't like to do that—influence. I can sense preternaturals. I have been able to destroy another's magic, but that was only once. And apparently, I can shift, but I don't recall doing that and have no idea if I can do it again."

"Truth," Yona murmured, though the corner of her mouth turned up slightly, her fear dissolving with each answer Vee gave.

"Are you a threat to us?" Long asked, now holding tightly to Bao's forearm, as if that was keeping her in place and from attacking. Vee looked deep into Yona's eyes. She felt the tension in the three men behind her, as if they were springs, coiled and ready for any move to harm her.

"Only if you are a threat to us," Vee said, her voice low. For a moment, Vee felt an instinctual urge to *push* them. She wasn't sure what she would be pushing their way, only that she could barely contain it once the feeling was there. Yona's hands tightened a little on Vee's; she felt a little of it.

"Truth," Yona whispered shakily.

There was silence for a few moments. Vee waited for the next question, but they all just looked at her. Bao was still tense beside Long, but she didn't resist the hand on her.

"Go now … your pack needs you," Urmah said, breaking the tense silence that had enveloped the small clearing. Yona pulled her hands away from Vee's. Vee expected her to step away, but instead, she put both hands on either side of Vee's face, came forward, and kissed her on the forehead.

"You are a gift," Yona whispered, once she brought her gaze back to Vee's.

Vee wasn't sure what Yona had seen or felt when she touched Vee, but the relief she felt was palpable.

Shane approached, slipping his hand into Vee's once more as Yona stepped away. Long pulled Bao out of the way of the path so they could pass, but she managed to shoot her hand out to Aho, halting him.

"This is unacceptable," Bao hissed. Her face was distorted slightly, the bones having shifted a little to give her a more feline-like appearance.

"They aren't a threat to us. What I did is in the past, and your pain should never have been allowed to punish the rest of us this way. We all miss him. Your pain … I understand it. I *know* how it feels to lose your mate. You mustn't continue to drag the rest of us through it with you," Aho told her. Though his words cut at her, his voice was still soft. She looked at him, shocked, her hold on his arm releasing. Without another word, he gave her a nod, turning to follow the other three through the path in the trees.

CHAPTER 21

M in was racing through the town center on the ATV. There were very few people out at that point in the night, as Vee had no idea how late it was now. The moon was high in the sky, waxing gibbous. A few days and it would be the full moon. She recalled thinking Patrick and Lori had one more run before school started the week before, but it had gotten buried in the sea of other pressing matters that had come up. She gripped tightly to Shane, who sat beside her in the second row of seats, Aho beside Min in the front.

They came upon the gate much more quickly than they did when they'd arrived. She wasn't sure if that was still the effects of her vision warping time or if Min was just pushing the ATV to the limit of its capacity. With no warning and no signs of slowing down, they flew through the gate, the magic sliding over Vee like a warm waterfall, and they were suddenly back in the much cooler air of Breckenridge. But before Vee had even a moment to collect herself, after the disorienting feeling of moving from one place to another, the ATV came to a sudden, jerking halt.

She looked up, and there was Durran standing before the ATV in their full Watcher glory. The only other time Vee had seen them this way was when they were battling the Witches. Durran had transformed into their androgynous form, but they were still Durran. Durran's subtle feminine curves were now a lean, long torso and narrow hips. Two black strips of leather-like material crossed over their chest; strong, long legs covered in the same material, with a hilt at their hip, while their black, feathered wings expanded fully out on either side of them. Durran looked beautiful and deadly.

Min and Aho growled, undoing their harnesses and jumping out of the ATV ready to defend.

"It's Durran!" Vee yelled, scrambling to undo her own harness straps and climb out of the vehicle. Shane had already gotten out and was coming around the front to stand between Durran and the two Sha before Vee had even stepped out.

"It can't be here," Min said, his voice raspy and on the precipice of a change.

"I felt Vee's fear and had to find her," Durran said. Their voice sounded much deeper, odd and echoey as they spoke.

"I'm fine," Vee hissed, walking up to Durran and ignoring Aho, as he tried to reach for her. "We're leaving anyway."

"It knows about the gate," Min continued, eyes blazing amber as the air shimmered around him, his change only a breath away.

"I care not about your gates, Sha. Only Vee's safety," Durran snapped, not taking their eyes away from Vee. There was no visible damage, though Durran could smell the blood and magic still clinging to her skin.

"Just a little vision quest and getting pulled into the pack," Vee said in response to Durran's searching eyes as they roamed. Vee was trying to keep her voice casual, even though all four of her companions were nearly about to lose it.

"Durran is an ally. Vee's Watcher, remember?" Shane said gently. She didn't know how he managed to keep his voice so calm when Vee knew he was also close to losing control. Their bond was giving her insight into just how difficult it was for him to achieve it. He was sending so much to the pack to help them with John, he was much more easily influenced by the power coursing through the others.

Min pulled his gaze from Durran and looked at Shane. Shane was not challenging but reminding and requesting that Durran be left alone. Aho became calmer almost instantly as Shane said the words. The immense pressure that all the magic, power, and dominance had brought forward went down a few notches.

"A Watcher for our Vee, hm?" Aho mumbled curiously, stepping a little forward but now completely lacking aggression. He went back to his youthful, casual nature, as if there hadn't been an imminent threat moments ago. "I haven't seen a Watcher in many, many years."

"Much like you, we keep to our duties and ourselves," Durran said, their voice still a bit rough, but feeling much better now that Vee was safely nearby.

"Yes, many things changed during the war," Aho said with a nod, sadness coming over him briefly before he turned to Min. "This Watcher is no threat so long as they are bound to Vee."

"Our gates are only known to those we trust," Min said, his intensity only slightly going down with his father's change of tone.

"And those we trust," Aho gestured to Vee and Shane. "They trust this one."

Vee looked up at Durran. This version of them was much taller, their face a bit more angular than the one she knew, shoulders broader and seemingly more muscled, but the eyes were still Durran. She touched their hand and gave it a reassuring squeeze.

"I'm okay," Vee told them.

Just as the words left her mouth, they could all hear, very faintly, the sound of movement in the woods. Everyone immediately went back on alert; that was not the normal night sounds of animals. Something was moving ... fast. Vee felt an icy chill begin to fill her mind. The unmistakable and unfortunately familiar chill of Lazare Duflanc.

"Vampire," she whispered, that being the only word she could reasonably get out. Suddenly, the text message from the mysterious number made so much sense. The moment she said it, they all shifted positions, Aho and Min letting their beautiful and almost immediate change take them. Two magnificent and massive wolves stood in their places, Aho with his crispy white coat and Min with a silvery grey coat. Both of their eyes burned amber. Durran pulled their hand away from Vee's to pull their sword from their hip.

Shane snatched Vee and placed her beside him, but he was still a step closer to the sound of the approaching movements. Just as Shane turned his eyes away from her, a blur exploded from the trees and rammed into Shane, subsequently knocking Vee a few feet away into a tree. Duflanc rolled through the tackle, easily coming to his feet and turning to her.

"Vee, I've been looking everywhere for you," Duflanc said, grinning as he stepped closer. Aho and Min leapt toward him as Shane was standing up, but he maneuvered around them to where they skidded through the dirt and pine needles littering the floor, narrowly avoiding a few trees that would have undoubtedly come down had they hit them.

Durran moved swiftly over to where Vee was, standing in front of her with their sword pointed toward the Vampire.

"Not a step closer to her," Durran spat.

"Her scent … her blood. It calls me. She has to be mine," Lazare said, shivering a little where he stood. He took a step closer, eyes trained on Vee's, just as Shane came at him from behind. His hands had become elongated and dark, with talon-like claws protruding from the ends of his fingers. He dug them into the fabric of the Vampire's chest, sinking deeply into his skin. Duflanc made a strange sound, like a roar but it seemed oddly bird-like. It rang in Vee's ears long after he had stopped, him having elbowed Shane hard in the ribs, and yet Shane didn't move.

"Killing me would mean war, wolf," Duflanc said in a shallow hiss, his voice unable to carry since he couldn't get enough air to speak with the lung having collapsed against Shane's claws.

"Your plans for Vee are enough for war," Shane growled in response, digging his claws deeper.

"And what if she were to choose me over you?"

The words sounded laughable to Vee as she finally stood. How on earth did he think she would ever choose him over Shane? But as she thought that sentiment, Duflanc caught her eyes in his gaze.

Come to me, his voice said in her head, more of an icy chill running from her crown and down her spine.

"What are you doing?" Shane snapped, his tone causing Aho and Min's wolves to growl and whine.

Come to me, Victoria Malone, he said again.

She could feel him pushing at the corners of her mind, see the magic in him flowing from his eyes, creeping steadily toward her. He was trying to enthrall her, the same way Holly, the intended at his house, had been enthralled. She tilted her head slightly and looked at him with interest. She could certainly *feel* his attempt, but it held no weight in her mind. The push was there, but she easily brushed it off.

"I don't think that's going to work on me," she said, surprising even herself with her words.

Duflanc breathed raggedly through his nose. She could feel his power building in him as his anger took the place of the addictive desire he'd felt before. With a movement so quick and fluid Vee wouldn't have seen it if she hadn't been staring directly at Duflanc, he raised his hands up and smashed both elbows into Shane's

ribs. This time, the distinctive sound of bones breaking could be heard, and Shane let out a gasp as the wind was knocked out of him.

Duflanc took the opportunity to rush Durran, blurring past them to get to Vee. But Aho came just as fast, clamping his jaws around Duflanc's shoulder and ripping him away from her and into a tree. Its trunk splintered, a huge piece missing where his body hit, but the tree didn't come down. Min tried to bite his leg before he thought to move, but Duflanc was too quick. He jumped up into the trees above, disappearing into the night-darkened greenery. Shane was still shuddering where he was kneeling into the ground.

Vee could feel him drawing on his power to heal himself, his breaths coming in shallow pants since his broken ribs prevented him from taking in any more air. His eyes turned to look into hers. The expression on his face told her everything. It would have even if she didn't have a bond or her own abilities. He was going to kill Duflanc and start a war if he had to … for her.

Durran's focus was on the trees. Every now and then, a bit of needles would fall from the branches above, keeping their eyes trained on the darkened canopy above.

"He's outnumbered, and he'll wait until we've separated before he tries it again," Shane managed to say quietly through gritted teeth.

"We need to move," Min growled. He had transformed back into his human form and was now beside Shane. Aho huffed in agreement, nudging Vee's shoulder with his nose for her to go ahead of him. The touch caused pain she hadn't been expecting, and she looked down at her arm, which was covered in blood. Her blood … and there was a large gash on her shoulder that she could see through the tear in her sleeve. It must have happened when Duflanc tackled Shane and sent her flying, but she hadn't noticed it in her adrenaline-fueled state. Preternaturals were rough on clothes.

They moved back to the ATV, Min hurriedly putting on his pants that had somehow survived his change and climbing into the driver's seat. Aho changed back as well and also found his pants only partially ripped on one side, good enough to stay on for the time being. Durran had followed them back but still had their eyes above, listening and watching as Vee got Shane to his feet. He was breathing better, but his hands were still in their half-changed state.

He flinched away from her when she reached to touch one of his claws and gave her a look that she could only imagine meant, "I'm a monster. Stay away." She gave him a rueful look back and grabbed his right claw, lacing her fingers through. *"Mine,"* her eyes and the push through the bond said. He may have thought he was a monster, but Vee knew better.

"We don't have time," Min said, starting up the vehicle. They all climbed back in, except for Durran, who perched on top. Vee wasn't sure it could hold their weight. It groaned a little, but otherwise held.

The ATV came to life and Min gunned it, tearing through the woods toward civilization, though Vee wasn't sure that was the best idea. Normally, preternaturals of any kind would shy away from a full-blown fight so near humans, but Duflanc seemed to have no sense of preservation of self or of the community as a whole at the moment. He was fanning the flames of potential war between his nest and Shane's pack and seemed to have no qualms about it.

They broke through the trees into the open area surrounding the Quicksilver SuperChair. There were still spotlights on, illuminating the lift but no humans in sight. The bright spotlights made the area outside of their beams appear darker.

They were about halfway through the clearing when something hit the ATV from the side, causing it to roll. Its previous high speed, and the force of the hit, caused the ATV to begin rolling down the hill closer to the spotlights.

When it finally stopped moving, Vee was hanging upside down from her harness, looking at the empty seats around her. The others hadn't buckled in. Horror and pain ripped through her, both her own and the feelings she felt from the others. They weren't terribly far, but far enough that she knew they wouldn't make it to her before Duflanc did. She began trying to unbuckle the harness at her chest. The pressure of her own body on it was preventing it from unlatching. Panic, deep and visceral, was settling in.

The sound of Shane's howl broke through the loud thumping in her ears. It was a bone- chilling sound of anguish.

She finally got the harness unbuckled, her body falling into the hard backs of the front seats. She knew she was going to bruise from the blow, but she pushed the thoughts of how injured her body was from her mind. She had to escape. She had to free herself, or she

CHAPTER 22

Vee hadn't felt the presence of the Fae that now stood a few paces from Durran's body, but it could have been because she was still so overwhelmed with all the other emotions and minds that she was feeling, along with her own. Pain was powerful and often took over other perceptions, especially when she was in just as much shock from her own experience. But she wasn't usually taken aback like this, and her head turned abruptly to see where the blast had come from as the Vampire flew away from her.

Duflanc was thrown over a hundred feet away, closer to the blinding spotlights than Vee was comfortable with. They didn't need anyone seeing this.

"*Fée*," hissed Duflanc, once he deftly used the momentum of the blast to land gracefully to the ground. Ness stood proudly, her skin dark grey and silky, pulled over lean muscle, eyes huge and menacing with hatred as she looked upon the Vampire. It was much scarier seeing her wholly in her true form than the slivers of the creature beneath what Vee was used to seeing.

"You should never have been allowed to taste her. She saved you, and *this* is how you repay her?" Ness asked, her hands balled into fists, which seemed to radiate a glow of their own. Ness was referring to Vee's mother, she assumed. Vee had not allowed Duflanc to feed from her, and, she hoped, never would.

"She shouldn't have left me," he hissed, turning his attention to Ness. The way he said it made it seem like Fiona and Duflanc had been lovers, though Vee suspected this was some sort of misinterpretation on his part. She didn't know her mother, but if she had such a sense of self-preservation to hide for the last thirty years, Vee felt certain she would not be allowing a Vampire to attach themselves to her.

"You're too old a Vampire to succumb to such an addiction. You know better than to taste the blood of a magic-bearer," Ness said, her lips twisting into a snarl.

"She offered it willingly," he growled.

"The once. And then fled when you couldn't contain yourself," she spat back.

Vee wasn't sure how wrapped in their conversation either of them were. She wanted to get to Durran and see if they were alright. She needed to figure out where Shane was. And she had no idea where Aho and Min were. She was a little closer to Ness than she was to Duflanc, but she knew she was not, by any stretch of the imagination, fast enough to outrun him.

She began trying to move very subtly closer to Ness and subsequently Durran as the two continued arguing about the past, and, by context, her mother. While she was infinitely interested in her mother's past, she had much more important things that needed to happen right now, like making sure her people were okay. She managed to get close enough to Durran and was behind Ness before Duflanc realized she had moved. She had a split second to see that Durran was breathing before she felt Ness drawing on her power again, the feel of it surging through Vee's mind.

Vee didn't have a chance to watch what happened next, because Duflanc had apparently dodged the second Fae blast, moving effortlessly around the now useless Fae, and tackling Vee to the ground, fangs penetrating the flesh of her neck like icy knives. Her breath caught in her throat, vision growing dark as she stared out into the grass before her, unable to move. He was touching her skin, with his lips and his hands. His body hard and heavy on top of her back as he pinned her to the ground.

Her pain, coupled with the pain of her friends … her Shane … was the only thing she could conjure to *maybe* push him away, but she also knew it would be too late when she did. She had already lost so much blood, and she was still not up to full strength after her vision and the shock of becoming pack soon after. But there was no other choice. No other defense against the long, deep draws of his mouth, as her blood surged from the punctures in her skin.

She sent him it all, pushing the pain and exhaustion she felt through to him just as quickly as he was draining the blood from her body.

Duflanc's eagerness and lust were instantly gone, replaced by a horror of emotions he hadn't felt with such intensity since he had been human. He unlatched his teeth from her, rolling over so he was beside her and screaming. The sound was not a human sound, nor was it anywhere close to the sound of a Werewolf in such a state of pain. It was a spine-tingling sound that made every hair stand on end. He stood, the scream still tearing from his throat, and ran out of sight into the thick wood they had just come from.

The last thing Vee saw before her eyes drifted closed were the golden eyes of Shane's wolf.

Shane watched in horror as the scene played out before him. He had been thrown, like Aho and Min, who still lay unconscious near him, from the ATV when Duflanc hit it from the side. A shoulder check at high speed was like a car getting T-boned at one hundred miles per hour. Vee, having been harnessed, was trapped in the vehicle as it rolled to a stop. Durran had faired a little better than Shane, having slid off the top and rolled, still injuring their leg and a wing, but was now standing ready to battle the Vampire. Duflanc had gracefully jumped through the air following the hit, landing on Durran's broken wing and biting their neck savagely.

It was that moment, despite what injuries he had, Shane knew he had to change. He was far from his pack, injured, and emotionally exhausted from the events of the day. This wouldn't be fast, but it was necessary if he was going to protect Vee. He let a howl full of pain, and determination rip through his chest as he summoned his wolf to the forefront, willing himself to transform. He had broken bones, but those would heal in time. Faster with his transition.

He couldn't move, his claws digging into the earth, tearing at it, as Duflanc tore Vee out of the ATV and threw her, the sound of a bone snapping and the feel of her silent scream through the bond, setting his hackles on end. He couldn't hear what Duflanc was saying to her; his ears were ringing with the effort of his change and the absolute rage that was consuming him.

His wolf eyes never left Vee as he struggled though. This change was slow due to his wounds. Too slow. She needed him *now*.

He barely saw it when the Fae appeared. He had not yet met this creature, but he assumed it was the Fae-woman Vee had mentioned. This was no old woman though. Her glamor was gone, and the blast of Fae magic burst forth from her hands like the wave of a stormy sea. He could tell, even without being able to fully hear the conversation, that this woman was stalling him while she recharged. She was not a powerful enough Fae to battle continuously and had only defensive magic.

Vee was smart, using the distraction to move away from Duflanc, but he could feel how preoccupied she was. She was overwhelmed with her own pain and the emotions of everyone else around her. If he could have focused on more than his body shifting, he could have helped her push through those distractions, even if it was momentary. The pack could have helped her, but there was no way he could teach her that right now.

He was very nearly finished, the last few bones still moving into place, when he saw it happening. The Fae wasn't ready to defend again, and Duflanc took the opportunity. He moved around her before her weaker blast hit him and tackled Vee to the ground so hard, Shane knew she took even more damage. Her body hit the ground with a pop of air being expelled and more bones breaking, and then he smelled her blood hitting the air, fresh and flowing.

He snarled, starting to move, but his wolf legs weren't quite working yet. This had happened in mere minutes, his changing being pushed faster than he thought it could with the urgency he felt, but it didn't matter. He felt that surge of power not as strong as it had been when Vee had fought Gwen or when they were in the dome hours before, but she was gathering it up into her for a moment before she pushed it back out. The push went directly into Duflanc. Duflanc released her, his inhuman scream echoing around the open space of the clearing, so loud it was overwhelming to Shane's sensitive ears.

The Vampire writhed on the ground beside her for a moment before he bolted, one moment lying on the ground and the next on his feet and running away, his voice still echoing as he went. Shane could finally move, though not as quickly as he would have liked. Despite his instinct to chase after the monster, he had

to see Vee first. He made it beside her, looking into her glowing amber eyes before they drifted closed.

Her pain was chilling, her face odd as he pressed his nose to her. He had just changed, but as the Fae approached him, he desperately wanted to change back. He had to. Through sheer will and grief, he lay beside Vee's too still form, his body molding back into the human shape he had just left behind. He needed his mouth if he was going to save her. He needed his voice, if he was going to do something he never thought he'd do.

He was going to beg.

As soon as he was human enough, he panted, looking up at the Fae who had approached and knelt on the other side of Vee.

"Can you fix her?" he asked, his voice rough as his body continued the change. Ness's black eyes assessed him for a moment, thoughts clearly swirling behind those eyes, but he wasn't sure what they were. Frankly, he didn't care. He just wanted to know if she could. If there was any chance that Vee could be saved. A rumble came from his chest after several long moments passed, and she still said nothing.

"For a price, I might be able to fix her, wolf. There must be balance," the Fae said, eyes gliding over Vee's body.

"What price?" He didn't care what price he had to pay, he would pay it for her. He would do anything for her. The Fae looked up from Vee and at him.

"You would take any price for her, wolf?" she asked, a glint of hunger in her eyes.

"Name it," he growled. She crouched low, sitting on her heels so she was level with him and stared into his wolf-gold eyes for a moment.

"We will call it a favor … I will call on you when I want repayment," she said, her voice and eyes having turned darker. "I cannot do it here," she murmured, glancing around and noticing the still bodies of the others scattered across the open area.

"Durran has a hotel room," Shane said, his change now complete as he sat naked in the grass, his hand gently resting on Vee's cheek.

"No … we'll go to my house," she said.

With no moment for further argument, there was a faint popping sound, and they were suddenly in a very strange house. There was nothing overtly strange about it to an untrained eye, but Shane found himself on the floor of a staged living room. Every expected piece of furniture was there, but the feeling it gave off was an odd perfection. No one had lived here in a very long time, and no one had ever actually used this furniture. The distinct lack of living scents that usually lingered on the fabrics were rather off-putting.

Vee was still on the ground before him, but Durran, Aho, and Min were all still unconscious, now lying on the plush white couches instead of scattered on the ground in the grass as they had been.

"Where are we?" Shane asked, having pulled Vee into his arms, but still looking around at the strange and uncomfortable room.

"Still in Breckenridge. I can't travel far with others. I don't have enough power. If I went much further, I wouldn't have enough of anything left to help her," the

Fae murmured. She had put on her glamor, one he realized he recognized, having seen her around Kansas City for years. He had known she was Fae; part of being a pack leader was making sure he knew what other preternaturals frequented or lived in his city. This one had stayed low on his radar. He had assumed she was just one of the Fae that desired to live her life as a human. She left others, human and otherwise, alone, and they did so in return.

"I know you, Fae," Shane said, slowly regaining enough control to have his voice sound more normal.

"Everyone knows you, Shane Keenan," she said, with a soft smile on her wrinkled, grandmotherly face. "Quiet now, wolf, so I can heal your broken mate," she said, kneeling on the floor before Vee with a grace that did not match her outward appearance.

He watched her move her hands over Vee, her breath hitching slightly as she built her power up, seeming to draw it from the air around them. Shane saw in his peripheral Aho had begun to stir. He couldn't concern himself with it though; he was too focused on Vee, whose color had faded to a sickly grey, her breaths coming in short, uneven pants. Duflanc had broken parts of her body and taken so much of her blood, he could hear her heart slowing as the minutes passed.

As the Fae hummed and murmured words in a language he couldn't understand, it wasn't just Aho who was starting to wake, but Durran and Min too. Aho sat up quickly, eyes amber and adrenaline pumping as he looked around the room. From the moment of the crash to when he awoke, it had only been ten minutes, maybe, but he was clearly disoriented. His eyes settled on the three on the floor. Immediately, they centered on Vee's neck, which looked like it had been ravaged.

"What did he do?" Aho growled, dropping from the couch to his knees before Vee.

"The Fae is fixing it," Shane said, a growl in his own voice.

"Should have killed him…" Aho said, echoing Shane's own thoughts. They had all held back, despite the danger. No one wanted war, but they wanted Vee dead even less.

"I won't give him another chance," Shane said, his voice quiet and cold. No, Duflanc would never get a chance like this again. Not with *his* Vee.

Durran and Min finally woke and for fifteen minutes, they all sat in a silent vigil, watching. Slowly Vee's color returned, the wound on her neck and shoulder healing before their eyes. The Fae finally stopped her song, which is what the murmurs had become, looking exhausted and very much the age of her glamor. The scent of magic and Fae that had filled the room fading.

"We all should rest here for a few hours. Dawn approaches, and the Vampire will no longer be a threat to us then."

Shane nodded, curling up around Vee's still unconscious form, Aho taking her other side, though careful not to touch her. Durran, who was slowly healing themselves, remained sitting at Vee's head on the couch, while Min got up to pace before the front windows. Only the Fae and Vee slept. They simply listened to the stronger thrum of Vee's heart and her breaths that were slow and steady, instead of the labored pants they had been.

CHAPTER 23

I'm dying.
Not yet.

Vee woke, but her lids were too heavy to move, choosing to stay firmly closed as she used the rest of her senses to tell her what was going on around her. Five other minds pushed at hers, familiar minds, but still overwhelming with the way she was feeling. The aftereffects of adrenaline seemed to leave her raw, as the last year and various conflicts had shown her. Shane's mind was the only point of comfort, his scent and the feel of his warmth surrounding her, keeping her from tensing.

She was expecting to feel the cold, hard ground beneath her, but instead she felt carpet. She could also feel light hitting her eyelids in a very unpleasant way. Hadn't it been night when they were battling Duflanc?

"Where are we?" Vee asked, voice raspy as she turned her head to press it more into Shane's chest.

"Still in Colorado," Shane murmured into her hair. His tone was matter of fact, but she could feel the sheer relief coming over him at the sound of her voice. "The Fae's house here."

"Durran?" she croaked, realizing the last thing she remembered was her friend's deathly still form.

"I'm here," came Durran's velvet voice, from somewhere behind her.

She opened her mouth to ask about Aho and Min, but Aho beat her to the punch.

"We are fine, Vee."

She took in a deep breath, letting the solace brought by knowing no one had died settle over her before she finally opened her eyes. The sun was coming through the window. It was still morning, she could tell; the east-facing window was taking in the sun with very little to block it through the thin curtains. Min stood at the window and looked at her with an unreadable expression, though she could feel concern still radiating off him.

"I need to go back to the site. It's early enough the humans might not have seen it, but —"

"The vehicle is all that remains. I brought everything here when I brought you," Ness said, interrupting Min as she came down the narrow stairs to Vee's right. Vee turned her head, which took more effort than she liked, and saw her and Shane's bags sitting beside the couch Durran was evidently sitting on. Her companions having not noticed them sitting there either meant they hadn't been there long, or they were much more absorbed in something else that was concerning. Given they were all surrounding her, she supposed *she* was what had distracted them.

She moved to sit up. She was exhausted, achy, and moving made her body want to rebel, but she forced it anyway, feeling Shane's body tense as she did so.

"I'll be fine," she said dismissively to the worry she felt from everyone in the room, with the exception of Ness.

"The Vampire should be dormant now. You should go home. Long journey awaits," Min said, his eyes tight. His emotions were conflicted, as if he was concerned about letting them go home alone. They *did* need to go home. Their pack needed them, but she needed a minute to regain her composure and sort out how awful she was feeling before she could focus on doing anything physical … like standing.

"I didn't call on you," Vee said, ignoring Min's statement and staring at the old Fae, who was deceptively fragile looking in her glamor. Ness flashed a smile and walked to take a seat in the armchair closest to her.

"My duty left me with little other choice than to follow along," Ness said, clasping her hands together on her lap. She was urging Vee to continue her questioning with her eyes.

"Your duty?"

The Fae stared at Vee for a moment, as if assessing her.

"I was never quite sure for this last decade. I stayed close because I could feel it there, but I wasn't sure until the veil was lifted with the wolf's claim. Your mother's protections were much stronger than I could penetrate," she started, eyeing Vee warily. "I come from a long line that are bound to the service of the Morrigan. There aren't many of us left; the wars wiped most of us out. I was handed to Fiona, as her protector." She turned to Durran, her expression cool. "Much like your Watcher."

Durran returned the gaze with an equal coolness, but no aggression.

"I lost her after she bore you. First time in nearly a thousand years I could not find her …or you, for that matter. She left me wandering, until I went home and realized she was there."

"Home? The realm of Faery?" Aho asked. He had the familiar air of casualness about him, but Vee could feel the eagerness in his voice. He still loved Fiona, even after all these years. To know where she had been all this time made him tingle with anticipation.

"No. Where the Morrigan dwells. It is not Faery as you all consider it … or what the humans imagine it to be. There are different realms. The Morrigan has their own, and that is what we call home," Ness said, causing Aho's eyebrows to rise with interest. Many secrets were being shared that had not been before.

"The Morrigan's realm, then?" Vee confirmed.

"Yes. My mistress extended my duty to protect the one whose thread may bend to its own will—" Her voice had become echoey and deep with the last few words, eyes far away. She blinked, shaking her head for a moment before she continued. "But your mother's protection held in such a way that I couldn't find you. Not until you revealed yourself."

"In charge of your own fate, indeed," Shane murmured with amusement, as he kissed the top of her head. Vee narrowed her eyes at the woman, glancing at Durran briefly.

"I think I have enough protection for now," Vee said calmly. She didn't want to insult the Fae, but she also didn't need more than her two protectors. A Watcher and her mate were quite enough.

"There is nothing to be done. I am bound to protect," Ness said, standing to approach the large window where the light poured in. Vee glanced at Min, who had taken a step away from her and continued to eye her suspiciously. Though there was no lie to her words, Vee knew the Fae were tricky and often used half-truths.

Vee moved to stand, taking her time and grudgingly letting Shane help her as she did so. The stiffness and aching of her body was oddly something she was getting used to. Was it age or was it that over the last year, she'd had a few times where she felt this way? She supposed age wasn't really something to worry about much now. Despite how she may have been raised and how she had lived the past few years, she was not even partially human. Most likely, she would live to be quite old.

She looked at everyone a little more closely once she had gotten her bearings and her legs didn't wobble. Aho was still in the torn pants he had been in; Min's didn't look much better; Shane was stark naked; and they all, except for Ness, were covered in blood. She could see the faint remnants of healing wounds on everyone, including Durran, who still sat quietly on the couch, eyes trained on the Fae.

"Get cleaned up," Ness said, her eyes also sweeping over the dirty men and Watcher for a moment. Shane stiffened, his grip on Vee's waist tightening slightly, reluctant to let go of her.

"Bathroom?" Vee asked, understanding that now was not the time to assert her independence. Too soon since everything had happened. If it hadn't been from the battle, she would have still been reeling from the events back on the Sha's domain anyway. She needed Shane close, just as he needed her.

Ness bobbed her head toward a door behind the stairs, and Vee weakly pulled Shane to their bags and then to the bathroom. Once the door was closed, Vee leaned against the counter, turning to Shane, and taking in his appearance. His shoulder had a dark bruise that reached down to his pectoral. The blood around it seemed to indicate it had been a large gash at some point earlier. A lot of the blood on his hands and arms, she could tell, was not his, though.

He put his hands on either side of her face, pulling her gaze from his previous wounds and his blood-darkened arms to his eyes.

"I could have lost you," he whispered so quietly, she knew only she could hear his words.

"But you didn't," she whispered back, reaching up to touch the soft skin under his eyes. He closed them, leaning forward to press his head to hers and breathe her in. Though he had held her for the last few hours, he desired nothing more than to find a quiet place and curl around her. Quiet and far from anyone else.

She pulled back first, looking at him for a long moment with an unreadable expression, even through their bond, before she gave him a quick kiss—more would have led to things she didn't think their

CHAPTER 23

companions needed to be privy to—and turned to get a washcloth wet in the sink so they could start getting most of the blood off of them.

Once they were clean enough and dressed in fresh clothes, they returned to the living room. Almost immediately, Shane and Vee froze with a sudden rage that was not from anyone in the room.

"John," Shane growled, eyes turning golden from one moment to the next. The pack bonds lit up again, and this time, Vee felt them much more than she had before. She couldn't pinpoint who the rage came from like Shane did, but it was enough to make her audibly gasp.

"We won't make it back in time," Vee said, her voice hushed with the newest spike in adrenaline. Suddenly, her exhaustion and soreness meant nothing. They were too far from the pack to help with whatever situation was going on that would make John's rage so palpable from this distance.

"How far is it to the hotel?" Shane asked Durran, who had stood with Vee's strangled sound.

"Ten minutes by foot," Durran told him, their glamor moving over them from one moment to the next.

"Ten hours," Vee said, her heart pounding. Whatever was happening back in Kansas City was very likely to be over, and not by way of the best possible outcome.

"Use Fiona's key," Ness offered.

"What?" Vee asked, hand unconsciously going to the key hanging on Shane's chain. But she remembered then, as she touched it, feeling the hum of magic at her fingers and what she had *known* in her vision. This key, not made from silver or iron but bone, would

277

open any door for her. It would even open a doorway to somewhere else.

She pulled the chain over her head, staring for a moment at the simple key before she turned to Durran.

"Bring the Jeep back for us?" Vee asked, suddenly understanding exactly what she needed to do.

"Faster than you would have," Durran said with a smirk, letting their eyes rest on Shane for a moment only half-teasing.

"What do you—?" Shane started as Vee turned back to the now closed bathroom door. It had no keyhole for her to put the key in, but it didn't seem to matter.

"Think of home," Vee said to Shane, her voice a little eerie, making the hair on his arms stand on end. She closed her eyes, picturing Shane's front door, the way her tension faded when she walked through the threshold, how odd but right her things were sprinkled about the house ... *His* home that he had happily, if not eagerly, brought her into. She let out a breath, opening her eyes and watching the magic, her own magic, flow out of her, making the key come even more to life. It glowed and vibrated in her hand.

She put the key carefully into the faceplate and aperture that had suddenly appeared and turned. Shane's fingers threaded through hers, his other hand holding their bags, as she opened the door. They hadn't been able to go over everything she'd seen in her vision. They hadn't had much time for anything since it had happened, but he trusted her. She could feel his trust, not only through the bond but through the sureness of his touch.

The door opened, and on the other side lay their center hall, the stairs before them as if they had simply opened the front door. With a tentative step, Vee crossed the threshold, stepping through the invisible barrier that separated Shane's home in Kansas City from where they stood in Breckenridge; Shane followed closely behind her. There was a moment when she turned back around, eyes falling on Aho, her father.

"Don't worry," he said with a twinkle in his eyes. "I've found you now. You'll see me again."

"I have more questions," she said with a raise of one brow.

"And if I know the answers, I will give them to you," he assured her with a nod. With one last sweeping glance at Durran and Min, she closed the door, feeling the magic that made the doorway possible, dissolve away.

She could have stood there for a while, contemplating all that had happened in just a brief time, but she didn't have the chance as they finally heard the commotion below them in the basement. Shane abruptly dropped their bags, racing through the dining room and kitchen to the stairs. Vee followed behind almost as fast.

Most of the pack was somehow in the basement, all of them struggling to put John in the cage. He wasn't cuffed, but his body was twitching underneath the skin, at the precipice of change, as he fought his pack mates for freedom. For a moment, once Vee and Shane entered the room, his power as their leader sweeping over all of them, John's fighting died down, but when his eyes landed on Vee's face, he let a snarl come from his lips.

"*Her!* I can feel her, and I can't even feel my own *wife*," he roared, managing to knock Thomas, who was nearest to him aside, giving him enough room to leap forward toward her.

Shane was a few steps ahead of her though and caught John by the throat.

"She's my mate, and she's pack. We don't harm our own," Shane said, his voice too calm. Deadly calm. Vee knew Shane wouldn't want to harm John. He was not a pack leader who hurt his wolves for control. But John's seemingly unrelenting hostility toward Vee, hostility she hadn't realized even existed until a few days ago, was something Shane would not tolerate.

"She harms us with her presence. She brings nothing but danger to us and our own. She *insults* me by being able to mate with you, to join our pack," John spat, stepping away from Shane, who let his throat go without hesitation.

"She is my *True Mate*. Fated, John. If her presence in this pack strikes such fear in you, you are welcome to leave," he said, his eyes burning as they stared down the lesser wolf.

Silence like there was in that basement shouldn't have been possible with so many Weres in the room, but no one so much as breathed once the words left Shane's mouth. Leaving a pack like this, a leader like this, would be foolish. So many packs were run by leaders who didn't bat an eye at the suffering of their wolves, while Shane made it his duty to not only protect his pack, but to make sure they thrived. With such

a simple sentence, Shane had not only told John he
had to adjust his thinking, but also made it quite clear
to the rest of them that if there was a choice between
them and Vee, he would choose her.

"I…" John started, his eyes downcast as he felt the
power of Shane's dominance and the magic that made
him leader flow over him. His aggression and anger
melted, shame taking its place.

"Go to your wife. Make a decision. Either you learn
to cope with your own feelings of inadequacy, or you
move on. Leib may be willing to take you. He owes us
a favor," Shane said, his voice not changing from the
cool calmness that was somehow scarier than when
he yelled.

John nodded once, still not meeting Shane's eyes,
as he made his way to the stairs. He didn't so much as
lift them to look at Vee as he passed, though she could
still feel a trickle of hatred from him, muddled by fear
and sadness. They all turned back to look at Shane
once John was up the stairs and out of sight. As usual,
Tommy was the first to speak.

"How'd you get home so fast?"

"We'll have a real pack meeting once Vee and I
get some rest … it's been a rough few days," Shane
told them all, since they all looked at them eagerly.
Yes, a vivid retelling was in their future, although some
things she planned to keep between them, at least until
she understood the implications.

Completely opposite to the reaction she was
expecting, especially given John's clearly negative one,
the pack gathered around them, pushing Vee close to
Shane, not that she minded. Now that the adrenaline

of the John Meyers encounter was subsiding, she was very aware of how overwhelming the vibrations of the Weres were in her mind. Touching Shane, she had found, helped with that.

They surround them, but not in any sort of threatening way. Everyone reached out to touch her. Most preternaturals, it seemed, were big on touch. A pat on the shoulder, a ruffle of her hair, a squeeze of her hand before they ascended the stairs to make their way out. Patrick, who had been hovering back as the other members approached and welcomed her, came up with a smile flashing in his eyes.

"From one battle to another with you. *I* managed to not get into any trouble while you were gone," he told her mischievously.

"I'm not sure if you've noticed, but trouble seems to find me," she said back, smiling a little. Once Patrick was close enough, Shane pulled him to them. The three of them stood, holding each other for a long moment.

"I'm glad you're okay," Patrick murmured once he finally pulled away.

"I could probably sleep for a week, but yes, we're okay," Vee said tiredly.

CHAPTER 24

It seemed like Vee and Shane slept for a full day. Once the pack had departed, they ate an odd mixture of leftovers. Shane even thawed out steaks and quick-fried them in a skillet even after they had cleared the refrigerator. Vee had never had a steak so rare, but she couldn't be bothered to care. Shane needed food after so much healing and changing he'd had to do, and Vee had suspected her loss of blood earlier was what made her so ravenous. Once they were overly full, they practically crawled into bed and slept from the afternoon to the next morning.

Despite the urge to go into the shop, being that it was Tuesday morning, Vee decided to let Patrick and Lori have one more day in charge. She hadn't shared her intentions with Patrick, though he seemed to understand, since she heard him moving and getting ready not long after her alarm went off. She quieted it with a rough tap, rolling a bit away from Shane to do so. He let her turn the offensive sound off, but immediately pulled her back to him once she had managed to accomplish the silencing.

She drifted for a while, her dreams filled with snippets of her vision, as if her brain was trying to make sense of it. She finally relented to waking, sighing as she sat up in bed, Shane's arm still draped over her waist.

"You know, we could stay in bed all day if we wanted," he grumbled, also having been awake off and on. Each time he had woken from his dreams, his fear and sadness pulling at the edges of her mind as his hands tightened around her. She knew he was having nightmares about her state after Duflanc had nearly drained her.

"Isn't there a house we need to see?" she asked, turning to him and looking down at his face. His eyes were still closed, but his mouth quirked up in a small smile.

"Mmm," he mumbled, pulling her down to him before he rolled on top of her. "That's right. We should go see our new house," he said quietly, looking into her emerald eyes, still wide with surprise for the suddenness of the movement.

"Wouldn't want to keep George waiting," Vee said, her voice husky, knowing very well that George was not waiting on them.

Shane touched his lips to her ear, making her shiver as he ran his nose down the side of her neck.

"No, wouldn't want to keep anyone waiting on us," he whispered, letting his hot breath wash over her skin.

She greedily pulled his face to hers, bringing their lips together feverishly.

This kiss, though it had started out playful, became more out of a need. Shane kissed her tenderly, savoring her, looking into her eyes as he touched her to make sure she was still there. His head occasionally traveling to her chest, not only to kiss the smooth skin there but to feel the strong beat of her heart that he had heard slow down as she lay fading in his arms only the day before.

I'm right here, she let flow through to him.

They let any worries they had from their dreams melt away, falling into the solace of each other's touch.

Later, Shane and Vee pulled into the cul-de-sac of their future home. There were only three houses that sat on the round, the center one being the house they were under contract with. They parked in front of it, the realtor sign in the front boasted "pending" instead of "for sale." Vee, in her nicest pair of black jeans and an oversized sweater (which was far too hot to wear in Mid-August, but she didn't have anything nicer) got out of Shane's car and simply stood there, looking at the beautiful, massive house before them.

Durran had called and confirmed they would be getting back to the city with the Jeep in the afternoon. Apparently, she had taken some time to heal herself fully before she headed home. She was still making better time than Vee had expected. The three of them needed to talk about everything that had happened, then there would need to be a pack meeting, but for now, Shane and Vee could take the time to see the house they were about to purchase.

Vee swallowed dryly as she looked upon it. Her feeling of inadequacy urging her to make herself smaller. A poor runaway locksmith shouldn't be even considering living in a house like this. She didn't even have nice clothes to wear, and her messenger bag that she was worrying with her fingers had seen better days.

"You deserve this, but this isn't just about you and me. This is perfect for all of us," Shane murmured in her ear, having come up behind her. He wrapped his hand in hers and used his other hand to raise her chin so she could look at the building instead of the sidewalk where they stood.

It was more stunning in person than the pictures on Shane's laptop had been. The grey stone complemented the sage green paint of the stucco, as soft arches held up the roof that made up a front patio. The landscaping in the front was minimal, which she appreciated, since she didn't have an ounce of green thumb in her. The only plants that had ever survived her were succulents and cacti, since she didn't have to water them often.

Shane's confidence helped her some, but she still felt uneasy as the large structure seemed to loom over her.

George pulled up behind Shane's car and got out with flair. His full realtor garb on, complete with perfectly styled hair and artfully selected accessories. She hadn't had much of an opportunity to get to know George yet, but he was unmistakably alluring. He probably could have been a male model if he wanted to be. It wasn't too curious why he had struggled in other packs. People were drawn to him: he was beautiful, more submissive, and gay, all things that tended to make the more traditional pack leaders turn a blind eye to abuse.

"You ready, Vee?" he asked, humor in his tone as he walked past her toward the front door.

"As ready as I can be," she said uncomfortably as Shane squeezed her hand, urging her to follow.

They walked through the large front door, leaded glass beautifully set in at the top. The entrance was big; the walls antique paneling in dark wood; the hall went all the way through to the back of the house, with the wide staircase greeting them and curving delicately up to the second floor. To the right was the massive dining room, big enough for nearly the whole pack. They'd have to get another long table like the one at the Pleasant Hill property. Vee smiled, thinking they could have a pack meeting without the numerous card tables and folding chairs.

To the left was an equally large room with a great fireplace; it must have been the living room. The built-in bookshelves made from the same wood as the paneling intrigued her the most. She'd never had so much space to fill with books before.

"We can get to the kitchen from the dining room or the hall," George told them as he centered himself in the middle of the entry.

Vee didn't say anything as they moved through the house. Each room was much bigger than she had imagined from the pictures, except for a few hidden, little treasures, like a half bath that's door blended into the wood paneling so well, you wouldn't be able to spot it unless you knew it was there. Or a small nook in the wall that had been specifically designed to hold a house phone. The office Vee had noted would be perfect for Shane, was situated directly on the other side of the living room's fireplace, having its own smaller fireplace on the other side.

The second floor had so many rooms, Vee wasn't sure what they would do with them all. She supposed it would be good to have plenty of beds in the event the pack had to stay there with them, but she was blown away by the primary suite. It had its own sitting room and sun porch, not to mention the bathroom and walk-in closet. The suite alone was bigger than her old apartment had been.

"What would we even do with this much space?" she murmured to herself, as she walked through to the sunroom and looked out the windows.

"We'll manage to find some way of filling it up," Shane assured her, following behind and watching her reactions with interest.

"Shopping," she said, cringing and glancing at him. He laughed at the pained look on her face.

"We can probably do most of the shopping online," he said, grinning as she continued to cringe. "If you don't take part in the shopping, you can't complain when the house *feels* like it's mine." His words recalling her earlier sentiments about why she never felt like Shane and Patrick's house was hers once she'd moved in.

"Fine," she grumbled, stalking back through toward the hall.

They finished the tour; the basement having been completely finished and lavish with its theater room and home gym space. She both felt overwhelmed and excited by the house. She had slowly felt less self-conscious about it once she started envisioning it as she thought it could be, with pack members in and out. It was *much* different than any home she had ever imagined herself in, but it had the space that they needed, was charming, and, more importantly, it suited not just Shane but herself as well.

"I sent you the inspection, so unless there's anything you want them to do before we sign the papers, I can get that set up quickly. They've already moved into their new house and are eager to wash their hands of this one," George told Shane, while Vee peeked once more into one of the many empty rooms that flanked the main space down here.

"I think I'd rather have what little renovations we want done to be handled by the pack or our guys," Shane said, not really paying much attention to the way Vee had wandered away from him.

An excitement came over Shane. Vee knew possibilities were running through his head, the idea of renovating the space to their needs and their liking settling something within him. Vee let the vision of pack members and their families lounging on non-existent furniture around the empty room before her enter her mind.

Yes, this house was perfect.

Vee managed to make it to the shop by about 3 p.m. Not much of a workday left, since the reduced hours only had it open for one more hour, but she wanted to get her bearings back, and part of that was making sure her shop was still standing. Shane came with her. He had cleared his schedule for the week, since they weren't sure how long they were going to be with the Sha, and even though it was daylight, the fact the Duflanc had survived their encounter made him uneasy about leaving her alone.

"Don't you have other things to do?" she asked, playfully grumpy.

"Do you prefer Tommy over me?" he asked, pretending to be offended, a mild shimmer in his eye. She could see him fighting to contain his smirk as he unbuckled his seatbelt.

"He's not as pushy," she said, leaning over the console with a grin spreading across her lips.

"Hard to resist you, but I'm better at it than others," he murmured, pushing a lock of hair behind her ear.

"Are you?" she asked, trying not to lean into his touch as she teased; it would ruin the fun. He let a small chuckle rumble in his chest before he leaned forward to take her mouth with his. The kiss was brief, though, as they were interrupted by a harsh tap of metal on glass from the passenger side.

Vee turned, cheeks hot with excitement and embarrassment, to find Lori's smiling face peering through the window.

"Officially official pack," Lori said as Vee stepped from the car.

"Yep," Vee said, trying for nonchalant but failing as Lori's face beamed at her.

"What did you do? I heard John lost it," Lori said as they walked to the door of the shop.

"Not sure what I did to the pack, but everyone seems to be alive, so I'll take it as not the worst thing that could have happened."

"Fair enough," Lori agreed, waiting as Vee took a quick, assessing glance at the show room. It was cleaner than it had been when she'd left, and there were more custom pieces out on display than there had been before. A few things she didn't think were fine-tuned or polished enough to be displayed for customers to purchase, but she wouldn't pester the youngsters for trying to help.

She eyed the inventory room door warily. It seemed like it was a magnet for disaster, and she had learned not to be fooled by how nice her showroom seemed. Patrick walked out, the flash of the storeroom behind him seemed to be in order.

"Welcome home," Patrick said, his words ringing in more truth than Vee was ready for. It startled her for a moment. This shop *was* her home, which was why it had been so hard for her to hand it over to their care while she was away. Even though it was difficult, they had clearly taken as good, if not better, care of it than she normally did.

"Alright, let me see the numbers," she grumbled, walking past him with a facade of irritation into the back to the computer. She looked through the numbers from Saturday and Monday. Even with the lack of house calls and reduced hours, it looked like they had come out nearly as good as she would have if the shop had been business was usual.

"Does it look okay? We did have a few house calls that I called back this morning and set schedules for since you're home now," Patrick murmured a little nervously. Maybe her performance of irritation had been too good. She turned to look up at his worried face. Shane had parked himself leaning in the doorway.

"It's perfect. Better than I could have done, I'm sure. What will I do without you and Lori to help me after next week?" she asked.

There was a strange rush of emotions that flooded through Patrick. His worry wasn't just because of her reaction. He had sat with them while they cleared the house of food, hearing the tale of their journey to see the Sha before the rest of the pack. She could tell he had been so happy when Vee was integrated into the pack, taking the magic she had shared with them all as truly part of himself, but with that, the whole pack had felt their pain ... her almost death.

Patrick fell to his knees, having kept his emotions at bay for nearly two days, but he couldn't anymore. Vee turned to him, reaching out her hands as if she were going to catch him, but he pressed his face to her chest, muffling the sob that had risen from his throat.

"You almost died," he whispered, after several moments of shaky, heaving breaths.

"I'm still here," she whispered back, pressing her cheek to the top of his head as she wrapped her arms around him.

"You can't die, Vee."

She smiled a little, looking over at Shane, who still stood in the doorway. It was no trouble for him to watch Vee holding their son and comforting him. *Their son.* That fact settled in both of them as he thought it. The mild pang in his heart at the thought of Patricia didn't change the truth in it though. Vee had chosen Shane. All of Shane and with that came Patrick, who had clearly accepted her with open arms.

"I'll try my very best," she whispered.

CHAPTER 25

Durran and Vee sat on the patio of the new American restaurant Durran had selected for their dinner that evening. Despite being fully integrated into the pack, Vee wasn't quite ready to join a run. It had only been a few days since they'd returned from Colorado, and she had no idea if she was capable of changing shape. She hadn't tried, and still didn't recall it even happening. Previous runs over the past six months she had stayed home like this, but Shane had only agreed to go the first night as long as Durran stayed by her side.

The pack meeting, as promised by Shane, took place just before the run. John had made an appearance, but it seemed to be begrudgingly. She had looked at him with sympathy while Shane somewhat explained what had happened with the Sha. The whole of what she had experienced was only something they had made Patrick aware of, but they did reveal her parentage to the group, which seemed to excite some of them while John continued to grow more closed down.

She had decided at the end of the meeting she would need to go to him and his wife on her own at some point. Shane was clearly not getting through to him. But right now was not the time.

The full moon shone brightly over their heads, their conversation about the food she had missed out on in Breckenridge having dwindled. For the first time, she felt the surge and tingle of pack magic move through her as they all changed under the pull of the bold white beauty above them.

"You're glowing," Durran murmured, eyes trained on her with both concern and curiosity.

"They're changing," Vee said, glancing down at her skin, which did, in fact, have an odd glow about it, but she suspected the light not far from their table would have distracted the humans from it. Or if not, she, for some reason, was unperturbed.

The night was comfortable. Not too humid or hot. Perfect for sitting out and watching the moon. The food had been good, and even though there was a sense of foreboding since nothing that had transpired was completely wrapped up, she felt oddly at ease. Perhaps it was the protection and sureness that Shane was pushing through the pack, or maybe the knowledge that even though she didn't fully understand everything she had learned, she would someday.

"Let's get you home," Durran said, breaking her from her thoughts. Perhaps Vee's glowing was becoming a bit more noticeable.

Durran paid inside, so Vee didn't draw any attention, and they walked back to the van. They had taken Vee's when they left the shop, Durran's conveniently left wherever it was she lived when she wasn't watching over Vee.

"You changed me too," Durran said out of nowhere, while Vee was slowing to a red light.

"What?"

"When Shane took you into the pack ... you said you changed them somehow. You changed me too. I felt it when it happened."

Vee turned to look at Durran, her eyes scrutinizing the expression and emotions she was feeling from her. How could that be?

Guilt.

"How could I have changed you?" Vee asked, eyes narrowing.

"There's a bond between Watcher and ward. Only a one-way bond so I can feel when you need me," Durran confided. She hadn't told her because it was forbidden. Watchers weren't supposed to reveal these sorts of things to their ward, but with Vee, all the rules seemed to be different.

The light turned green, and Vee pressed her foot to the pedal, her hands tightening on the steering wheel as she processed what Durran had just said. Durran sat in the tension like a priest taking penance. Though Vee had hidden for many years from others, she had opened herself up to Durran before she had anyone else. Every time Durran revealed something new, she felt like she was driving a wedge between that carefully crafted trust that Vee had once had in her. A trust no one else had garnered until Shane.

They pulled in front of Shane's house, Vee still silent as she turned the van off.

"It took a lot for Shane to leave me here with only you. He trusts you because I trust you," Vee said quietly, her voice even, not giving away what she was feeling. Durran quelled the immediate fury she felt at those words. Durran had been here first. It taking a lot of *trust* for Shane to leave Vee with her was ridiculous. But her jealousy and frustration about that would not be helpful; Vee's eyes didn't change as Durran sorted through her emotions.

"I have been bound by rules," Durran admitted.

"Are you not now?" Vee asked.

"Like I said … you changed me too."

Vee's eyebrows shot up. She wasn't expecting that. Magic was unpredictable, chaotic. Most magic creatures were bound with limitations, rules that they learned quickly how to adapt to so they could use it to their will. Vee had only scratched the surface of what magic she could wield, and whatever she had done when she came out of that vision was still revealing itself to her, as she imagined it would be for some time.

She was about to say something snarky to lighten the mood, as Durran hadn't necessarily wanted to keep all these things from her; she had been bound by the rules and magics of the Elders. She didn't like it, but she understood how difficult that would make things for Durran. However, before she could say anything more to Durran about it, she was suddenly aware of a void approaching the van. Not Duflanc's now familiar and unwelcome mind, but another Vampire.

"There's a Vampire," Vee said, eyes moving past Durran's head to the house.

Durran turned to where Vee's eyes drifted, seeing the woman standing there in the lawn. Vee began to get out of the van, coming around to Durran's side of the car, but staying quite a few paces away. The Vampire was petite, but Vee knew size made no difference when it came to the strength and speed a Vampire could wield. Her dark hair fell straight over her shoulders, pale green eyes peering curiously at Vee.

"You are the one who kept warning me about Duflanc," Vee realized, this Vampire's mind feeling somewhat familiar in its alertness. She had been the one to puppet Holly, though that felt like ages ago now. The Vampire smiled lightly and nodded.

"I am Antonella, but you may call me Anton," she said, eyeing Durran, who was tense at Vee's side.

"Why have you come here?" Vee asked, carefully. While this Vampire may have tried to warn her, she certainly didn't step in and help her. Vee wasn't certain that this Anton was an ally yet.

"Lazare Duflanc still lives. I can still feel my connection to him, though it's faint."

"Yes. He attacked, but my companions didn't want to start a war," Vee told her. Anton nodded thoughtfully.

"How much do you know about Vampires, Vee?" Anton asked after a pause, her eyes glowing slightly. Vee merely shook her head. She knew very little about them in comparison to other preternaturals.

"A Vampire nest must have a master or mistress. Without one, there is little control over the younger ones in the flock. The intendeds begin to die, and they begin *hunting*. If Lazare doesn't come back soon, the flock will soon crumble. He has not returned to hand over the reins of the nest to any of the other older Vampires here, nor has he taken back his place. It is very unlike him to be gone so many days without prior planning."

"What does that have to do with me?" Vee asked. This sounded like a Vampire problem, something their own kind needed to handle. Duflanc had created this problem himself when he decided to follow and attack them.

"He will not stop until he has your blood, your power ... *you*," Anton whispered.

"He already took her blood," Durran snarled beside Vee, causing Anton's face to shift into one of utter surprise.

"Not good..." she mumbled to herself, her eyes darting back and forth rapidly in thought.

"What does that mean?" Vee asked, her hands dropping to her side as she looked up at Durran, who was vibrating with anger.

"He didn't give you any of his blood, right?" Anton asked, ignoring Vee's question as panic set in.

"He didn't get a chance," Vee told her.

Suddenly, Anton was only a few feet from Vee, her eyes clear pale green, like pieces of jade, as she gazed into Vee's.

"It took him nearly forty years to recover from the last time he had a taste of blood like yours. It made him powerful and ruthless. He searched for her, leaving the younglings to go wild, and when he returned, he would kill them all. He will not stop coming after you. Now that he knows you are here, now that he's tasted you, he will do everything in his power to keep you."

The sick feeling of dread settled over Vee as Anton spoke. Not a single twinge of a lie hit behind her eyes.

"The one he tasted before ... she was my mother," Vee said, recalling the strange conversation between Ness and Duflanc. From what Vee gathered about that conversation, Fiona had offered her blood to save him, and he went mad from it by the sound of it. Durran stiffened even more, if it was possible, beside Vee, eyes glowing crimson.

"I do not wish to be the mistress of this nest, but I cannot let Lazare pull us down with him like he did before. It will start to fall apart soon, and the world is much more ... well, it might bring unwanted human attention that will be harder to avoid this time around. It's not just about us. You and yours may well be exposed too," Anton said hauntingly, stepping back a few paces.

"If we kill Duflanc, that will mean war," Durran said.

"Not necessarily," Anton told them, nodding one final time before she sprinted away faster than any of the humans on the block could see.

AUTHOR BIO

Chelsea Burton Dunn is a Kansas City native—the Missouri side, not the Kansas side. That matters to locals. Where is that you might ask? Right, smack-dab in the middle of the country. She has two beautiful children and is married to a superb partner, but let's not forget their two snuggly cats and eager-eater of a dog.

Having always been a little strange herself, she instantly fell in love with paranormal, supernatural, and fantasy books, movies, and TV shows as a child. Did everyone think it was a phase? Absolutely. Was it? Absolutely not. Being weird is a blessing, not a curse. She's always embraced that part of herself and those around her.

She started writing from a very early age, initially starting and completing one of the Deadman's

Handbooks in high school. She is a lover of music, having her other love and talent be for singing. She performed on main stage operas in the children's chorus from grade school to high school.

Chelsea loves to delve into the difficulties of life, love, and loss, while spicing it up with a little magic and monsters. As she liked to say when she was younger, "The monsters in my head need to come out to play every once in a while," so giving them life on the page seemed appropriate.

You can see more about Chelsea, her projects, and find her social medias by going to www.chelseaburtondunn.com.

SNEAK PEEK AT NEW MOON RISING
BOOK 4 OF BY MOONLIGHT

It was loud. Shouts, banging, the unmistakable sound of something being dropped and broken filling the still unfamiliar dwelling where Vee sat. Too much sound, too many people, and far too much commotion for Vee who was, instead of directing all these people to where things should be going in the new house, she was staring fixated on the ornate front door lock she had just pulled out. It was a good distraction. A needed one too. This move had been far from easy, and they weren't even finished with it yet. She was struggling through this day for many reasons, the first of which was the sheer number of people and all their emotions. Mostly frustration and fatigue.

Being an empath in a crowd was hard enough. Being an empath in a crowd of Werewolves was harder. Their emotions seemed heightened with their intense buzzing presence and the chaos of moving day was not helping with that intensity. Since she had been folded into this pack by way of the bond with their leader and by, quite literally, being made pack with blood magic, she had grown much more accustomed to their presence, but this day was overwhelming enough as it was. And their spiking emotions certainly didn't make her own easier to handle.

So she was doing what she did best, distracting herself with locks. Being a locksmith, she was very good at using her work as a way of blocking out her abilities.

"What are you doing on the floor, Vee?" came a familiar voice from above her. Apparently she was blocking a bit too much. Normally she would have been able to anticipate this intrusion, but she had been lost in the metal pieces that made up the old deadbolt in her hands.

She glanced up, looking into the face of Toby Curtis, her friendly acquaintance who kept her shop supplied with antique locks that needed restoring. His renovation company was working on a few modifications that Shane had requested on the new house, but they hadn't quite finished one of them before the move-in date, hence why he was there on moving day, thrown into such chaos and standing in the open doorway, looking down at her.

"Looking at the lock?" she said back, a question in her voice, since it seemed obvious to her. She was, after all, holding the lock's innards before her.

"Why?" His boyish sideways smile crept onto his face. There it was, that thoughtless flirtation she hadn't noticed until recently. Her almost-stepson, Patrick, and her semi-frequent bodyguard and friend, Tommy, had enlightened her to his very obvious feelings for her a month previous, something she had clearly and

willfully ignored for some years. She fought back a
bodily cringe.

"Because I'm trying to figure out if I can adjust the
tines and make a new key. Don't need old neighbors
or a maid just waltzing into the house," Vee told him,
eyes darting back down to the lock itself.

"Why not just replace it?"

Toby was under the false impression that Vee was
only here to change the locks and other fixtures in the
house. She had been, off and on, taking various knobs
that she had found particularly wobbly and fixing
them to put back in place. A few fixtures that had
been replaced over the years with unfortunate modern
pieces, she had swapped out for refurbished antique
ones that matched, or matched closely enough, from
her inventory at her locksmith shop. No one had mentioned to Toby that her presence there was for anything other than working purposes, and he had simply
assumed she was hired on, just as he was.

Toby knew she did work for Shane and others in
his employ. He also knew that Patrick, Shane's son,
worked for Vee at her shop. What he didn't know was
that Vee and Shane were a couple, engaged to be married, and had bought this house together.

Why did that matter?

Toby was in love with her. She couldn't help but
notice it now that it was pointed out to her. She had
no idea how to break the news of her relationship to
him without losing a friend and a business associate
who helped her bring in a decent amount of money.
For years, Toby had been bringing her antique locks to
refurbish and sell from houses he was remodeling. She

had never noticed his feelings before, either because of utter stupidity or because she simply didn't want to know, but Patrick and Tommy had pointed it out to her, and now she couldn't unsee it.

"Shane likes it," she said, her words true but not completely. Yes, Shane did like old things and was happy to let her keep it or swap out any locks that she chose in their house. He wasn't so much concerned about keeping the front door lock though, and had told her if it was too difficult to adjust, he would rather her replace it. She had seen that as a challenge, but not one she had been originally planning to do in the middle of move-in day.

"Did you convince him to keep it? I feel like his security-obsessed self wouldn't want to waste the labor it will take you," Toby said with a grin.

That laid-back grin and the amusement flickering within him told her all of her suspicions of how much he knew were correct. Toby had no idea. No idea at all that Vee and Shane were not just together, but engaged. *She* wasn't going to be the one to break it to him, at least not today. Her anxiety about everything going on today increased significantly.

"He likes old things," she murmured, trying very hard not to let on what she was thinking. This sweet man deserved so much, and his feelings for her, which she had willfully ignored, were only growing. He had been quite bold, for himself, the week before, when he was dropping off broken antique locks and had brushed her hair off her shoulder. She sucked in a breath at the recollection. She felt nothing but friendship for him, but because of that, she worried about hurting him.

Waiting to tell him about her and Shane was probably not the way to go about it, but she couldn't. She couldn't get the words out when his eyes sparkled as he smiled down at her.

"You seem a little overwhelmed," he noted. She firmly kept her eyes on the lock. The house was chaotic, but his presence there was far more anxiety-inducing than the rest of it had been.

"Noise," she murmured, hoping it was dismissive but not cold. She didn't want him to wrongfully assume she was angry or displeased with him. It wasn't *his* fault, but she doubted Shane would see it that way if he was in the presence of both of them for more than a minute. Shane would most certainly notice Toby's feelings for her, and Werewolves tended to be ... well, overprotective would be putting it mildly.

"Hm..." he mumbled, his look showing his doubt at her words as clear as the emotions she felt from him. He wasn't buying that noise was the only thing wrong. It made her feel oddly transparent. But he didn't have time to speculate or question her further. One of his men hollered his name from somewhere in the house, and he rushed to wherever the voice came from, leaving Vee to her very helpful distraction. Thank goodness.

This day was stressful enough without having male postering to add to the mix. Durran, though usually in female form, and Shane did enough of that already. Durran, her best friend and Watcher, had decided to make herself scarce for the move. It had been for the best. High tension and preternatural creatures didn't mix well on the best days, but Shane and Durran had a very tentative balancing act when it came to Vee, since they both wanted to protect her: Durran being charged with doing so by the Elder Watchers and Shane having bonded with her initially as a vow of protection. But they were also both in love with her.

Vee got lost in the old lock for a moment, seeing exactly how she would adjust it and envisioning what the new keys she would make would look like to accompany it. The beautiful faceplate would be gleaming by the time she brought it back to the house. Now if she could figure out how to slip away from all the chaos to retreat to her shop.

Her sanctuary.

She glanced around; no one seemed particularly interested or concerned at her whereabouts at the moment, shuffling boxes to and fro or tramping up the stairs with furniture held in ways no human would be capable of managing alone. Her van was parked on the street just before the cul-de-sac her new home sat in the center of. She had parked it there so as to avoid it getting in the way of the moving vans and work vehicles. She could very easily just wander there and drive to her shop, hopefully not returning until most of them were gone.

She swiftly wrapped the lock in the towel she had set the pieces on while she was removing it and tucked it in her messenger bag, before getting to her feet and heading straight out of the house toward her van. Shane was at the other house, directing the next load to be hauled, so she was certain she would get away without being noticed, until Lori stepped out of the house next door, eyes like a hawk and trained on Vee.

"Vee!" she shouted, now moving rapidly to intercept Vee's path. Her curls bouncing with each step, the locks fading from the once vibrant purple of the month previous to a still rather pretty, pale lavender.

"Hey Lori," Vee said back, waving as she tried for nonchalance.

"Shane said you'd be directing everything being unloaded," Lori said once she caught up with her. Her curls bounced lightly as her rapid footfalls slowed to match Vee's pace.

"I just need to grab something from my car. Aren't you supposed to be helping your mom?" Vee asked, watching Lori's face blanch at the mention of her mother.

Thomas, Shane's second and Lori's father, had purchased the house next door. While Shane had ordered some renovations done to the house they were currently moving into, Cora, Thomas's human wife, had much more drastic changes in mind. This took much more planning, something Lori, normally, would have loved to take part in, but she was clearly cowed at the way her mother had transformed into a monstrous version of herself once set on her new mission.

"I needed a break," Lori admitted, glancing behind her at the house, as if her mother would burst out any minute. Vee smiled sympathetically.

"Me too," Vee whispered, grabbing Lori's hand and tugging her toward the car.

"Grabbing something from your car isn't going to be much of a break," Lori grumbled as she allowed Vee to drag her along.

"We're making a break for it," Vee hissed, quickly rounding the end of the street and seeing her van waiting. Their sweet, escape chariot.

"Oh!" Lori said with a grin, happily climbing into the passenger seat while Vee started it up on her side.

Steadily, to not attract attention, Vee made her way through the neighborhood, turning north shortly into Ward Parkway to head back toward Westport and to her shop. They were a good distance from the house now, both having been holding their breath expecting to be caught, when they finally let out a giggle.

"So why did you need to escape? This is *your* moving day, after all," Lori said, once the giggle subsided. Vee shot her a glance with her eyebrow raised.

"Too much going on there," she murmured.

"Weres and humans running around. Grumbling and complaining." Lori's eyebrows shot up. "Yeah, that sounds like a Vee nightmare."

"You have no idea," Vee said, a bite in her voice as she turned to park the van in front of her shop. It was a Sunday, so the shop was closed. She had planned this, hoping Toby's crew would be taking a day off for the weekend, but Shane had insisted and paid them extra to get the unfinished project done.

"What project is Toby finishing?" Lori asked, as she watched Vee unlock the front door.

"I honestly don't know. I'm sure Shane told me at some point, but this week my brain has been all over the place."

"Oh, I know. I had three papers to write this week, but I stayed up late instead of skipping helping you here just because it's been…" Lori trailed off, looking at the papers scattered over the front counter. Normally Vee was very precise in how she kept her paperwork. She was quite precise in how she kept everything in her shop, really. This chaos across the normally pristine counter showed exactly how frazzled Vee had become.

"You've put off school?" Vee asked, whipping around to give Lori an accusing glare.

"It got done! Nothing a little coffee couldn't fix the next morning," Lori insisted, eyes turning away from Vee's piercing emerald orbs to see what papers were left out and where she should put them.

Vee's eyes narrowed slightly, but she took a deep breath and moved to the inventory room door to grab the supplies she'd need to adjust the tines on the lock tucked carefully in her bag. She had relied heavily upon Lori this last week. Patrick had also been quite busy with the packing to be of any extra assistance to her. She cringed thinking of Lori staying up late to finish her schoolwork. The school year had only been in session for a month. As usual, when chaos came to call, it came in droves.

Vee and Shane had purchased the house that was currently filled with irritable Werewolves carrying large things, because their previous home had been compromised. Vee had been followed—scented home by the master Vampire of the local nest almost a month before. They also had, sort of, solved the mystery of what Vee was preternaturally. Though it had been an intriguing mystery to Vee, one she absolutely had planned to eventually get to the bottom of, they had not been given the choice of her finding out at the slow pace she'd had in mind.

The Elder Watchers and the Sha had both demanded to know who and what she was, and that had been put at ease, for the time being, by their trip to the Sha realm at the same time. She had met her real father, been brought into the pack, and also been attacked and nearly killed by the Vampire who had endangered their home and pack headquarters. All things culminated in the very harried life Vee had led since. There had been a whirlwind of activity, and she scarcely felt like she could catch her breath, let alone feel any sort of normalcy and cadence to her new life.

Originally, when she had moved in with Shane, she had reasoned that she would find a new sort of normal that she would become accustomed to if she had allowed herself to feel comfortable, but now, especially with the revelations they had most recently had about who and what she was, she wasn't sure a calm and uncomplicated life was in the cards.

It was unlikely someone who was destined to hold their own fate in their hands and had prophecies foretold that her choices would change the course of the world would be capable of hiding away and living simply as she once had.

But she still had her distractions. The lock before her was a task she could easily lose herself in and let the troubles of her life fade, if only for a time.

"You thought anymore about your birthday?" Lori asked, as she separated the once scattered papers into more cohesive piles on the counter so she could file them away appropriately. Vee's eyes snapped up to glance at Lori from over her magnifiers.

Her birthday was only next week. This would be the first birthday she had even considered celebrating since her adoptive parents died. No one had been pressuring her, but they all wanted to do something, anything other than pretend it was just another day like she typically did.

"Too much going on," Vee murmured back, looking back at the lock before Lori's sympathetic eyes met hers. Lori didn't push, which was somewhat unlike her, turning to take the papers into the inventory room and letting Vee zone into the lock.

"Patrick texted a minute ago. Said he and Shane are headed back to the new house," Lori said when she reemerged, causing Vee to straighten up. She had, only moments before, finished adjusting the tines and only needed to put the plates back over it.

"They'll wonder if I'm not there," Vee grumbled, realizing there was still the matter of making the keys. No way for them to get back before Shane got there; that could either be good or bad. Maybe Shane would be able to send Toby away before she returned, or perhaps Toby would be finished. She could hope.

"And Shane and Toby will both be in the house soon," Lori said, seeming to have read Vee's thoughts. Vee glanced at her guiltily. Ever since it had been brought to her attention the truth of Toby's affections, she had been uneasy. Shane had a hard enough time grappling with the fact that Durran was in love with her. She wasn't sure how well he would handle the same being said for her work acquaintance. She didn't want to hurt Toby's feelings nor did she want to push away the delight and additional income of restoring the old locks he brought her, but she knew Shane.

"I don't want to hurt his feelings," Vee said, looking up at Lori's sympathetic face.

"He has to know eventually," Lori said, with far more wisdom to her words than a girl of nearly seventeen should be able to muster. Vee nodded, giving Lori a weak smile before she snatched the uncut keys she had decided matched well enough to the lock from their spots along her key wall and went to the back to cut them. Vee had just finished the first key and came back to try it in the lock when her phone rang.

"Hello, Shane," Vee answered, wedging her phone between her ear and her shoulder as she resumed the fitting. It was a little stiff; just a slight adjustment needed to be made.

"Why, if I may ask, are you not here?" Shane asked, not bothering to greet her, simply straight to business as usual. She let a small smile grace her lips at the sound of his deep voice, velvet, even through the phone. If there was one thing she didn't feel any trepidation about, it was her feelings for him.

"Adjusting the lock," she told him. Truth. Not an ounce of a lie in that, since that was, in fact, what she was doing. She just didn't mention she was doing it to avoid everything else.

"There's about twenty boxes that are stacked in the entryway because someone wasn't here to tell them where to put them."

"I'll move them when I get back," Vee promised, trying for nonchalance, but clearly failing. Shane knew her too well.

"Got a little overwhelmed?"

"Needed a more … quiet project," Vee told him with a bit of hesitation, as she moved back to the inventory room to shave down a few rough spots on the new key. The bond between Shane and Vee opened up a bit, as she felt Shane's reassurance, comfort, and love warming her. She didn't realize she had needed it until then, both of them having shut their end of the bond down over the course of the last week with all the chaos. Each of them had been tense on their own and hadn't wanted to increase the anxiety of the other by combining it.

They had become like two separate islands joined by a watery land bridge. They could feel each other, could tell the other one was still connected and within them, but they were cut off beyond that. Vee didn't realize how much she had missed the full bond until she felt it open on his end, blossoming within her. She could almost smell him surrounding her.

"How much more time do you need?" Shane's voice had grown much softer now, and she suddenly didn't care what awaited her at the house; she wished she could fold herself into him. The comfort of his voice and the open bond felt so good, she didn't want to think about anything else, but she knew realistically they needed keys and a functioning lock.

"I need to make at least two more keys, and then Lori and I will head back," she told him, taking the now much smoother key back to the lock for another test.

"I'll get these things unloaded and try to send everyone home before you get here."

"I think that's the most romantic thing I've ever heard you say," Vee murmured with a smirk.

"Romantic, was it?" he asked with a chuckle. His laugh was rare, and the deep vibration over the phone made her face feel hot.

"Mhm. Almost seductive," she said, trying not-so-subtly to do to him what he had unintentionally done to her. She was rewarded with a deep growl from the other end.

"I will make them all go home before you get here," he amended, his voice still nice and gravelly against her ear.

Lori made giggling faces from the other end of the shop, but Vee only grinned. There hadn't been much opportunity for alone time between her and Shane the past week, and she was now eagerly awaiting going home.

Home.

Shane's house hadn't felt like hers, but this new house, though it was much grander than her old tiny apartment by a mile, something about being able to choose it, knowing she, Shane, and Patrick would be putting it together, made it hers, made it home.

"Good," she said, but just as the word left her mouth, she felt something at a slight distance from her shop. A Were.

All the pack wolves were busy helping in the move, helping Cora with demolition, or at their human jobs. Not one pack member was free on this chaotic day to be roaming about Westport. Vee shot Lori a glance and moved her eyes to the front windows, indicating which direction she felt the presence coming from.

Lori immediately straightened, her body going on alert as she moved silently toward the windows, peering out briefly before stepping through the door.

"What is it?" Shane said quietly, having been clued into her sudden change in emotion.

"There's a Were here. Lori's taking a look," Vee said, quietly enough that only Shane would be able to hear, as her eyes focused unblinkingly at the teenager who had just stepped out, without hesitation, to protect her. Shane's breathing changed on the other end of the phone. There was nothing he could do from where he was.

Lori and Vee were, unfortunately, alone.

BOOK CLUB QUESTIONS:

1. Now that we know Vee's origins, how do you think that will manifest in her powers?
2. Vee is opening up more; her attitude to her old self-isolation is changing. In what way may that change how her abilities are expressed?
3. Fiona O'Morrigan remains a mystery. What chance do you think there is that Vee will eventually find her? What do you think will be revealed if she does?
4. Ness, the Fae, was brought fully into the story this time around. What about her version of how she lost track of Fiona, and subsequently Vee, would you like more of an explanation about? Do you believe her story is exactly as she said?

5. Vee changed into three different animals when she was in her vision. What creature do you think Vee will choose to change into, if she manages to change again in the future?

6. Durran was changed by Vee when Shane brought her into the pack, as were the Weres. Do you think Durran is able to confide more in Vee now that this change occurred, and if so, why?

7. How do you think Vee's magic somehow changing everyone in the pack and Durran will show itself? What exactly did she change?

8. Vee now knows what preternatural types are in her makeup. Do you think that simply knowing will be enough to keep the Watcher Elders satisfied, or will there be more problems that come from this revelation?

More books from
4 Horsemen Publications

Fantasy, SciFi, & Paranormal Romance

Amanda Fasciano
Waking Up Dead
Dead Vessel
The Dead Show
Dead Revelations

Beau Lake
The Beast Beside Me
The Beast Within Me
Taming the Beast: Novella
The Beast After Me
Charming the Beast
The Beast Like Me
An Eye for Emeralds
Swimming in Sapphires
Pining for Pearls

Chelsea Burton Dunn
By Moonlight
Moonbound
Bloodthirsty

D. Lambert
Rydan
Celebrant
Northlander
Esparan
King

Traitor
His Last Name

Danielle Orsino
Locked Out of Heaven
Thine Eyes of Mercy
From the Ashes
Kingdom Come
Fire, Ice, Acid, & Heart
A Fae is Done

J.M. Paquette
Klauden's Ring
Solyn's Body
The Inbetween
Hannah's Heart
Call Me Forth
Invite Me In
Keep Me Close
Heart of Stone

Jessica Salina
Not My Time
To Be Normal

Kait Disney-Leugers
Antique Magic
Blood Magic

KYLE SORRELL
Munderworld
Potarium

LYRA R. SAENZ
Prelude
Falsetto in the Woods: Novella
Ragtime Swing
Sonata
Song of the Sea
The Devil's Trill
Bercuese
To Heal a Songbird
Ghost March
Nocturne

PAIGE LAVOIE
I'm in Love with Mothman
Dear Galaxy

ROBERT J. LEWIS
Shadow Guardian and the
Three Bears
Shadow Guardian and the
Big Bad Wolf

T.S. SIMONS
Project Hemisphere
The Space Between
Infinity
Circle of Protections
Sessrúmnir
The 45th Parallel

VALERIE WILLIS
Cedric: The Demonic Knight
Romasanta: Father of
Werewolves
The Oracle: Keeper of the
Gaea's Gate
Artemis: Eye of Gaea
King Incubus: A New Reign
Queen Succubus: Holder
of the Crown
Val's House of Musings: A
Mixed Genre Short Story
Collection

V.C. WILLIS
The Prince's Priest
The Priest's Assassin
The Assassin's Saint
The Champion's Lord

DISCOVER MORE AT
4HorsemenPublications.com

Printed in the USA
CPSIA information can be obtained
at www.ICGtesting.com
LVHW050356090224
771184LV00040B/561

9 798823 202558